BLOODY BAY RUM CLUB

AJ BAILEY ADVENTURE SERIES - BOOK 10

NICHOLAS HARVEY

Copyright © 2021 by Harvey Books, LLC

All rights reserved. This book or any portion thereof may not be reproduced or used in any manner whatsoever without the express written permission of the publisher except for the use of brief quotations in a book review.

Printed in the United States of America

First Printing, 2021

ISBN-13: 979-8507883936

Cover design by Wicked Good Book Covers

Cover photographs by Drew McArthur

Cover location; Macabuca, West Bay, Grand Cayman

Mermaid illustration by Tracie Cotta

Author photograph by Lift Your Eyes Photography

This is a work of fiction. Names, characters, businesses, places, events and incidents are either the products of the author's imagination or used in a fictitious manner unless noted otherwise. Any resemblance to actual persons, living or dead, or actual events is purely coincidental. Seven Fathoms name used by permission from Cayman Spirits.

DEDICATION

*For Cheryl, my mermaid.
Home is wherever you are.*

MAP

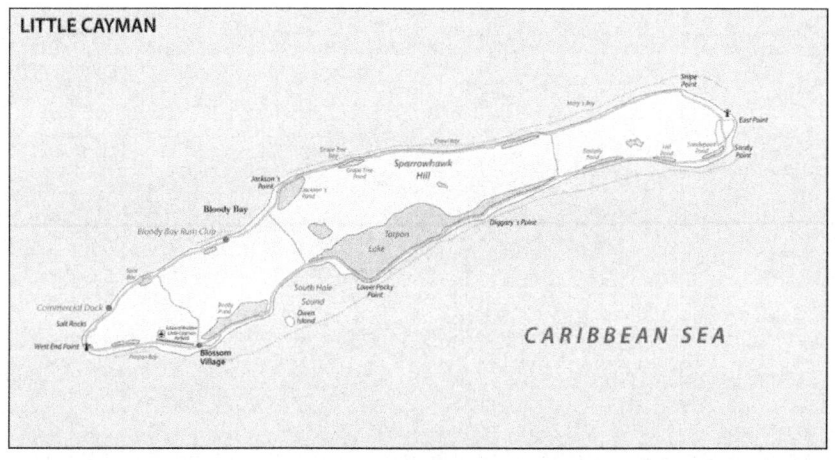

1

WEDNESDAY

Connery O'Brien piloted the 102-foot aluminium hulled, twin-engined catamaran away from the dock at Dodge Island in Miami. Pointing the bow south, he brought the Caterpillar C32s above idle and aimed for the William M. Powell Bridge which carried Rickenbacker Causeway over Biscayne Bay. All was still and quiet in the early hours of the morning – or middle of the night, as most people would describe 4am. Bright lights from the shoreline reflected off the calm water, and the only movement came from a handful of cars cruising over the causeway ahead. The roadway appeared like an illuminated stripe against the dark sky of Biscayne National Park to the south.

A wiry man, no more than 5 foot 8 inches tall, the fifty-one-year-old Irishman enjoyed the peaceful hours before dawn. The Miami night crowd had found their way to someone's bed, and the early bird fishermen were still an hour away from leaving their marinas. Radar showed the Rum Chaser was alone on the water as it passed below the bridge into the wide expanse of the southern part of Biscayne Bay. Just the way he liked it. Connery sat back in the helm seat and took a long swig of coffee from his mug. A week at sea and three weeks at home, a schedule that suited him just fine. He had spent too many years in foreign lands, living wherever the job took him, which was mostly the deserts of the Middle East for the latter part of his military career. Bosnia and Kosovo before that, back in the nineties. He had helped design his stateroom on the custom-built cat; it wasn't luxurious in anyone's eyes, but it beat a tent in the middle of some hellhole, where it always seemed to be stinking hot or freezing cold. Back then, he was paid to make trouble, and now he was paid to avoid it. Paid well, too.

Once clear of the Causeway, Connery eased the throttles forward and brought the big boat up on plane. Sixteen to nineteen knots was her sweet spot, depending on the seas. At that speed she sat up nicely on the water and made her best fuel efficiency. Across the flat calm bay, the Rum Chaser felt like a racehorse begging for the reins to be slackened, but once they hit the swells of the open Atlantic Ocean she'd be working harder, the broad 32-foot beam of the twin hulls offering a stable platform for the freight she would carry later in the journey. They would spend the better part of the next two days on the open seas, running along the western edge of the Bahamas and around the eastern tip of Cuba to their first stop in Montego Bay on the north side of Jamaica. From there, it was a much shorter run of 145 nautical miles to Little Cayman with their heaviest load, and then the long trip around the western tip of Cuba and through the Straits of Florida back to Miami.

The forecast was for exceptionally fair conditions, so if all went well, Connery would be back in his condo by Sunday night. An extra day in Little Cayman wouldn't disappoint him any. There was a young lady he didn't mind spending time with, but unnecessary delays were unnecessary risks, so Sunday was his goal. After all, there were plenty of women in Miami, although none of them hung in his thoughts like the redhead on the island. He slipped the straw fedora from his head and ran his hand over his freshly shaved scalp, taking a deep breath. Risks were something they paid him to avoid when possible, and manage when not. This morning he expected to manage an unavoidable risk, something he usually took in his stride. But this one was different.

He glanced at the radar and noticed a small blip returning off his starboard stern, less than half a mile back and gaining. Maybe a fisherman making an early start, he pondered, keeping an eye on the radar screen. Whoever it was didn't seem to be giving him a wide berth, and they'd have to be blind not to see the Rum Chaser's lights up ahead. During the day, the weekend boaters and renters were unpredictable and reckless, but a fisherman ought to know better and give the larger vessel plenty of room. Connery felt a familiar tingle through his body as his lean muscles tensed in anticipation. As a man who had spent his life walking towards trouble that most people would run away from as quickly as they could, he had a keen sense of looming threat.

He pushed a button on the intercom. "Shake your lazy arses and get up here now. We might have company."

After a few moments of silence, a sleepy Hispanic-accented voice replied, "On our way."

Connery looked over his shoulder out of the back windows of the pilothouse and picked up the boat's running lights. It had slowed to the Rum Chaser's speed and sat off her starboard side, slightly astern. If they were pirates looking for a score, they were in for a surprise, he chuckled to himself. The first reason being they had nothing of value aboard the boat.

Two men came up the stairs from below, one a stocky young Cuban American in his early twenties, followed by a slim dark-skinned man in his forties.

"What's the trouble?" the Cuban asked, looking out of the front windows.

"Maybe nothing, maybe something," Connery replied. "We got someone on our tail. Small craft, sitting off our stern."

"Could be Mason," the lad said, swinging around to look out the back.

"Mason coming from der south," the Jamaican muttered, already staring at the lights of the boat behind them.

"Most likely it's FWC or the like," Connery said, glancing down and verifying he had the VHF marine radio on Channel 16.

The Cuban turned back to the helm. "What's the FWC? Some water cop?"

"Florida Fish and Wildlife Conservation Commission," Connery replied quietly. "And yeah, they're like cops."

"Want me to bring up..." the kid started.

"Hell no," Connery interrupted. "Dunno, head to the stern and see if you can make out who it is."

The Jamaican nodded and started towards the door at the back of the pilothouse.

"Let me go, man," the Cuban pleaded. "Let me do the cool shit for once."

Connery nodded for Dunno to continue before answering, "Look at yer arms, Jay-P."

"What about them?" the youth replied, looking at his toned, light brown forearms, tightening a fist to flex the muscles.

"Now look at yer shirt," Connery continued.

Dunno slipped quietly out the door into the night as his co-worker looked down at his bright yellow shirt with 'Miami Boy' written boldly across the chest.

"Do you see Dunno?" Connery asked.

The kid looked out of the window but couldn't see the man. "Where is he?"

"Exactly," Connery growled. "Unless you're gonna turn black and change that stupid shirt, you ain't going out there, Jay-P."

Alejandro Pérez mumbled something to himself and looked disappointed, or mad, or something else, but Connery didn't care. The kid might be the boss's relative through a gene pool connection he cared even less about, but the idiot wasn't going to compromise an operation Connery had worked tirelessly over the years to perfect.

A voice came over the VHF radio, startling Jay-P. Connery listened carefully to the man's confident tone amongst a background of crackly static. "Rum Chaser, Rum Chaser, Rum Chaser. This is Special Agent Kurt Hunter with the National Park Service.

Please come to a stop for a safety check. I repeat, please come to a stop. Over."

The door to the pilothouse opened, and Dunno slipped back inside.

"Centre console, no markings. Just da one man aboard. Looks like he wearing a shirt wit badges an' all."

Connery nodded and thought a moment before easing the throttles back and picking up the radio microphone from its cradle. "Mr. Hunter, this is Rum Chaser, good morning. Once I'm stopped pull to the stern and my lads will tie you in. Over."

"Rum Chaser, acknowledged. Over," came the brief reply.

The big catamaran came off plane and slowed quickly, the broad hulls creating more drag as they bit deeper into the ocean.

"Alright lads," Connery instructed. "Head back and tie this guy in. You know the drill, say as little as possible, we've got nothing aboard to worry about."

Connery flicked a couple of switches and bathed the wide, flat rear deck in light as the two left the pilothouse. He took a last glance at the radar screen to verify there was no one else around. They were in the middle of Biscayne Bay with another 10 miles to their rendezvous point, and the screen showed the waters were clear. He put the diesels in neutral and the boat coasted to a stop. Connery needed to get this nosey guy on his way. He opened the door to leave when the radio crackled again.

A distressed-sounding man was shouting. "Mayday, mayday. This is Perfect Distraction. We're taking on water. We need immediate assistance. Over."

Connery paused and grinned before leaving the pilothouse and strode across the deck to the stern, taking a cursory glance at the ten stacks of empty wooden pallets tied down off to the side. His two men had the 24-foot centre console tied to the stern cleats and as he walked up the agent keyed the mic on his VHF.

"Perfect Distraction, Perfect Distraction, Perfect Distraction, this is the National Park Service, what's your location. Over."

Connery nodded a greeting to the tall man at the helm of the centre console, who looked his way while waiting for a response.

"Hey there Park Service guy, this is Perfect Distraction. We're moored off Dinner Key. Please hurry, we're sinking fast. I don't know what happened, but we've got no power and we're taking on water."

Kurt Hunter keyed the mic. "Perfect Distraction, Perfect Distraction, Perfect Distraction, this is the National Park Service. You're on your radio therefore you have power from somewhere."

The man shook his head and looked up at Connery again. "Your stern light is out," he said, pointing to the offending lens. "You'll want to get that taken care of."

Connery nodded. "Appreciate you noticing. Probably the LEDs are dead; we'll replace it."

The agent surveyed the unique catamaran. "Another time, perhaps?"

Connery smiled. "Another time, indeed. I look forward to it. Our fine protectors of these beautiful waters are always welcome aboard the Rum Chaser."

Hunter eyed the Irishman suspiciously as Dunno and Jay-P hastily threw his lines clear.

"'Till then," the agent said and fired up the twin outboards.

Connery touched the brim of his hat as a farewell and watched the man pull away into the darkness.

2

FRIDAY

Hazel's Odyssey, AJ Bailey's 36-foot Newton dive boat, carved through the open water of the Caribbean Sea. At the helm, the 31-year-old owner soaked up the morning sun and the cooling breeze rushing over the fly-bridge. Her purple-highlighted, shoulder-length blonde hair fluttered in the wind, and a pair of wood-framed sunglasses shielded her eyes. Either side of her, on the deck of the fly-bridge, lay two men with their heads resting on rolled-up sweatshirts, fast asleep. Her boyfriend, Jackson, was on her left, his long dark hair tied back in a ponytail, spilling to the floor from his makeshift pillow. On the opposite side was Thomas, the young Caymanian who worked with her at Mermaid Divers. The dark skin on his legs glistened in the sun where the sides of the fly-bridge ended and a railing backed the bench seat.

AJ shook her head as she looked at the two of them and tapped her foot to the The Cat Empire singing about 'Days Like These' on the boat's stereo. They were two hours out of Grand Cayman with another three to go until they reached the sister island of Little Cayman. Everyone had been chatty and excited for the first hour, but now the guys had crashed out and her good friends Reg and

Pearl Moore were on the main deck under the shade of the flybridge, leaving her alone and bored.

The boat was designed for coastal dive trips, not open ocean passage, without autopilot or radar. All she had to do was keep the vessel steered along the line on the chart plotter, which was simple, but tedious once everyone else had left her alone.

The plan had been to fly over for three days as Pearl, a musician who usually played a few nights a month at their local pub, the Fox and Hare, had a gig at the Bloody Bay Rum Club. The manager of the resort segment of the rum distillery had invited her to play a guest spot. They decided it would be a fun long weekend, so AJ and Jackson said they'd tag along. As the day approached and the forecast was for calm seas, Reg suggested they take the boat over so they could dive as much as they liked while there – a fun 'road trip', he claimed. AJ borrowed Carlos, who worked for Reg, along with her friend Nora, to cover her clients for the weekend using her smaller boat, Arthur's Odyssey, which allowed Thomas to join them too. Reg almost cancelled when he realised he couldn't bring his dog, Coop, along, but they convinced him that Nora and her boyfriend Ridley would take good care of him. Now, as AJ bounced across the endless ocean with no one to talk to, she started thinking that plane flight might have been just fine.

AJ unzipped her hooded sweatshirt and slipped it off, dropping it over the back of the helm seat. The heat from the sun was beginning to override the breeze. She wore cotton shorts, no shoes, and a Mermaid Divers long-sleeved sun shirt to protect the ornate tattoos on her arms from the UV rays. Her standard daily work uniform. She was about to nudge Jackson with her foot and force him into sharing the boredom with her, when Pearl came up the ladder with a Thermos of coffee to refill AJ's stainless-steel travel mug.

"Thank you, thank you, Pearl," AJ beamed. "You're an angel, I was starting to go stir crazy up here," she said, talking softly in her English accent.

"I see the boys are good company," Pearl said, laughing as she looked at the sleeping bodies on the deck. "Reg is sawing logs on the bench down there too."

"Men. Useless beasts most of the time," AJ chuckled as she poured some of the hot coffee into her mug.

"That is true, my dear," Pearl agreed. "Until they're not, and then they're really nice to have around."

AJ grinned and looked down at her boyfriend who had moved to the island earlier in the year to be with her. "You can say that again."

Pearl leaned on the back of the helm seat to steady herself as the Newton rolled and dipped across the light swells. In her late fifties, she could easily be mistaken for a younger woman, and while her curvaceous figure wasn't as slender as in times past, she still turned heads. She wore a headscarf to keep her long blonde hair in check, and her lightweight flowery summer dress clung to her figure in the breeze.

"I think we've done pretty well for ourselves, I must say," she said in her London accent that remained strong after years away from England. "You gonna make an honest man out of this one, or what then?" she added, nudging AJ in the shoulder.

"Hey, bloody hell, Pearl," AJ laughed. "There's no reason to mess with something that's doing just fine the way it is."

Pearl laughed with her. "You know I'm just messing with you. Still," she continued after pausing a moment, "if you were to think about having some nippers and all…"

AJ turned and batted her friend across the arm. "Hush up Pearl, you're worse than me mum."

Jackson stirred on the floor and turned over with both women looking down at him.

"See, you've got him frazzled too."

Pearl laughed again. "It's the mention of making babies that does that to men – they like the making part."

"Well, we haven't really talked about the offspring question," AJ said. "Suppose it's something we should discuss at some point."

"Probably worth talking about," Pearl replied. "You know, see if you're on the same wavelength about it."

AJ reached back and touched her friend's hand. Reg and Pearl had wanted kids but weren't able to. They had practically adopted AJ and become her island parents, in regular contact with her actual parents back in the UK. Sometimes AJ wondered if they didn't talk to Bob and Beryl more often than she did.

"So how long have you known this manager lady at the rum place?" AJ asked, keen to move on to another subject.

"Can't say I really know her, to be honest," Pearl explained. "She contacted me well over a year ago about playing at the resort, and we've stayed in touch ever since. This just worked out that Reg felt he could get away for a few days when they had an opening. I think they have a house performer that's taking a holiday."

"I've seen their rum for sale, but I didn't know they had a resort at the distillery," AJ said. "I briefly looked at their website and the place is really nice."

"It does look lovely," Pearl agreed. "It's a boutique type of place, just a handful of guest cottages, but they have a restaurant and a bar overlooking Bloody Bay. I'm playing two evenings then Sunday brunch."

AJ made a small correction to keep them on the route shown as a line on the GPS screen. "This is going to be so much fun. I can't wait to dive the wall. I came here years ago for a quick trip. It must have been before they built the distillery, as I can't remember seeing anything along the Bloody Bay shoreline."

"I don't think there's much there now, just the distillery and its little resort," Pearl replied. "All the other places to stay are on the south side of the island."

"I stayed at Little Cayman Beach Resort," AJ recalled. "They're a dive resort on the south side, but we made most of the dives on the north. They brought the boat around each day. This will be mega; I reckon we could even shore dive the drop-off."

"I might have to join you on a dive or two this trip," Pearl said, resting a hand on AJ's shoulder. "Sounds like my kind of relaxing diving, not these crazy adventures you and my Reg like to do."

They both turned when they heard heavy footfalls on the ladder.

"Anyone ready for a snack?" Reg's deep voice boomed.

The big man clambered up to the fly-bridge with a Tupperware container clutched in his hand and his unruly salt and pepper hair blowing in the wind.

"What are these two bums doing sleeping on the job?" he growled, and gave Thomas's foot a firm kick. The Caymanian didn't wake, but Jackson stirred and sat up before Reg could get to him.

"Hey," Jackson said sleepily in his soft Californian accent, "guess I nodded off for a bit."

"Fine bloody co-pilot you are," Reg scoffed, "leaving her ladyship alone at the helm."

Pearl laughed and took the container from Reg. "Don't listen to him, Jackson, he only woke up a few minutes ago himself."

Within a second of the lid coming off the Tupperware, Thomas was awake and pulled himself to his feet, stretching out his long, lean limbs and eyeing the food.

"Blimey," AJ said, shaking her head, "Reg nearly booted you over the side and you didn't even stir. Open a tub of Pearl's currant scones and you're wide awake."

Thomas grinned. "Be rude not to sample Miss Pearl's fine bakin', seeing as she went to all dis trouble."

Pearl held out the container and Thomas scooped up a pastry. "Thank you, Miss."

Thomas eagerly chewed on his treat. "Let me take the wheel for a spell, Boss," he said, and AJ stepped aside while Pearl offered the tub around to the group.

"I need a break, thank you, Thomas," AJ replied. "I've been dying to pee for a while."

Reg shook his head. "Nice going you two," he said, looking between Jackson and Thomas.

"She could have woken us up," Jackson said. "You know better than anyone, she's not shy when she wants something."

"Fair point," Reg admitted.

"I was letting him get some sleep," AJ said, "and don't worry, you'll make it up to me," she added, giving him a quick kiss as she passed by on her way to the ladder. She decided the fact that she'd been about to wake him up didn't need to be discussed.

"Don't reward him for sleeping on the bloody job," Reg roared, sneaking a second scone from the tub.

"Hey, look at this," AJ called from the ladder. "We have friends."

She pointed off the stern where a pod of dolphins were swimming along the edges of the Newton's wake, dancing in and out of the surf thrown up by the broad hull. They all stood in amazement and watched the show as several of the graceful creatures moved to the bow. AJ slid down the ladder, hopped up on the gunwale, and ran along the edge of the railing to the bow pulpit. Below her, several dolphins were speeding through the clear blue water, blurry grey streaks effortlessly pacing the twin diesels that propelled Hazel's Odyssey. Every few seconds they leapt clear of the surface, dipping their noses to duck back below with barely a ripple.

"This has to be a good omen, my girl," Reg called down from above. "Reckon this might be a trip we'll never forget."

AJ looked up and smiled from ear to ear. "Bloody good start, Reg."

3

WEDNESDAY

Connery watched the agent's centre console disappear off the radar screen to the north and relaxed again. He was aiming for a GPS location in the bay, west of Billy's Point on Elliott Key, away from the cut they would be taking shortly. As he closed within a half a mile of the spot, Connery slowed the catamaran and scanned the empty waters for signs of any other traffic. Darkness enveloped the lower part of Biscayne Bay with the only lights coming from the Turkey Point Nuclear Power Station to the west, and Ocean Reef Club community to the south. The keys separating the bay from the Atlantic Ocean to his east were uninhabited national park, hidden in the shroud of night.

He came down to idle and gently eased up to the rendezvous spot, glancing between the windows and the radar screen. He took the diesels out of gear but left them running. Connery turned to speak to Dunno, who had been sitting in the back of the pilothouse, but the man was already heading out the door. He rarely had to ask the Jamaican to do the routine tasks. The man might be quiet, but he was sharp as the blade he carried tucked in his boot.

A small blip appeared on the radar screen, moving towards

them from east of their position. It had been nestled in the edge of Elliott Key and only showed once it began to move. Jay-P came up the stairs from below and Connery was pleased the young man had changed into a plain, dark, long-sleeved tee-shirt.

"They're coming," Connery said. "Go out and help Dunno at the stern."

Jay-P nodded and slipped out the back door into the darkness. Connery did not turn the deck lights on for this meeting. Once the speck on the radar was close, he too turned and stepped out the back of the pilothouse and carefully made his way to the stern. The big Caterpillar diesels rumbled in the engine shrouds on either side of the deck, nestled into the hulls where they drove the large stainless-steel screws via shafts to the stern. Connery stood next to the other two men and watched a nondescript 23-foot fishing boat pull up without running lights on, and the dash covered with a thick towel. The vessel was only visible from the Rum Chaser's stern light glistening off the water, both functioning after Dunno had effected repairs.

A Cuban man in his thirties grinned up at Connery, as a younger Caucasian heaved a sturdy black 24-inch duffel bag under the stern railing of the catamaran. Dunno held a mid-line wrapped once around a deck cleat, ready to release the boat at a moment's notice. Jay-P dragged the first bag clear while the next one was manhandled to the deck.

"Thanks for the help," Connery said to the Cuban at the helm. "Perfect Distraction was a nice touch. Not very subtle, but I enjoyed it all the same."

"No way," Jay-P said, pausing his work. "That was you guys?"

The man at the helm shook his head and grinned again at Connery. He started to say something, but decided against it and shrugged his shoulders.

"No shit," Connery agreed.

They loaded nine bags on the deck of the Rum Chaser, followed by a lighter duffel bag and a rucksack.

"Come on, Mason," Connery said sternly. "Let's get out of here before that agent comes sniffing around some more."

The young man climbed the ladder and slipped his rucksack over his shoulder, picking up a heavy duffel in one hand and his kit bag in the other.

"I'm good. Let's roll, dude," Mason replied, turning and nodding to the other man on the boat. "We'll drag this below while you take us through the cut."

Dunno released the line, and within a few moments the fishing boat was lost in the dark morning.

"Sure you have everything, Mason?" Connery asked.

"Yeah," the Californian replied. "Nine bags this trip."

Connery scooped up a duffel in each hand and started across the deck. Each bag weighed 56 pounds, but he wielded them as though they were filled with feathers.

"I'm just making sure you have everything you want aboard, didn't forget anything, or need to leave anything else behind?" Connery said as he lugged the cargo across the deck, followed by the three men.

"Dude, what's got into you?" Mason answered. "What's with the weird questions, man?"

Connery looked over his shoulder and smiled. "Just want to make sure you have everything as you'd like it to be."

He continued across the deck without waiting for a response. Dropping the bags near the deck door leading to the cabins below, he entered the pilothouse and left the crew to finish. He could hear Mason outside as the American swung open the heavy metal door to the stairwell.

"What's eating him, man?"

"He's always riding my ass – seems normal to me," Jay-P replied.

Mason turned to Dunno. "Don't suppose you can shed any light on the boss's shitty mood?"

The Jamaican shrugged his shoulders. "Dunno."

"That's what I figured," Mason replied, managing a laugh as

they all banged and crashed their way down the narrow metal steps.

Connery took a deep breath and exhaled slowly. He dropped the motors in gear and the big boat eased away as he checked the chart plotter. He brought up a programmed route through Caesar Creek, between Elliott and Totten Keys, leading to the Pacific Reef Channel, a natural pathway into the deeper water of the Atlantic. Their two-day journey was under way and he and Mason would each take turns at the helm, Dunno filling in occasionally. Jay-P would beg to take a turn at the wheel and Connery would probably let him on this trip, under close supervision. Better to have the fool play captain for an hour or two than whine to his father's cousin and cause problems. Connery had worked for Dayán Castillo for nearly twelve years. Over that time they had built a trust, but blood was always thicker than water, and there was only so much faith a Cuban immigrant from the Mariel boat lift in 1980 would put in a former mercenary from Ireland.

Mason came up the pilothouse stairs from below and put a Thermos of coffee in a cup holder by the helm. He sat in the second helm seat, stared out the window at the crack of light forming on the eastern horizon, and sipped coffee from his mug.

"Should be a smooth ride, man. Weather report I saw looks golden."

Connery nodded and made a small wheel adjustment to keep them in the centre of the channel. Unladen, the catamaran drew a shallow draft with its 7-foot-wide hulls designed to carry a payload of 170 US tons. Even at low tide the boat could safely wander from the channel without bottoming, but there was no reason to discover an unmarked or newly sunken hazard in the shallows. Risk management.

"How do you want to split the shifts?" Mason asked.

Connery glanced over at the young man, faintly lit by the instrument lights and the breaking dawn. Mason had been part of the team for four years, and Connery had taken a mentoring role as the streetwise kid had matured into a responsible adult. Raised on the water in Long Beach, California, Mason had a natural affinity for the ocean. Connery had no qualms in promoting him to first mate two years back when the previous man was assigned to another role in Castillo's vast operation. Mason was a reliable seaman, but more than that, he understood the boat and how she functioned. Between the two of them, there wasn't much they couldn't maintain or fix themselves, from the diesels to the marine heads. The modern electronics were about the only systems they needed outside help with.

"I'll get us to the Gulf Stream," Connery replied, "then I'll have you take the wheel for a while. I have something I need to take care of."

"Split it four hours apiece after that?" Mason asked.

"Sure," Connery replied.

The catamaran was riding high in the water, up on plane at 18 knots and gliding effortlessly through the light swells of the open ocean. They would traverse the strong, warm water current of the powerful Gulf Stream, taking the shortest route across towards the Bahamas. The Gulf Stream swept through the Straits of Florida between Cuba and the Keys, turned north and ran up the coast of America, before heading across the northern Atlantic towards Great Britain. They wanted to head south-east but would burn up twice the diesel fighting the Gulf Stream so it made more sense to cut across east and turn south once clear of the northbound current. The big boat would yaw out as much as 20-degrees to maintain its easterly heading.

The sun rose above the horizon, throwing yellow and orange hues across the water before it climbed in the sky and the temperature inside the pilothouse soared. Connery turned on the air conditioning, which he liked to keep at 78 degrees. Enough to knock the humidity out of the room, but not so chilled that the heat bowled him over when he stepped outside. He used to keep it at 80 degrees, but maybe he was softening in his old age.

Once he felt the current pick up and he needed to point the boat farther south to keep on their heading, Connery stood up and nodded for Mason to take the wheel. The Irishman stood at the back of the pilothouse and watched his protege settle in at the helm. He hoped he was about to prove himself wrong, but he was sure that wouldn't be the case. Connery quietly left the pilothouse down the side stairs to the narrow berths in the port side hull.

4

FRIDAY

Everyone gathered on the fly-bridge as Reg piloted Hazel's Odyssey around the west end of Little Cayman and approached Bloody Bay. The island was similar to Grand Cayman in as much as it had very little elevation. Two mountain peaks that barely broke the surface in a vast sea. The third island, Cayman Brac, less than 5 miles east of Little Cayman, had dramatic bluffs on the south side reaching 141 feet above the water. As seas continued to rise, Brac would become the only remaining Cayman island at some point in the future.

    Bloody Bay was more of an indent than an actual bay, with the shoreline curving east to Jackson's Point. The Bloody Bay Rum Club was nestled amongst the low trees and shrubs growing along the ironshore coast, and the dark green metal roof of the tall distillery building was the first structure they could see. The resort bar and restaurant were built on a small natural spit of ironshore extended into the crystal-clear water, and beyond that was a pier stretching out across the shallows. Brightly coloured cottages surrounded the restaurant, splaying rearward in a vee to afford each dwelling a magnificent view of the ocean.

    Reg pulled up to the west side of the pier, carefully watching the depth as he approached. A pontoon boat with the resort logo adorning its helm bobbed on the east side. AJ and Thomas hopped to the jetty as they pulled up, and tied the Newton into a pair of cleats that were mounted every 10 feet along the pier. AJ looked over at the bar and saw a red-headed lady waving to them. She waved back.

"Pearl, is that the manager you were telling me about?"

Pearl passed a guitar case over to Thomas before turning to look. "I'd say so," Pearl said, also waving to the woman, who was making her way down the pathway to the head of the pier. "I've only seen a picture of her."

Reg helped Pearl bring the rest of her gear up from the bow cabin while Jackson passed up their luggage.

"Wow," Thomas said quietly, and AJ noticed he was looking down the pier. She turned and saw the woman approaching.

"Cool your jets there, Romeo," AJ whispered with a grin. "Jacqueline will have your guts for garters if you start ogling the talent as soon as you hop islands."

Thomas laughed. "I'm just appreciatin' our welcoming committee – nuttin' to get all fussed about."

The redhead strode confidently up the pier wearing a pleasant smile and white silky trousers billowing in the breeze. She was taller than AJ – although most people were – slender, and very pretty. Her long curls bounced and fluttered as she walked, the light glistening off her copper tones.

"Hi everyone, welcome to the Bloody Bay Rum Club," she said with an American accent, extending her hand to AJ.

"Thank you," AJ replied, and shook her hand. "I'm AJ, and this is Thomas," she said, stepping back so they could greet each other. "This is beautiful."

"This sure is," Thomas said as he shook hands in turn, and AJ tried to hide her smirk.

"I'm Madison Reed," the woman announced as Pearl stepped to the pier, "but everyone calls me Mads."

"Hello, dear," Pearl said as they too shook hands. "Thank you for inviting us. We've been quite excited about coming here."

Pearl turned and pointed to her husband. "This is Reg, and the good-looking fellow over there is Jackson."

Mads waved to them. "Hi, welcome. This is really special for us," she said, returning her attention to Pearl. "I'm a huge fan, so I'm honoured you agreed to come."

Pearl waved her off, slightly embarrassed. "Pleasure's ours," she said looking at the idyllic location and the beautiful island style cottages. "I don't think we'll mind staying here at all."

Two local men wheeled luggage carts down the pier and they all helped load their bags and Pearl's gear aboard. The musical department took up most of the space. As they ambled towards the buildings, Mads continued her welcome speech.

"We have you and Reg in a one-bedroom cottage, and the rest of you in a two-bedroom next door. I've put you on this side of the restaurant building so you'll have a view of the pier and your boat. We have a resort boat that's available for divers and snorkellers, and you're welcome to take advantage of that if you'd prefer, but I'm guessing you'd rather take yours out as you brought it all this way.

"We're all-inclusive and you'll find the mealtimes in the welcome folder in your rooms." She glanced at her watch. "Lunch will be starting in a few minutes, in fact."

Thomas's eyes lit up and AJ nudged him with a grin.

"Entertainment usually plays between 6:30 and 8:30 in the evening, which catches the sunset when the bar is the busiest, and then continues through dinner. Feel free to break up your sets however works best for you," she said, looking at Pearl.

"And here's the two-bedroom cottage," Mads continued, pulling three key cards from her pocket and handing them to AJ. "Make yourselves at home and call me if you need anything. My card is with the welcome folder inside."

"Thank you," AJ enthused, handing keys to Jackson and

Thomas. "I read about a distillery tour on your website. Can we do that at some point?"

Mads smiled. "The tour is all part of the package, but we have something a little special for you guys."

Reg leaned in a bit closer, keen to hear this part.

"Our head distiller, Walker, will personally give you your tour, but before that, we have a unique dive planned for you. Something only staff members get to experience. I'll explain a little more at dinner tonight."

Thomas dragged his bag from the luggage cart as the bellboy hurried around to help him.

"No problem, man, I got this," Thomas assured the man and strode to the door of the cottage.

"Somebody's ready for food," AJ laughed. "Thank you, Mads. We'll get settled in and perhaps you can join us for lunch?"

"I would love to if I'm not intruding?" she replied.

"Of course not," Pearl assured her. "We want to hear all about this place."

"Are you a diver?" Jackson asked as he slid his and AJ's bags from the cart.

"I am," Mads answered. "Not to the level of you guys, but it would be sad to live here and not dive, right?"

"It would be," Jackson agreed. "Maybe you can come out with us while we're here. I'm sure you can show us the cool spots."

Mads laughed. "Walk down the pier, jump in, and swim anywhere you like. It's all amazing and so close to shore."

"Can we shore dive the wall?" AJ asked.

"You certainly can," Mads replied. "It's a little under a quarter of a mile out there, but there's plenty of mooring balls and only a few dive operators on the island, so I'd take the boat and save yourself the swim."

"We're excited to see it again, so I'm sure we'll go out this afternoon," AJ said, grinning at Reg.

"Why you looking at me?" Reg countered, chuckling behind his shaggy beard. "It's your bloody boat."

"True," AJ declared. "What I mean is, we're going diving this afternoon, so why don't you join us?"

"I'd love to, but I do have to work, I'm afraid," Mads replied. "We're expecting our supply boat this evening and I know the guys at the distillery are behind on the shipment. They had some trouble with the label machine or something I don't really understand."

Thomas reappeared from the room, having changed from his board shorts into cargo shorts and a collared shirt.

"Bloody hell, Thomas," Reg laughed. "I thought it took a wedding or a funeral to get you spruced up."

"Nah, just a pretty lady and an offer of lunch," AJ said, and elbowed Thomas as she headed into the cottage.

Thomas looked around awkwardly and blushed. "I thought I should make an effort, this place being so nice and all."

AJ and Jackson threw their bags onto the king-sized bed in one of the bedrooms and looked around, admiring the rustic island theme. Rather than the standard floral prints and bamboo furniture of most island hotels, the rooms were furnished with richly coloured solid wood pieces and hand-painted murals on the walls. Only one framed picture hung on the wall. A photograph of a bottle of rum atop a wooden barrel with a glass of amber liquid next to it, and stacks of barrels in the background, all marked 'BBRC'.

They splashed some water around their faces and quickly changed from their salty travel clothes. They had both packed light, far more concerned with practical comfort than fashion statements. AJ wore cotton shorts and a thin, blue, long-sleeved hooded Mermaid Divers tee-shirt, and Jackson decided on plain dark-grey board shorts and a black Sea Sentry golf shirt. A reminder of the non-profit marine conservation organisation he spent several years working for.

AJ slipped her Rolex Submariner back on her wrist, an extravagant 30th birthday gift from her family and friends, and pulled the privacy curtain back on the bedroom window. Thomas was outside, pacing around impatiently, which made her smile.

Every window in the cottage faced the ocean, and each building angled to give the occupants an unobstructed view of the sparkling blue water. AJ's tiny cottage in the grounds of a large holiday home overlooking Seven Mile Beach had a magnificent view itself, which she marvelled over every day. Sometimes she felt like pinching herself. Growing up in the rolling countryside of Sussex, England, the life she had built for herself in the Caribbean was a far cry from her childhood. It had taken one family holiday to Grand Cayman, back when she was a teenager still in school, to forge her love of diving and seal her connection with the Caymans. That first experience underwater, in the capable hands of Reg Moore and his then fledgling dive operation, Pearl Divers, was forever tattooed in her memory. She never could have guessed, sixteen years later, she would be sharing the same idyllic existence.

"Ready?" Jackson asked, standing by the door to the living area.

AJ tore herself away from the window and smiled at the man she had fallen completely in love with. He was another part of her life she had begun to think would never happen. She walked over and threw her arms around his neck, planting a soft kiss on his lips.

"I'm very ready," she whispered.

5

WEDNESDAY

The 102-foot catamaran had been specifically built for carrying a hefty payload across the open ocean at a decent clip. To accomplish that goal, the vessel needed to be light, buoyant, and powerful. Broadening each hull from Austal's standard design helped the buoyancy. The two 1450-horsepower Caterpillar diesels took care of the power, and a lean, no-frills construction kept the vessel's weight down to a minimum. The only structures above the deck were the pilothouse, crane, and the two engine cowls. Each hull housed the motors themselves, fresh water, grey and black water tanks, and the berths. The massive pair of 4,000-gallon diesel tank systems were a unique long, low design, built into the deck above the hulls and partway across the cargo deck structure. They were actually a series of bladders between the lateral I-beam supports, linked by lines and pumps. Collector tanks in the engine room assured the fuel made it to the motors without interruption, even when the huge bladders were nearing empty. Stairs led from the rear corners of the pilothouse down to the living quarters in the hulls, and a second set of enclosed stairs led from the deck to the port side hull.

Connery's stateroom and the galley took up the starboard hull living space, and the port side housed four narrow berths, a shared shower and head towards the bow, and a storage locker between the sleeping area and the engine. Each berth was accessed through a sliding door, contained a single cot, sink and hanging locker. A small porthole made the space feel a little less like a cell; they were tight quarters, but at least each person had their own space and the extra berth was used for storage.

Connery quietly slid the door open to berth four, nearest the bow, stepped inside and closed the door behind him. He looked around the tiny room and noticed Mason had already unpacked and stowed his gear. His kit bag was under the cot and his toiletries were secured in the rack by the sink. The Irishman opened the locker and thumbed through the neatly hanging clothes, sorted in order by garment type, shirts first, trousers farther back. A pair of deck boots and a pair of trainers were on the floor of the locker above two built-in drawers. The boots would be worn while they loaded and unloaded in port, the trainers would have no use on the boat and would only be worn if the crew went ashore. Connery slid his hand inside one of the trainers and found what he'd hoped wouldn't be there.

As he exited the berth, Dunno poked his head from his door and stared blankly at his boss. The Jamaican liked to keep himself to himself, but Connery knew he would be curious why the berths were being searched.

"Wait ten minutes, then roust up Jay-P and meet me in the pilot-house," he instructed and Dunno nodded before ducking back inside his door.

Connery went back up the stairs, across the back of the pilot-house, and down the other stairs to the starboard hull. He walked through the galley to his stateroom, unlocked his door, and went inside. Without the need for a passageway, his berth was the full 7-foot width of the hull and spacious compared to the crew's quarters. A small dinette functioned as a desk with a storage cabinet against the dividing wall to the berth where his full-sized cot and wardrobe led to a private shower and head.

He took a stubby Phillips-head screwdriver from a drawer

under the locker and reached into the top corner of the wardrobe. Turning a large screw head one quarter turn released the lock on the light fixture above the sink on the other side of the wall to the head. Connery stepped around the dividing wall and lifted the three-bulb fixture which hinged at the top to reveal a hidden compartment. He took out a Smith & Wesson M&P 9mm handgun, tucked it in the rear waistband of his trousers and let his shirt fall over the weapon.

Mason sat in the helm seat, reading a book with the boat on autopilot. He glanced up as Connery sat in the second helm seat, then returned to the novel. Connery could only see the back cover, but it looked like a thriller of some sort. He pulled a brown paper bag from the cargo pocket of his trousers and tossed it onto the console where it landed with a dull thud. Mason looked up and visibly tensed. Connery said nothing, and the young Californian returned to his book, but was no longer reading the words on the page. The next few minutes ground by in awkward silence until the sounds of movement came from below and the other two crew members came up the stairs. They stood at the back of the pilothouse and waited for their boss to explain what was going on.

Connery pointed to the brown paper bag. "How about you open that, Mason. Show the lads for me."

Mason closed his book and put it down, turning to look at his boss. Connery could see the fear in his eyes.

"What is it?" Mason said, but his voice couldn't summon any conviction for the lie.

Connery stared at him coldly. "Don't belittle yourself with that bullshit, lad. I just pulled it from your kit."

Mason nodded, and his hand was shaking as he reached out and picked up the bag. He reluctantly opened it and took out two clear plastic bags and placed them back on the console. Each bag contained 500 grams of cocaine.

"I can explain this, dude, it's not what it seems," Mason said, shifting nervously in his seat.

"You can, huh?" Connery replied calmly. "You have an explanation as to how you brought drugs aboard my boat, knowing the rules? I'm all ears, lad, let's hear it."

Connery heard someone fidgeting behind him and knew it was Jay-P. The kid would be loving the drama unfolding and likely wanted to see blood. Some people could operate around violence and handle themselves when faced with violent situations, such as well-trained soldiers like himself. Then there were people who enjoyed violence and soaked up the pain of others, relishing another's anguish and suffering. Jay-P would have clamoured for a front-row seat in the Roman Coliseum.

"I'm sorry, Boss," Mason started. "This dude in Jamaica promised me a huge score on a kilo. It was too good to turn down, man," he said, as though he'd hardly had a choice. "I figured one run wouldn't do no harm, man. I'm sorry, Connery. I know I screwed up, but I swear it'll never happen again."

Connery took a deep breath and thought a moment. Four years he had put into this guy. Four years of training, teaching and mentoring, yet he still broke the rules. He had begun to think of Mason like a son he'd never had, and now his anger was only surpassed by his disappointment. Not that he let any of it show, and he continued to stare coldly at the young man. The final straw was the lie. This wasn't the first time. Two trips ago, Connery had become suspicious of something going on in Jamaica and found a stash of cash in Mason's berth. Last trip he found the coke on the way out and followed the kid to his meet with the dealer. He had hoped in some optimistic way that Mason would figure out to stop himself, but of course he didn't. Or couldn't. Once that cash flowed, it was hard to turn a back to it. So here they were, a basic rule had been broken, and now they would both suffer the consequences.

"This was at least the third run," Connery said solemnly.

Mason started to defend himself but stopped, "But I..." He hung his head and his breathing quickened to short pants.

"Put those bags in your pockets, lad, and let's go outside," Connery said as he stood.

"Coño, let's do this, man," Jay-P exclaimed, and swung the door open.

Connery ignored him and watched Mason slowly rise from the captain's chair and shove the bags of cocaine in his shorts pockets. They both walked across the pilothouse and out of the door, past the grinning Cuban. The salt air whipped around them as the Rum Chaser continued on its trek across the Gulf Stream, and the hot mid-morning sun made them all sweat.

"It don't need to be this way. Connery, you know me, dude," Mason pleaded. "I know I screwed up but I'll make this shit up to you, man."

Connery nodded towards the stern and Jay-P gleefully shoved Mason across the deck.

"Lay another finger on him and you'll be swimming home, you little shit," Connery growled and Jay-P quickly lost his grin.

Dunno followed along but kept his distance and Mason stopped at the gap in the stern railing where the ladder hung down towards the water. The lower section of the ladder was folded up and locked in place so it didn't drag in the water while the boat was running, and a safety line was strung across the gap. Mason looked back at Connery, who stepped around him and unclipped the safety line, letting it drop to the deck.

The Irishman stood close to his protege and spoke quietly, close to his ear. "You're gonna want to fight this, lad, you'll try and hang on, but there's no point." He rested a hand on the young man's shoulder and felt his body trembling. "This is the end of the line on this go-around. Let it happen."

Mason's voice was broken and shaky. "I'm sorry, Connery," he managed weakly. "You deserved better from me."

"I don't deserve shit, kid," Connery replied. "But I'll see you on the other side one day, and I'll be looking forward to it."

Mason nodded and Connery took his hand away as the young man took one step and dropped to the ocean below. The current immediately swept him away to the north as the Rum Chaser continued ploughing east across the Gulf Stream.

"What the hell, man," Jay-P yelled. "Why didn't you blow his brains out? What if a boat finds him or some…?"

Connery had Jay-P pinned to the railing before he could finish his sentence, his legs shoved wide and his arms over the top rail before he could grab a hold of it. Connery's left forearm shoved the Cuban's neck over the stern and the 9mm was leaving an indent in the back of his scalp.

"You want to see some brains in the water, you worthless piece of shit?" Connery snarled as the kid flexed his muscles and fought to get free without success. "What putrid muck you have instead of good sense will be floating before your eyes if you don't learn to keep your mouth shut."

He pushed Jay-P's head down harder with the barrel of the Smith & Wesson to a groaning response.

"Wait till Castillo hears about this, man," Jay-P squirmed. "He ain't gonna be happy."

Connery laughed. "That's funny, 'cos Dayán told me if I couldn't straighten you out then I should toss you over the side and let the sharks have you."

He felt the fight go out of the kid and he let him go, stepping back, tucking the gun back in his waistband and looking out across the water. All Connery could see was endless swells of deep blue leading to a clear sky dotted with wispy white clouds. He turned and walked towards the pilothouse, glancing up at Dunno as he passed by.

"You've just been promoted to first mate."

Dunno nodded, never changing his stern expression, and dropped in step behind his boss.

6

FRIDAY

Pearl walked to the end of the dock with the other four to see them off. She was skipping the afternoon dive in favour of preparing for her first evening performance. They all moved a little slowly, full from their incredible lunch. The special was fish tacos made with that morning's fresh catch of hogfish, which suited AJ, who had been a pescatarian since she was young. For Jackson, the vegetarian in the group, the chef prepared breadfruit tacos filled with roasted veggies and a mango salsa. The starchy Caribbean fruit was thinly sliced, boiled in salt water, then fried to form the crispy shells. AJ stole one of those from him too. Thomas ate everything placed within his reach.

The restaurant was busy with current guests, along with several groups of visitors from other resorts, and a handful of local residents. According to Mads, the evening would be packed to capacity with the promise of new entertainment in town.

They cast off the lines and AJ reversed Hazel's Odyssey away from the pier until the depth showed 5 feet, then spun the boat around and pointed the bow towards the open ocean.

"Where to, Reg?" she asked.

Reg shrugged his shoulders. "From memory, every site along here is incredible."

AJ picked up her Reef Smart waterproof dive map for Little Cayman and studied the sites in Bloody Bay.

"Thomas and Jackson haven't been here before," she thought aloud. "So we should give them the ultimate Bloody Bay Wall experience to kick off the trip, don't you think?"

Reg nodded. "I reckon that sounds good."

AJ steered the Newton slightly to starboard, aiming directly north, and eased into the throttles. They glided smoothly over the calm sea and within a few minutes she coasted towards a Cayman Islands Department of Environment buoy marking a dive site. Thomas was ready with the gaff and hooked the mooring line that drifted lazily in the water from the buoy. Looping the boat line through the eye of the mooring rope, he secured it to a cleat on the bow and made sure the line lay in the chock as he dropped it over the side. As AJ shut the motors down, Hazel's Odyssey settled against its tether in the soft, easy swells.

"Right then," she announced, scampering down the ladder to the deck, "we're on Great Wall West. Well, I'm pretty sure we are, but we could be on East. Either way, I promise you this will be a breathtaking dive."

As they were recreational diving without paying customers, they weren't required to leave anyone aboard the vessel, so everyone eagerly geared up. They had brought their tank racks full of nitrox tanks, a blend of breathing gas with a higher percentage of oxygen versus nitrogen. To equalise against the increased surrounding water pressure at depth, their regulators delivered much higher volumes of gas than normal breathing at sea level. The body dealt with dissolved nitrogen by dispersing it through tissues via the bloodstream, but the onslaught of much higher levels pushed the tissues towards saturation, limiting dive times when going deeper. Using a higher percentage of oxygen slowed the nitrogen accumulation and allowed the diver to stay down longer before going into 'deco' – the slang term used to reference the saturation point, requiring a series of timed stops at shallower depths to safely 'off-gas' before surfacing. In recreational diving, the rule was to always stay within 'no deco' limits and their dive computers constantly monitored their depth and time to alert them of their progress.

"Okay, if everyone's ready, let's go," AJ announced, looking around to make sure they were all prepared. "Should be around 25 feet deep under the mooring," she grinned, "and then we'll move north and it'll get a lot deeper, really quickly."

They shuffled to the swim step at the open transom and one by one each took a giant stride into the clear, warm water. Looking down from the surface, the reef below was alive with movement and colour. They descended and after making sure everyone was comfortable, AJ finned towards the deep blue expanse of open ocean.

The transition from the shallow reef to the drop-off was immediate and dramatic. On land, it would be considered a sheer cliff, which is exactly what it was, only submerged. One moment they were cruising across the reef at 25 feet and next they were staring down a coral-encrusted wall that plummeted vertically away hundreds of feet below them, beyond visibility. Thomas and Jackson were wide eyed behind their masks. Descending the face gave them an even more impressive perspective. Looking back up, the side of the mountain abruptly ended in the brighter water above them, yet all around, to the sides and below, all they could see was the massive face. Reg and AJ had experienced the awe-inspiring sight before, and still they were dumbstruck all over again.

They levelled off at 100 feet and gently finned east. Large barrel and tube sponges grew straight out from the wall in search of sunlight from above, interspersed with radiant sea fans fighting for their own UV rays. The usual assortment of fish flitted along the face from one recess to the next coral outcrop, and the antennae of an occasional lobster probed the water from their hidey-holes.

AJ turned with her back to the wall and gazed out into the

Caribbean Sea, a pale, translucent blue near the surface, slowly deepening to the blackness of the depths far below them. Specks of reflected light revealed the movement of larger ocean fish in the distance, perhaps ocean triggers, permits, or jacks. It was hard to tell. She sensed Jackson beside her and turned to face him. He held a thumb to his chin, then swiped his fingers in a circular motion in front of his face, using sign language for beautiful. AJ smiled and returned an okay sign, her mask leaking at the edges from her cheeks creasing as she beamed. It dawned on her that this was the first trip they had taken anywhere together. Before he moved to Grand Cayman, it had always been quick visits when his Sea Sentry boat passed through on its way somewhere else. Since he had been living with her, travel outside the islands had been restricted, but the sister islands weren't a problem. She looked forward to meeting his family and visiting Northern California's Bay Area where he grew up. But for now, their little jaunt felt like a wonderful way to spend their first holiday together.

They spent twenty minutes at depth before the group began to ascend in a gentle angle while still heading east. A clumsy green sea turtle with its smooth, exquisitely patterned shell clung to a huge barrel sponge and crunched off pieces with its powerful beak, entertaining the divers for several minutes. Eventually, they reached the corner of the drop-off at 25 feet, which was just as acute as where they had begun. AJ turned and led them west, back towards the boat at a slow, leisurely pace, taking their time exploring on the way. For a big man, Reg was effortlessly graceful underwater and seemed to move with almost no effort at all. His size meant more fuel to keep his engine running, so he would always use more breathing gas than a similarly skilled diver of a smaller build. He made up for it by making minimal, efficient movements, keeping his heart rate at a Zen-like crawl. Jackson lived every moment of life in a Zen-like state of chill, so he was no different diving, soaking up the gorgeous environment and enjoying every second. Thomas was more of a golden retriever. He tended to dart from one exciting discovery to the next, eager to show everyone something that would bring a smile to their face. Fortunately, he was in great shape, so his energetic exertions were all carried out with a minimum of effort, but he was still the first one to go through the gas in his tank.

They spent the final part of the dive near the boat, staying above 20-feet depth to off-gas some of the nitrogen build-up in their systems. When Thomas reached 500psi in his tank, they ascended to the ladder and climbed back aboard.

"That was a stunning dive site," Jackson enthused as he shed his gear. "Everything you hear about Bloody Bay Wall still doesn't prepare you for how immense it is, and how sheer the drop-off just falls away."

"Dat was amazing," Thomas agreed, still too excited to take off his BCD, the vest divers used to carry the tank. "We don't have a place quite like that at home."

AJ couldn't stop smiling. "Glad you enjoyed it," she said, sliding out of her gear. "Neptune's Wall is vertical like that but it starts from a gently sloping reef down to 70 feet before it drops away. The square edge at 25 feet here is what makes it so overwhelming."

"That section we just dived is the really spectacular part," Reg added. "When we go farther east or west the wall slopes a bit more and the reef leading to the drop-off is deeper and broken up with canyons and cuts. Much more like back home."

"I figured we start with the mind-blowing dive before we did the simply epic stuff," AJ laughed.

"I wonder what Mads has in store for us tomorrow, den?" Thomas mused. "I hope we didn't just dive her special treat already."

"I reckon I know what she has in store," Reg replied, "and I'm guessing it's a bit farther along the coast from here."

"What is it then?" AJ asked.

"Didn't you go to their fancy website and read all about their rum?" Reg queried by way of a reply.

Thomas shrugged his shoulders. "I don't drink, so I didn't see much point," Thomas laughed.

"I looked at the resort bit and the virtual tour of the cottages," AJ said. "I figured we'd do the tour and learn about the rum part."

Reg looked at Jackson, who grinned. "Yeah, I checked it out and my guess would be the same as what I'm certain yours is."

Reg nodded and turned away, dropping his rig into an empty tank holder, saying nothing.

"Well?" AJ blurted, looking between the two men. "What is it?"

Reg's broad shoulders shook and she could tell he was laughing to himself. "You miserable old goat!" she shouted at him. "You can't tease us like that then keep it to yourself."

"I can't now?" he replied, turning around with his beard and scruffy hair dripping water everywhere, shaking from his laugh. "And yet I think I will. I'd hate to spoil Miss Mads's lovely surprise."

AJ whipped around and stared at Jackson. "You better tell me, or you'll pay for it, mister."

Jackson just grinned. "I'm with Reg on this one, be rude to ruin the surprise."

"What!" she said, throwing her hands in the air. "I'll get the info out of you, Yank, just wait till I get you back to the room."

Thomas roared with laughter and covered his ears. "Come on now, Boss, I can't be hearing such things about the lady I work for."

Reg kept chuckling behind his beard and Jackson went from a grin to a big smile. "I think I might enjoy this interrogation."

AJ turned bright red and stomped up the ladder. "That's not what I meant."

"We not doing another dive?" Reg managed to say between laughs.

"Hell no," AJ yelled down. "I'm taking you two buggers back to the dock, then my good friend Thomas and I are heading to the bar so I can have a drink, and he can get something to eat."

"I like that plan," Thomas said, rushing to the bow to release them from the mooring.

7

FRIDAY AM

The run to Montego Bay, Jamaica dragged on for Connery. Once they had cleared the Gulf Stream, he and Dunno had traded shifts as he would have done with Mason. Wednesday ebbed into night, and Thursday crawled from daybreak to sunset. Moving the duffel bags from their hiding place to where they could be unloaded was their only task beyond piloting the boat. Each four-hour spell at the helm felt like an eternity, rolling on through the open ocean, but less than four hours made it tough for the other person to get any meaningful rest. Not that Connery was resting much anyway. He lay awake, tossing and turning in his berth, unable to put Wednesday's events behind him. He knew he had done what he had to do. It was expected in the circumstances, but nevertheless it haunted him.

Connery had joined the British army at nineteen years of age. A strange choice for an Irishman raised on the streets of Londonderry, especially in the late 80s when unrest in Northern Ireland was still dominating the headlines. Growing up poor, Connery learnt to fight for all he could get, and hang on to what little he had. Smaller than kids his own age, his speed, determination, and above all his smarts, were what kept him in one piece. He built a reputation as someone to avoid tangling with, and it wasn't long before men with IRA connections came recruiting. Connery had no interest in politics, and less interest in going up against the might of the British empire. It seemed like a battle that couldn't be won, and dying or being jailed for life as a hero to a portion of the Irish people was even less appealing. The impoverished streets of Northern Ireland were tense and violent, without an end in sight. He could be a big fish in a little cesspool, or he could find a way to get out.

Signing up for the army was the last thing his family expected. His father refused to speak to him and his mother had no idea how to balance her love for her son with the vitriol spat her way by neighbours and friends. She cried, gathered his three siblings close to her, hugged her eldest son, and watched him leave. It would be twelve years before she set eyes on him again.

Connery found a home in the army. Once he had adjusted to being told what to do every minute of the day, he found the life was one in which he excelled. His wiry, lean build developed into a compact, muscular, coiled spring of controlled aggression. He could handle much larger men in hand-to-hand combat using his agility and focus. Once through basic training he applied to the Special Air Service, or SAS, the elite unit known as the toughest selection process for any branch of the military, worldwide. He survived five months of intense survival and skills testing and endurance training to be one of the 10% that are chosen to wear the coveted beige beret. A year later, Connery would be putting his training to work behind enemy lines in Iraq during the first Gulf War. For a dozen more years, conflict, suffering and death became a constant companion, through multiple deployments to Bosnia, Kosovo and Afghanistan.

In 2002, persuaded by a fellow 'Blade', Connery retired from the British military and joined a well-organised and connected group of 'security contractors', known as PS1. Since the 1989 International Convention made the use of mercenaries illegal, many countries, including the US and UK, found various ways and titles to define their continued use of hired soldiers. PS1 had contracts with the US government and Connery quickly found himself back in Afghanistan, marching to the beat of a different tune. If the mission was unpalatable for the regular forces, then PS1 was assigned the task. The conflict, suffering and death was notched up several levels.

The blood of countless humans stained the Irishman's hands. Not all his targets were men, or even soldiers, and many happened up close, where he saw the life drain from the victim's eyes. But over the years, Connery had found a way to place the memories of his actions into a vault, deep in his mind, that allowed him to sleep with ease. Why, after all the lives he had taken, a young surfer from Southern California, who had broken one of the few unbreakable rules, should keep him awake was puzzling and unnerving. Was it age? He had quit PS1 in 2008, not because he was tired or burnt out, but because he had enough money to do whatever he wanted. He left, feeling like he was still on top of his game, but with the odds of his survival decreasing with every mission, it made sense to walk away while he still could. At some point, no matter how skilled or how diligent he was, the surrounding violence would encompass him. He had watched so many of his fellow soldiers open the wrong door, step on the wrong piece of desert, or drive down the wrong dusty road. All the money he had accumulated was no use to him if he didn't stop and take the time to use it.

Two years later, after travelling the world, staying clear of deserts and conflicts, he found himself drifting, lost without purpose. For twenty years he had been told where to go and who to shoot and who to save. Now, with money and time to do as he pleased, he had no idea what to do with his days. Meeting Dayán Castillo changed all that.

It was dawn on Friday morning as all three men gathered in the pilothouse while Connery piloted Rum Chaser into the commercial docks next to the cruise ships' berths of Montego Bay. Dunno and

Jay-P headed out to the deck and threw lines over to several dock workers who tied them in. Connery shut the diesels down and surveyed the dock from the pilothouse. He could see the pallets of molasses totes neatly arranged in a marked-off area waiting to be loaded. He recognised one of the dock workers from previous trips, but not the second man. The fellow he knew was Jeremy, who was on their payroll. Part of Jeremy's job was to make sure his co-worker wouldn't cause them any trouble. Connery trusted the man was diligent in his duties.

Connery kept looking around while Dunno manned the crane mounted behind the pilothouse. It had its own diesel motor to run the hydraulics which rumbled into life, and Dunno waited for everything to warm up and build pressure. Their dock worker drove a forklift over and began moving one pallet at a time closer to the edge of the dock where the crane could pick them up and transfer them to the deck of the catamaran. Connery finally spotted the man he was looking for. Dressed in a uniform under a bullet-proof vest, the Jamaican Customs Contraband Enforcement Team agent casually strolled towards the forklift. Part of the country's border protection agency, the contraband group were a lot more interested in what came into Jamaica than what went out, but it was common for an agent to be present at the docks.

Jeremy stopped the forklift and reached a hand out to the agent, who gave him a friendly fist bump. Connery couldn't hear their exchange, but they were both laughing and waving their arms around enthusiastically as though recalling a funny story. Jeremy offered the man a cigarette, and they both took their time chatting and smoking while everyone else waited patiently. Finally, the agent slapped Jeremy on the shoulder and sauntered down the dock, away from the Rum Chaser. Connery stepped outside as the loading process began once more. Dunno used the crane to offload the stacks of empty pallets, setting them down on the dock near where Jeremy was lining up the heavy pallets laden with molasses.

The dense, sticky by-product of sugar production was shipped in 275-gallon bladders known as totes. Placed on a pallet with thick, industrial cardboard sides to contain each bag, they were then swathed in clear shrink-wrap to protect the contents from the elements. Each pallet was 4 feet square and exactly 102 of them fitted on the deck of the catamaran, with a few feet of walking space around the perimeter.

Bringing the first pallet aboard, Dunno carefully set it down at the forward location on the port side, right behind the door leading below deck, with Jay-P guiding him by hand signals. The next pallet he brought over he placed behind the first, starting a row down the port side. On the dock, Jeremy took a break from lining up cargo and used the forklift to carry the empty pallet stacks into a warehouse. He hustled quickly and efficiently to remove all ten stacks from the dock front while the second worker stood by and kept watch. Dunno and Jeremy worked steadily to bring all the molasses aboard, the last pallet craned over and set down directly in front of the crane itself. Dunno shut down the crane, leaving the forks under the final pallet.

"Stay up here," Connery said to Jay-P. "We'll only be a few minutes."

He nodded to Dunno to follow him and jumped the few feet from the catamaran to the dock, ignoring the sullen pout on Jay-P's face. Jeremy stepped down from the forklift and walked over to meet them.

"Where's this guy?" Connery asked without wasting time with salutations.

"Come with me," Jeremy replied, then turned and walked towards the warehouse, signalling for his co-worker to stay put and keep an eye out.

They strode across the large open concrete dock space and through a large roll-up door into the warehouse that seemed dark after the bright morning sunshine. A van was backed into the far side of the warehouse and several men were pulling apart the pallet stacks Jeremy had unloaded. They lifted off the first four on top of each stack then reached in and retrieved a black duffel bag before replacing the top four pallets once more. The duffel bags were loaded into the van and hidden beneath large cream-coloured laundry sacks. By the time the three men had reached the van, the process was complete, and the doors were closed.

Jeremy looked at one of the men from the van, who nodded to a dark corner of the warehouse. Connery spotted a figure lying on the floor, tied at his hands and feet and with a hood over his head.

"You sure that's the guy?" Connery asked.

Jeremy shrugged his shoulders. "They says he is. I know he's a local dealer, man. He bin around for years, dis one."

Connery sighed and thought of Mason stepping from the stern of the Rum Chaser in the middle of the Gulf Stream. It was unlikely his body would ever be found, but if it was, it would match the missing persons filed in Miami Wednesday morning. An unfortunate boating accident while out fishing. Before him was the man that had promised Mason a lure rich enough to cross the line that had cost the kid his life. Part of him wanted to make the drug dealer suffer for the length of time he guessed it took Mason to succumb to the waves. He was trained in horrific ways to make other humans confess their deepest secrets, but torturing this man wouldn't change anything. Mason was still gone.

Dunno slipped the knife from his boot and looked at Connery. The Irishman shook his head. Dunno put the knife away and stood back, understanding that this would be personal for his boss. Connery pulled the hood from the man's head to reveal someone older than he'd expected. The man blinked and tried to focus, grunting behind the duct tape across his mouth, his eyes darting around, assessing his options and no doubt attempting to plead for his life. There were no options. Connery straddled the man's chest, which brought the man's focus solely to him. Connery watched the fear, laced with a sprinkle of hope, evaporate into the realisation that these were his final moments. Connery clenched his jaw, set his hands around the drug dealer's throat and squeezed the man's future into oblivion.

8

FRIDAY

AJ sat at a table in the shade of the covered outdoor bar and restaurant area, overlooking the water. She sipped from a sweaty glass of a concoction from the menu she hadn't been able to resist, once the barman had told her they didn't have Strongbow cider. It was called a Scuba Libre and contained their signature Seven Fathoms rum, topped with cola and a twist of orange. In the hot, humid late afternoon, the cool drink tasted so refreshing she was tipping it down too quickly, and as a light drinker, the generous rum pour was already giving her a slight buzz. Thomas drank his cola and Reg had joined them after helping Pearl carry all her gear down, ready to set up on the little stage. Jackson sat next to AJ and he and Reg were tasting the rum neat, over a large, single ice cube. From their expressions, they were both enjoying their drinks.

"How was your diving?" Mads asked, walking up to their table.

"Hey," AJ replied, turning to face her, "it was mega. Ask these two, it was their first time here."

AJ looked at Jackson and Thomas, who both enthused about the dive.

"Got time to join us for a drink?" Reg asked.

Mads glanced at her watch, which AJ noticed was an elegant

Breitling Navitimer Chronograph 41 in stainless steel and red gold. Not a cheap timepiece.

"It's almost 5 o'clock, I guess I can knock off for a bit," she replied and Thomas pulled a seat out from the table for her.

"Do you keep set hours?" Jackson asked. "I would imagine it's variable in the hotel business."

Mads sat and thanked Thomas, who scowled at AJ for grinning at him knowingly.

"No, especially here where most of us live at the resort," Mads replied. "The hours are whatever it takes to get everything done. It's good and bad really. Good, in the fact we get to be flexible, and bad as we're never far away from the job."

"Do you live in one of the cottages?" AJ asked.

Mads laughed. "No, I wish. There's a handful of apartments in the back of the property where some of the staff live. They're nice, but small, and they don't have this view," she said, waving a hand at the sparkling blue water. "But then again, I get to enjoy this view every day anyway, so I'm not complaining."

The waiter stopped by and placed a drink in front of Mads before asking the rest of the table if they would like anything. Everyone politely declined, and he moved on to other customers. The patio was getting busier as folks arrived from their daytime excursions.

"Guess you're a regular here," AJ chuckled.

"And predictable, apparently," Mads laughed.

"Do you manage the distillery as well as all the resort stuff?" AJ asked. "Sorry for all the questions, but I'm fascinated by how this works. You know, a rum distillery tucked away on Little Cayman, with a resort attached."

"That's okay," the redhead smiled in return, and AJ noticed again how pretty the woman was. She had the fair complexion which came with her hair colour, but a light tan that she must have carefully encouraged and maintained. She wore very little make-up, and her hazel eyes exuded the kind of childish joy that made people smile for no reason they could pinpoint.

"I manage everything to do with the resort, which includes the cottages, restaurant and bar, plus any activities we run or facilitate for our guests," she explained. "Future plans include more guest cottages and a banquet room aimed at hosting retreats, presentations, launches and corporate events."

"And the distillery is separate?" Reg asked. "Who runs that?"

"Yup," she replied after sipping her drink. "The rum company is managed from Florida where the owner lives, and the distillery itself is run by a small group of experts headed by Walker, and then staffed with local labour. Between everything we do here, we provide around twenty to thirty jobs for locals, depending on the season."

"Thank you," Thomas said, the only one at the table born in the Cayman Islands.

"There's also a Caymanian co-owner, but he's a silent partner and I think that's to meet a government requirement for offshore ownership," Mads added. "I don't think I've met the fellow in the three years I've been here."

"I was going to ask how long this place has been open," Jackson enquired. "Obviously at least three years."

"Five years this summer," Mads explained. "But I joined them when the resort was built; before that it was just the distillery. It's been a progressive development with more to come, as I said. It's the expansion that really caught my interest," she said, looking out over the ocean again. "And living here, of course."

"While we're interrogating you," Reg said with a grin, "I have a question. Where does the sugar cane come from to make the rum? Can't be grown on the island here, right?"

"When you go through the tour tomorrow, our distiller, Walker, will explain the whole process, but the supply part I can tell you about, as it's a monthly routine around here," Mads said, taking a sip of her drink before continuing. "In fact, you may well see how it gets here tonight. Our boat is due in."

"Our boat?" Reg commented in surprise. "You have your own freighter?"

"We do, custom made for the purpose," Mads explained, "and it's on the way from Jamaica right now, with a deck full of molasses. It's not like a traditional tanker or cargo freighter, and its sole purpose is to run from Florida to Jamaica, pick up the raw materials and drop them here, before loading up with our export rum and taking it back to Florida for distribution."

"Bloody hell," Reg blurted. "I can't wait to see this thing. Where does it dock? No way it could pull up to your pier here, right? Too shallow."

"No, it goes to the commercial dock down the road that the barge from Grand Cayman uses," Mads replied. "It's deep enough there. But when I say 'commercial dock', what I mean is there's a small concrete pier with a narrow lane leading to it. It's our little island version of a port."

"I think I know where you mean," AJ nodded. "We passed it on our way. Maybe two miles west of here?"

"That'll be the international port of Little Cayman." Mads grinned.

"How big is this freighter of yours, then?" Reg asked, still sounding curious.

Mads shrugged her shoulders. "I've got no idea," she said, laughing. "It's much bigger than what you guys came here in, but it's not like those big container ships either. It has the two bits that go in the water, not just one big body like yours." She covered her face with her hands. "That all sounds incredibly rude!"

They all laughed with her.

"Well, you may have lost us there when you got into all the technical boat language," AJ recovered enough to say, "but I'm guessing you mean it's a catamaran with twin hulls, and I'm not sure what you think of Reg's body."

Pearl arrived as the table erupted into more laughter. "Blimey, leave you lot alone for five minutes and you turn into silly buggers," she said, smiling, "and what's this about my Reg's body? None of you lot need to worry about him, I'm the only one that gets to climb that mountain."

After another round of raucous laughter, the group finally settled down when Mads stood up and pointed out to the water. The sun was low in the western sky, causing sparkles of reflected light to dance across the turquoise water. Several hundred yards offshore, a silvery catamaran motored towards the sunset, and they all stared at the boat heading for the commercial dock.

"Incredible timing," Mads declared. "There it is now."

AJ couldn't take her eyes from the vessel. It was unlike any boat she had seen before. "Gotta be about a hundred foot long. What do you think, Reg?"

"I'd say," he replied, not taking his eyes from the water.

"Ever seen a boat like that before?" AJ asked.

"Not in person, but I read about a company based in Australia that builds boats for coastal law enforcement and military," Reg replied. "They also make offshore rig support vessels and I remember a picture of one similar looking to that."

"What's an offshore rig support vessel?" Jackson asked, "Like a supply ship for oil rigs?"

"Exactly," Reg said. "They have to move people back and forth all the time, as well as all the food and general supplies. I recall the Australian company built aluminium, high-speed vessels, and they looked a bit like this one."

They all sat down as the boat continued into the bright sun to the west.

"Usually, they take a few hours to unload and move the export aboard before they head straight out," Mads explained, "but I know there's a slight delay as I mentioned earlier, so you may get to meet the crew if they stay overnight. They'll probably come here for dinner."

"I wouldn't mind chatting with them," Reg commented. "Curious about that boat, I must say."

"How many crew are der?" Thomas asked. "Must be a few if dey normally sail through da night."

"Four," Mads said. "Been the same group for a while now. I'll introduce you if they come by later."

"Could we take a look at the boat?" AJ asked eagerly.

"That, I don't know," Mads replied carefully. "I'll ask the captain, but they stay on the boat so it's not something we've done before. Can't imagine why not though, if they're staying a day or so. Don't forget we're diving tomorrow morning. What time do you want to go out?"

Reg looked around the table. "We're all used to getting up early, so I don't think it matters to us."

Thomas frowned, AJ threw him an evil look and Pearl cleared her throat. "When he says it doesn't matter," Pearl corrected, "he means it doesn't matter what time you'd like to go after nine o'clock."

Mads smiled. "You're on vacation, well, some of you are," she replied, winking at Pearl. "Your tour is set for later in the morning at eleven, so if we leave at nine we'll easily be back by then."

"That sounds civilised enough," Reg said. "We can take our boat as all the gear's already aboard." He looked over at AJ, "Maybe we can sneak in a peek at the catamaran beforehand."

AJ groaned. "You're determined I'm not gonna get a lie-in, aren't you?"

"My mistake," Reg replied, throwing his hands up. "There was me thinking you were a real sea dog that wouldn't pass up a chance like that. But hey, if you're just a fair-weather sailor who was keen until she had to get up a little early in the morning, then the real mariners will go check it out, and we'll meet you on the dock at nine. You can have one of those nice fellows carry your beach towel down to the boat for you," he kept going, turning to Mads. "The bellboys would be kind enough to help the young lady out, I presume?"

The best thing AJ could come up with quickly was her twist of orange peel from her drink, which she flung across the table at Reg, who ignored it and belly laughed for over a minute.

9

FRIDAY

Connery squinted out of the front window of the pilothouse, the sun just above the horizon and dropping fast. He pulled up a saved number on his mobile phone and waited while it rang.

"Dis is Antoine," answered a man with a thick Caymanian accent.

"Evening Antoine, it's Connery, we're just pulling in now."

The man laughed. "Typical, you wait till I'm sitting down havin' tea wid my cousin, den you show up."

"Truth be told, mate," Connery replied, "we've been here for hours, but I sent one of the lads around and told him to call me as soon as you put a fork to your mouth."

The man roared with laughter and Connery had to hold the mobile away from his ear until he stopped.

"That doesn't surprise me," Antoine finally replied. "You're a devious Irishman, no fooling," he chuckled. "Can you hold up for an hour and I'll be there den?"

"You're killin' me, my friend," Connery said, laying it on thick. "Me and the lads have been at sea for three days straight. We were sure looking forward to a decent meal at the Rum Club. Why don't we do this," he continued. "We'll nip over to the resort, get us a proper meal and maybe a beverage or two. Bob's your uncle, we'll be back to the Chaser and stay on the boat like we always do. You come by about seven in the morning, and we'll do all the paperwork and get to unloading. How's that sound?"

The line was quiet for a few moments. "You know I'm not supposed to do dat, Connery, you can't be settin' foot on da island till I got you stamped in and what have you."

Connery stayed quiet and let the man think a moment.

"Tell you what," Antoine finally continued. "Me cousin have some fine coconut pie for dessert, and dat what make me decide, my friend," he laughed. "Best I know you tucked up tight on da boat till I get dere in da mornin', Connery. I'll get you all straightened out wid da papers den, alright?"

"Sounds perfect to me, Antoine," Connery replied. "Save me a slice of that pie and I'll see you at seven."

Laughter echoed from his mobile and Connery held it away again. "If you saw da faces staring at dis pie you'd know ain't gonna be no slices left by mornin'. Have a good night."

Connery smiled and ended the call. He put his mobile down and focused ahead on the small concrete dock nestled along the ironshore coastline. He kept the catamaran a hundred yards out until he was directly abeam of the dock, then turned hard to port and followed the natural channel of deeper water into the shore. Dunno and Jay-P were already at the starboard railing, both midships, with bow and stern lines in hand. Connery reversed the port engine and spun the wheel, gently rotating the big boat until the bow faced back out to sea and the catamaran drifted in against the dock, softly nudging its bumpers against the hard rubber edge bolted to the concrete dock. Dunno and Jay-P hopped off and Connery nudged the motors until the pilothouse was just past the end of the dock before they tied the lines to the bollards. The Rum Chaser was twice the length of Little Cayman's commercial dock, leaving the bow hung out into the sea and the stern overhanging towards the rugged ironshore.

Connery shut down the diesel engines, stepped from the pilothouse to the deck, and squeezed behind the crane to the starboard side railing.

"Alright, let's be quick about it, you two," he shouted to his crew. "Got us a good meal waiting."

Dunno scrambled back onto the boat and stood at the controls of the crane, firing up its motor. Jay-P came back aboard and disappeared down the steps below, returning a few minutes later with a large roll of industrial shrink-wrap and a cordless drill with a socket attached. The hydraulic pumps hummed and Dunno raised the forks, lifting the final pallet he had loaded straight up until it was clear of the others. Climbing up and hanging on the arms of the crane, Jay-P took a blade and sliced the plastic wrap, letting it fall away into Connery's hands, revealing the hefty cardboard which formed the tote.

Connery wished they could perform this task before docking, but even on the calmest seas, operating the crane was too much of a risk. Although they had never been disturbed in the past, he still kept a keen eye on the shore.

Dunno clambered up next to Jay-P, and taking the drill, began undoing a series of ¼" hex-head bolts in a vertical line by the corner of the tote. Connery stood below and caught each bolt as they came loose.

With all the bolts free, the cardboard hinged open to reveal the bladder containing the molasses. Except this tote had an aluminium frame in the lower half of the tote with a half-sized bladder sitting over it. Under the frame were black duffel bags, similar to the ones brought from Miami, which Connery began removing and handing to Dunno, who now stood behind the crane. He in turn passed them along to Jay-P who stacked them by the door to the stairwell. Within two minutes, all eight bags had been removed and the bolts replaced in the cardboard surround, which Connery had to shove hard against to push the bulging side of the bladder back in place. Jay-P climbed on top of the neighbouring tote and by passing the roll of shrink-wrap between them, the three men had the tote looking as though it had never been touched. Dunno lowered the crane forks back to the deck before shutting the motor down, letting a tranquil calm fall across the shoreline.

Connery dialled a number on his mobile and waited.

"Bloody Bay Rum Club and Resort, dis is Shawna, how may I help you?" came a young, female Caymanian voice.

"Shawna, it's Connery, have you been surviving without me, my dear?"

"Connery, welcome back," the woman replied gleefully. "Shall I send a golf cart?"

"You'd be a darlin' if you would," he replied.

He heard a muffled sound as he presumed she held her hand over the receiver and instructed one of the bellboys to come and get them.

"He's on his way, and no sneaking by straight to the bar," Shawna warned him. "You best come in and give me a hug."

"It's what I've been thinking about all day," he lied. "See you in a bit."

He finished the call and helped carry the last few duffel bags down to the port side hull passageway. Dunno already had the countersunk Allen-head bolts of a long overhead panel removed, and they laid the aluminium hatch to the side on the deck. Inside the hatch space was a black fuel cell bladder marked in white stencil with various standards and warnings. Dunno and Jay-P reached up and pulled firmly on the fuel cell, which came out of its slot and dropped into their arms. The two men lowered the bladder to the deck, liquid slurping inside, and one by one the three of them stuffed the duffel bags into an open space behind where the dummy fuel cell had been. Connery shoved the last duffel bag in place, stretching to reach inside the overhead opening, which was actually the deck structure. Beefy I-beam supports spanned the hulls and housed the real fuel cell bladders.

"Check they're all the way in," Connery said to Dunno, who was several inches taller with better reach from his long, lean arms.

Dunno shoved and nudged a few of the bags, then nodded his approval to Connery and picked up one end of the dummy fuel cell section. Water slurped inside the bladder as Dunno and Jay-P heaved the mass up into the opening, and with some effort, wriggled it back in place. Connery and Jay-P held the aluminium hatch panel over their heads in its machined recess while Dunno used the cordless drill to spin the bolts up and secure the panel.

Sweat dripped from each of the men as they put the drill and shrink-wrap roll away in a storage cabinet at the end of the passageway, then brushed themselves off.

"Alright, throw something presentable on and we'll leave in ten minutes, the golf cart is probably on the dock already," Connery said, and made a point of catching Jay-P's attention. "When I say something presentable, that means you wear clothes that normal people wear, not that daft shit with crap written all over it or them stupid colours, understand?"

Jay-P frowned and shook his head. "Ain't my fault you don't know what's in fashion these days, man," he mumbled.

"Fashion, my arse," Connery snapped. "We're not supposed to be seen, let alone stand out like a sore bloody thumb."

He left up the stairs to the pilothouse before Jay-P could protest anymore. He looked out the window towards the dock, which was bathed in an orange glow of the approaching sunset. A golf cart was just pulling in and Connery opened the door to the deck and stepped behind the crane.

"Hey mate," he yelled, "we'll just be a couple of minutes."

The man waved back, turned the golf cart around ready to leave and dug out his mobile to kill the time playing a game. Connery went back inside, down the steps and through the galley to his stateroom. Stripping off, he uncharacteristically tossed his work clothes on the bed and headed straight to the shower. One benefit of thinning hair and keeping his head shaved was cleaning up didn't involve any hair drying, preparation or maintenance. In three minutes he was washed and mostly dried, standing before his narrow wardrobe selecting a shirt. He settled on a long-sleeved, dark grey button-up, printed with a subtle darker grey paisley pattern. He hummed and hawed between jeans and a pair of black linen pants, settling on the lighter weight linen for the balmy evening. He slipped on his nicer pair of deck shoes and his straw fedora completed his outfit.

Connery stepped around the partition and looked into the mirror above the sink. Staring back at him was a man who was older than he felt inside. He shook his head and thoughts of years gone by flickered through his mind like a zoetrope stitching still moments in time together forming an animated picture. The movie was filled with dusty places, camouflaged clothing and people long buried in far-off lands.

He growled to himself and cursed, "Must be getting even older than you look, you dumb bastard. Enough of this sentimental bull-shit already."

Connery spun around and strode out of his stateroom, still berating himself. He paused at the bottom of the steps and took a few deep breaths. He softly closed his eyes and imagined he could see beyond his forehead to a source of light where the focus of both eyes met. Relaxing all the muscles in his face, he drew in a breath and smoothly exhaled in an even pattern, repeating the exercise until the function happened without his conscious thought. The chaotic mayhem of thoughts and images that bounced around his mind began to fall away until, finally, a vision of Mason stepping from the stern of the boat faded and a wave of release ran through him.

A fellow soldier had taught him the simple meditation in Afghanistan. The man's father was a Buddhist and his mother a nurse with the Red Cross. Connery never understood how a fellow from that background, who practised much of the peaceful teachings his parents had instilled in him, could engage in the violence they were surrounded by. After watching the man meditate every day for weeks in the tent they shared, Connery finally asked him to explain his process. He felt ridiculous and self-conscious at first, but after trying the methods for a while, in quiet moments alone, he found he could clear his mind and ease away some of the tension. After his friend was blown to pieces by an IED, Connery stopped meditating for years. After a particularly tough and violent mission in Iraq, he tried meditating again as a last resort to help him sleep through the nights. It did help, so he stuck with it.

Clanking feet on the metal steps from the other side of the boat shook Connery back to the present. He trotted up his stairs and met the other two in the pilothouse. He grinned when he saw Jay-P had managed to find a light blue sun shirt and a pair of royal blue cargo shorts. It was certainly toned down from most of his wardrobe. Dunno wore his usual nondescript jeans and a dark shirt. Connery figured Dunno was the perfect man for frustrating the police. No one could ever describe him. He had the unique ability of sliding by unnoticed in almost all situations. A sketch artist would be faced with a blank stare when the witness was asked to describe the man.

Feeling buoyed after his reflective moment, Connery led his reduced crew to the golf cart and took the seat next to the driver. He was looking forward to some fine cuisine after three long days at sea, and a glass of rum sounded good. But more than anything, he was hoping for company and pleasant conversation with a redhead that he thought about more than he'd like to admit.

10

FRIDAY

Pearl wrapped up her first set with Rod Stewart's 'Maggie May', her gritty, soulful voice bringing the packed crowd on the covered patio of the bar to their feet. Reg greeted her back at their table with a big hug and the others showered her with compliments as they all sat back down. Pearl blushed at the attention and waved them off.

"I can't thank you enough," Mads enthused. "We've never had the crowd this enthusiastic before."

Pearl laughed. "I had Reg pay them all before I started."

A waiter swooped in and began clearing the empty dinner plates and Mads put a hand on his arm, turning to Pearl. "Do you want something to eat now?" she asked. "We've all finished and you haven't had a chance yet."

Pearl thought for a moment. "Do you have something light? Maybe a salad would be good."

"The chef makes a marvellous tropical salad – it has mango, avocado and a lovely pineapple vinaigrette dressing," Mads replied.

"Perfect," Pearl said, and the waiter nodded.

Mads stood up and waved across the busy patio, and AJ looked up to see three men making their way to the bar at the back of the patio. The nicely dressed man in front waved back.

"That's the boat crew," Mads explained. "I'll introduce you to the captain."

The man said something to the other two before making his way towards their table, leaving his shipmates continuing to the bar. Mads stepped around the table and greeted the man with a hug.

"How was the trip?" AJ heard her ask.

"Smooth, we made good time," the man answered, and AJ detected an Irish accent.

Mads turned to the group. "Let me introduce everyone," she said, leaving a hand on the man's shoulder. "Connery O'Brien, this is Reg and Pearl Moore. Pearl is performing for us this weekend."

Connery reached out and shook Reg's hand as the big man stood up. "Pleased to meet you," Connery greeted them both.

Reg and Pearl shuffled down a seat to leave a chair open next to Mads as she continued introductions. "This is AJ, Jackson and Thomas. They're all over from Grand Cayman for the weekend. They made the trip on AJ's dive boat."

"Pleasure to make your acquaintance," Connery said, shaking hands with each in turn. "The Newton at the dock is yours?" he asked, looking at AJ.

"Yup, not really an offshore boat, but like you said the seas have been fair, so we thought it would be more fun than flying over," AJ replied. "I think we're all more interested in your boat, though. We watched it go by this evening."

They sat back down but Connery hesitated before taking his seat. "Are you sure I'm not intruding?" he asked.

"Not at all," Reg's booming voice came over the others, echoing the same sentiment. "We were hoping to get a chance to talk to you. Like AJ said, that boat of yours is pretty interesting."

Connery sat down. "Well thank you. Naturally, it's not my vessel, but I did have a hand in laying out the specs for it, and I've been the captain since we launched it."

"Hold up you lot," Pearl interrupted. "Before you bury the poor fellow in a million questions, how about we get the man a drink and I'm guessing he might be hungry?"

Reg and AJ both apologised and Connery insisted it was fine but Mads put her hand on his arm. "What would you like? I should have asked you already."

Connery laughed. "You're all too kind, but I have to say I'm a wee bit starved, so I would love whatever the fish special is."

"It's so good," AJ assured him, and Thomas waved from the other end of the table.

"I can second dat, I had it blackened, and it was delicious. Better than my Ma's, but don't tell her I said so."

Mads flagged down their waiter. "Could we get a fish special, please." She turned to Connery. "Blackened or grilled?"

"Sounds like I'd best get it blackened after that glowing review," he replied.

"Blackened fish special and a rum over ice, please," she said, turning back to the waiter.

"Anything else for the table?" the waiter asked.

Reg and Thomas both held their glasses up.

"Another rum over ice and a cola," the waiter confirmed. "I'll be right back."

As the waiter left, AJ noticed Reg looking at Connery and, following his eyes, spotted the tattoos just visible below his shirt sleeves.

"Military man?" Reg asked.

Connery paused a moment and smiled. "I was," he replied, glancing down at his exposed wrists. "Army, for a tour or two."

Reg nodded, and the men exchanged a look of respect. "Navy myself. Diver. Probably before your time though, mine was the Falklands."

"Gulf wars," Connery responded, "and a few other spots in between."

Reg smiled behind his thick beard. "Army the whole time?" he asked.

The corners of Connery's mouth turned into a slight grin. "Branches of."

Reg slowly nodded again, and he leaned back to let the waiter place the fresh drinks on the table. He picked up his glass and held it towards Connery. The Irishman raised his own glass, and they clinked them together.

"Cheers, brother," Reg said.

"Cheers, brother," Connery replied.

AJ looked at Mads and grinned. The whole table had fallen silent as they watched the two former warriors run through their sizing up of each other. She sensed a lot more had been assessed and communicated than the few words that were spoken.

"Okay, now you have to tell us all about your boat," AJ blurted.

Connery laughed, and AJ noticed it was a calm, relaxed and unforced amusement. Their group had known each other for a long time, and it pleased her to see how quickly and comfortably Mads, and now Connery, felt like they were among friends.

"Well, it started when our boss asked me how we could get the raw materials from Jamaica to Little Cayman, and then the rum from Little Cayman to Miami," Connery began, "which I replied to by asking him why he was choosing a remote island in the middle of the Caribbean with no commercial port and a tiny airport to build his distillery."

They all laughed, and Reg spoke up, "We were wondering the same thing. It does seem an odd choice to start an export business."

"Exactly," Connery agreed. "But he tells me it'll be on Little Cayman, or it won't be at all. He explained he had an opportunity to buy this incredible piece of land," he continued, waving a hand across the coastline where the lights from the bar twinkled on the water in the darkness. "And he wished to employ a unique method of ageing the rum, that wouldn't be available just anywhere. He went on to explain how he wanted to build the resort into a destination where the locally produced rum would be part of the experience."

"Wow," Mads said, smiling and nudging Connery. "You should be giving tours around here, you've got the spiel down."

Connery looked slightly embarrassed. "Sorry, I didn't mean it to sound like sales bullshit."

Mads put her hand to her chest and feigned offence. "Are you saying I'm full of bullshit?"

"Oh jeez." Connery shook his head. "I'm digging myself a hole here."

"The boat!" AJ dived in to help him. "This all started with you explaining about the boat."

Connery put his hands together as though he was praying to AJ. "Bless you, miss, the boat indeed."

Mads laughed. "Fine, insult me, but get back to telling them about the boat."

Connery and Mads shared a look and AJ smiled too. She couldn't tell if they were already romantically connected, but if they weren't, it was definitely in the works. He was quite a bit older than her, maybe ten years or a little more, she guessed, but they seemed a good fit together.

"So, anyway, that left me with the problem of figuring out how we could make all this shipping work," Connery continued, "as the boss was dead set on Little Cayman."

The waiter arrived again and placed food in front of Pearl and Connery, which she quickly tucked into and he ignored for the moment after thanking the man.

"The logistics were a bit complicated as we needed to look at the volume we expected to move, the time to sail the distances, and of course the cost involved. The first thing I tried was a commercial freighter service," he said and paused to look at the plate before him.

"But the problem was the dock here, right?" Reg commented. "You'd have to route everything through Grand Cayman and use the barge to get it to and from here."

"Let the man eat his bloody food, Reg," Pearl said, nudging her husband. "Poor bloke's starving."

"Yup," Reg apologised again. "Sorry mate, eat your food and we'll talk after."

"Thank you both," Connery replied, picking up his knife and fork. "If you don't mind me taking a bite or two, I'll promise not to talk with my mouth full."

He took a bite of the fish and savoured the taste, nodding at Thomas. "Good recommendation, thank you."

After another bite, he dabbed his lips with his napkin and set his silverware down. "You're correct, Reg, the barge was the only way and it added a lot of expense, but also a lot of time. That's when I first started looking at the possibility of shipping the stuff ourselves."

Connery picked up his fork and took another bite of his meal, slowly chewing and enjoying the kick of the spicy fish.

"Where did you find that boat?" Reg asked. "Is it an offshore rig supply vessel?"

Connery nodded and finished chewing his food before replying. "That's exactly what it's based on – good eye."

Reg beamed at AJ, who rolled her eyes. "Blind squirrel and all that."

"It came from a company called Austal, they're based in Australia, but they have several places around the world they build their boats, including America."

Reg chuckled and winked at AJ.

"He guessed that too," AJ said, shaking her head. "He'll be unbearable now."

Connery smiled. "Man knows his boats."

Pearl stood up and kissed Reg on the cheek. "Some of us have to go to work while you lot drink it up and blabber about boats." She grinned and started towards the little stage in the corner of the room.

"Knock 'em dead, love," Reg called after her before turning back to Connery.

"These Austal lot, do they make coastal defence and military boats too?"

"That's the company," Connery confirmed. "Even make small ferries and the supply boats. I was able to choose an existing hull design and then have them adjust a few things to suit us. We need a big flat deck for our load, so I chose a supply boat design and had them leave the passenger cabin off and slide the pilothouse forward. Picked the motors we wanted, which they guided us with, and then I sketched out the cabin space and they built it just like that."

"I bet that was cool, getting to design exactly what you wanted," Jackson chirped in having been listening intently.

"It was, I must say," Connery replied, picking up his fork again. "A bit nerve-wracking too, wondering if the multi-million-dollar boat you just spec'ed out for your boss will actually work."

"Any chance we could take a look at her?" Reg asked, keenly.

Connery chewed his food and thought for a moment.

"I did tell them I'd ask you if they could," Mads added. "I know we don't usually, but I figured it's because you're always in and out of here so quickly."

Connery looked at Mads and smiled. "Yeah, I suppose it would be okay."

The crowd cheered as Pearl's backing track played the saxophone intro to Bob Seger's 'Turn the Page'.

Reg shouted over the applause. "We could be there first thing in the morning?"

Connery nodded. "That would be fine. We have the customs guy coming at seven, so after that would be best. We're not really supposed to be on the island until he's stamped us in, so if you see him don't mention we met tonight."

Reg laughed. "No problem." He looked over at AJ and gave her a thumbs up.

"Fine," AJ mumbled, her shoulders slumping. "I'll go with you."

11

SATURDAY

AJ bounced along on the back seat of the golf cart as she and Reg were chauffeured to the Little Cayman commercial dock. The sun was rising before her alarm had gone off, so by the time she stepped outside the cottage at a few minutes before 7am, it didn't feel too early. On a regular day at home, she would have already been up for an hour, so it felt like a bit of a lie-in. Of course, she wouldn't let Reg know that.

The driver pulled off the narrow main road onto an even narrower single track towards the water. Ahead, the catamaran dwarfed the concrete pier which paralleled an indent in the ironshore coastline. Parked at the end of the road was a car and aboard the vessel, AJ could see Connery talking with a man in a customs uniform.

"Drop us off here, please," Reg instructed the driver. "We'll wait until they're done with the customs bloke."

"I can wait, no problem," the driver replied. "Dat way you have somewhere to sit while you wait."

He pulled over and stopped the golf cart well short of the parked car and AJ stared at the clear-coated aluminium finish of the big boat. Connery was laughing with the customs man and he looked up and waved. She and Reg waved back.

"Bet all that molasses must weigh a bit," Reg said. "Deck is packed with the stuff."

The customs man stood on the base of the crane to see across the cargo and pointed at each pallet as he appeared to count them. He wrote something on his clipboard, then smacked a stamp on the same page and handed a copy to Connery, along with several passports. At 7:12, the man stepped off the catamaran to the dock and nodded towards the golf cart on his way to his car.

"Come aboard," Connery shouted from the boat and AJ and Reg thanked the driver. After waiting for the customs inspector to drive past, they walked over to the boat.

"Morning," Reg said as they stepped through the gap in the railing.

"Welcome aboard the Rum Chaser," Connery greeted them.

"She's more impressive up close," AJ said, looking over the packed deck.

She recognised the two crew members from the night before, who now stood by the pilothouse. One looked younger and Hispanic, and leered at her with a smug grin that made her uncomfortable. The older dark-skinned man didn't look their way at all.

Connery glanced at his watch. "The truck will be here in about twenty minutes, so if you like I can give you a quick tour before then?"

"Lead the way," Reg replied, giving the Irishman a friendly slap on the shoulder.

Connery nodded to the two crewmen, who disappeared through a door and down a stairwell, the heavy metal door clanking closed behind them. Connery stepped towards the pilothouse door where there was a little more room for the three of them to stand. The loaded pallets came up to within a few feet of the crane and the extension off the back of the pilothouse, leaving a 6-foot by 9-foot space between them. The pallets were 4 feet high, neatly arranged, butted tightly together. AJ stood on her tippy-toes to see over the cargo.

"I suppose we can start here," Connery began. "As you can see, we're loaded full, and this is the molasses we picked up in Jamaica." He tapped the top of one of the shrink-wrapped boxes. "We call these totes. It's a basic wooden pallet with a large bladder full of the molasses. It's surrounded in heavyweight corrugated cardboard and banded to keep it secure, then wrapped in the shrink-wrap as you can see, to keep the elements out."

"What does each of these packages weigh?" Reg asked, "Got to be a hefty cargo on here."

"It is indeed," Connery acknowledged. "They weigh about 3200 lbs apiece. Each tote contains 275 gallons of molasses, and that stuff is dense. Best not to drop one on your toe."

Reg whistled. "No kidding."

"And this crane lifts them all on and off?" AJ asked, pointing to the deck-mounted device.

"That's right," Connery replied. "It runs off its own diesel motor to power the hydraulic pumps, and the crane is rated to 6,000 lbs at full extension. We had it built to precisely reach the back of the deck. The main arm telescopes out and you can see we use a pallet lifter hung from the hook. It travels under the last pallet loaded as there's no room to remove the forks. You'll see it in action once the truck gets here."

Connery opened the pilothouse door and held it for them to go inside. "The supply boat design had this cabin structure extend back to house the passenger section, which we didn't need, so we had them slide the pilothouse as far forward as we could and still have the stairs down to the berths," he said, letting the door close behind them and pointing to the steps in each rear corner of the room.

The back of the pilothouse was an open space between the stairs, and Connery pointed at two round receptacles in the floor. "There's a table we can mount here; we have used it for meals but found it's more in the way, so we took it out. Everyone grabs chow whenever it works for their shifts, anyway."

"How many crew do you have?" AJ asked.

"There's four of us," Connery said, moving forward to the helm.

"We saw the two chaps last night and this morning – you have one more?" she asked.

Connery paused and took a moment to respond. "Well, yes, our fourth didn't come on this trip. Just the three of us this time."

"Looks like you've got all the nav equipment you need," Reg said, looking over the array of instruments.

"Yes sir," Connery replied. "The usual radar, chart plotter navigation system and a pretty sophisticated autopilot with radar, weather and condition-triggered alarms."

After showing them the monitoring and control systems for the engines, Connery led them down the tight metal stairs to the passageway in the port side hull.

"Here are the crew berths, head and a storage room towards the stern," Connery explained, "and beyond that is the port motor. The storage room and some heavy insulation keep the sound down some, but as you can imagine, it's never quiet down here when we're at sea."

"Where are all the tanks on this thing?" AJ asked. "Being a catamaran I guess everything has to be in the hulls."

Connery pointed towards the bow. "Black and grey tanks are in the bottom of the hulls up front, a tank for both on each side. The freshwater holding tank is in the deck between the hulls and gravity feeds with on-demand heaters. Not that the heaters run much, the aluminium structure gets plenty warm in the sun and so the water comes out the cold tap hot enough to shower. We keep our ice maker busy. We do have a desalination system, but on our regular loop we don't need to use it."

"What about diesel?" Reg asked, looking up at access panels in the ceiling of the passageway.

"You're looking at them," Connery smiled. "We have almost 8,000 gallons capacity between all the cells. They're in two main sections running most of the length of the deck and 8 feet wide from halfway over each hull to over the first part of the decking," he said, pointing to the top corner of the passageway. "Running across the boat port to starboard are huge I-beam sections which take the weight of the cargo and tie the hulls together. The diesel tanks are between all the I-beams and we use a series of pumps and lines to connect them together. We can program which cells we pull from like they do on an aeroplane. That way we also manage our weight distribution."

"That sounds like quite a system," Reg commented.

AJ looked at the panels all snugly secured in place by a multitude of neatly countersunk bolts. It reminded her more of an aeroplane than a boat with the series of aluminium hatches. She noticed the screws in the one above her head appeared shinier and more worn than the others and wondered why this one saw more maintenance than the others.

"Does this one have all the pumps behind it or something?" she asked idly as Connery led them back to the stairs.

He turned back and frowned. "Which one do you mean?"

AJ pointed above her head. "This one. It looks like it gets used more."

Connery grinned. "Good eye. We take that one down for our monthly checks," he answered before continuing up the stairs.

The bright light of the morning streamed into the pilothouse after the dim and confined space of the hull, and AJ noticed a flatbed lorry pulling up to the dock.

"Stick your heads down the other side and you'll see the galley," Connery said, pointing to the stairs. "Beyond that is the captain's stateroom, which I'm not showing you as it's a bit of a mess right now," he added, laughing.

Reg went down the steps and had a quick look around while AJ stayed in the pilothouse. She doubted Connery's room would be untidy; he struck her as someone who liked everything in order. The pilothouse had been spotless, not a stray piece of paper or a personal item anywhere.

"Sorry to end the tour, but we have to start unloading," Connery explained. "We saw about everything there is to see, mind you. Rum Chaser is a simple boat really, with a handful of sophisticated systems keeping her running."

Reg trotted back up the stairs. "This was great; thank you for taking the time to show us around."

"Yeah, really interesting," AJ added. "This is a cool boat."

They made their way out to the deck and shuffled past the crane to the railing and stepped down to the dock. Behind them, AJ heard Connery call the resort and ask for the golf cart to come back. She looked at her watch; it was 7:45am and they were supposed to meet Mads at nine for their mystery dive. They would have enough time to grab some breakfast before then, and more importantly, coffee.

The diesel motor for the crane started, and she saw the older of the two crew members was manning the controls. She and Reg stepped back out of the way and the driver moved the lorry closer to the edge of the dock, ready for loading. The hydraulics of the crane groaned and the first pallet lifted swiftly into the air. Once clear of the others, the man rotated the crane and extended the arm until the pallet hung over the lorry. As the load was placed on the bed, the truck rocked and squatted slightly.

"Bet this will take a few runs to carry all this weight," Reg said as the crane arm swung back, the pallet lifter dangling from the hook.

The second crewman helped guide the forks of the lifter under the next pallet, and the hydraulics whirred again as the crane raised the pallet from the deck. This time the diesel motor noticeably laboured under the strain and the second pallet made the truck squat a lot more. The golf cart pulled up behind them, and Reg and AJ took their seats. Looking up at the boat, AJ waved to Connery, who briefly waved back, his brow furrowed. She wondered if they'd been a burden, holding up the crew's normal routine. The Irishman hadn't seemed as relaxed as the night before, but he was at work after all. Her mind drifted back to coffee as the golf cart motored far too slowly towards the resort.

12

SATURDAY

AJ and Jackson walked down the pier to Hazel's Odyssey to find Thomas had already warmed up the engines in preparation to leave.

"Thomas, you didn't have to get here early, you're on holiday too you know," AJ said as they stepped aboard.

He beamed back, "I had me enough breakfast for three people, so I needed something to get me away from dat buffet."

"The food is insane here," Jackson agreed. "The chef whipped me up an incredible omelette."

AJ looked up and Reg, Pearl and Mads were walking down the pier. Reg carried dive gear, decorated with pink accents, which she guessed must belong to Mads. Thomas took the gear from Reg as everyone greeted each other and came aboard.

AJ started up the ladder to the fly-bridge. "Okay Mads, where are we going?"

Mads followed her up. "Head east," she said and indicated towards the end of Bloody Bay where the land curved out to form a point. "That's Jackson's Point and we're going a little beyond that."

AJ laughed. "Hear that, Jackson?" she yelled down. "You have a point named after you."

"A valid statement, or a piece of land?" Jackson shouted up from the deck as he and Thomas cast off the lines.

AJ carefully reversed the Newton out towards deeper water, looking back over her shoulder. "Lump of old limestone by the look of it, but it's pretty at least," she said.

"So, you saying da man look pretty but have nuttin' to say?" Thomas laughed and slapped Jackson on the back.

AJ tried to stay focused as she spun the boat around but couldn't keep herself from laughing.

"You're a tough crowd," Mads chuckled.

With the bow pointed towards the deep blue of the drop-off, AJ eased away, picking the motors up only slightly above idle so the props didn't stir up the sand and turtle grass on the shallow bottom.

"We do like to rib each other," AJ grinned and glanced back, winking at Jackson, "and he is rather dishy."

"Oh, he's dishy alright," Mads added. "Seems pretty switched on too. He was telling me about Sea Sentry this morning at breakfast while you were checking out the Rum Chaser."

With 12 feet of water under them, AJ eased into the throttles and they were soon passing over the wall and the depth finder shot up to almost 1,000 feet. She kept going away from shore for another hundred yards before turning to starboard and aiming for Jackson's Point.

"Yeah, I feel a bit guilty as I'm probably the main reason he left Sea Sentry," AJ said, "and the work they do is so important. I know he misses it sometimes."

"He made the right decision," Mads replied. "You two are great together."

"Yeah, I kinda think so," AJ smiled. "I had a pretty good life, but everything's better with him around."

AJ looked over at Mads, her fiery hair blowing in the wind and her sunglasses hiding her expression, which AJ sensed held some sadness.

"What about you?" AJ asked. "Has to be difficult living in such a remote place. I'm assuming you're unattached as you haven't mentioned anyone."

"I am indeed unattached," Mads replied. "I wasn't when I moved here, but he decided not to come over as planned."

"I'm sorry," AJ said, feeling bad for bringing up what she guessed was a bad memory.

"That's okay. I thought he was the one, but by his decision he clearly wasn't, so better to move on," Mads replied, and AJ could tell she was forcing her optimistic tone. "So yeah, anything meaningful is pulling from a small pool of options around here."

They rode across the calm water for a few moments in silence before AJ spoke again, recalling the prior evening.

"Hey, what about Connery? You two had sparks flying everywhere last night. He seems like a nice guy."

Mads laughed. "Yeah, he's a great guy. Maybe a little old for me, but at thirty-seven my raising-a-family ambitions are probably in the rear view anyway."

"Age is what you make of it, right?" AJ said, "Ten years' difference when you're young seems like a huge gap, but as you get older, it has less meaning or consequence, I think."

"True," Mads agreed, "but I think it's more than ten years in this case, probably more like fifteen."

AJ shrugged her shoulders. "So?"

Mads laughed. "Okay, so the other problem is, he lives in Miami and swings by here for a day or two once a month. Hardly the basis of a steady relationship, even if he was interested."

"Oh, he's interested," AJ chuckled.

Mads nudged her. "Well, I know he's interested in that," she said, "but I don't want to start something frivolous with a co-worker – that can end badly."

"Have you asked him?" AJ probed.

"What? Whether he's okay rolling in the hay with a co-worker?" Mads laughed. "He's a man. Of course he is."

"No, silly," AJ clarified. "Ask him if he's interested in more than that."

Mads thought for a moment. "I suppose. I mean, I haven't asked him."

"Maybe you should," AJ added, "but for now, tell me where we're going next 'cos we're at Jackson's valid statement."

"Oh, right," Mads said, taking out her mobile phone and bringing up a map. "Sorry, I'm not allowed to give out the coordinates, so I have to guide us in. Okay, stay like you are offshore and keep going parallel with the beach. We're looking for the Central Caribbean Marine Institute building – it's just beyond that."

They both scanned the shoreline and Mads pointed to a beige two-storey waterfront building with a white metal roof a quarter of a mile away. "That's it," she said.

AJ stayed well clear of the shallow reef she could easily spot in the crystal-clear water and noticed the sandy bottom sloped far more gradually to where she had 60 feet underneath Hazel's Odyssey. A big difference from the abrupt wall by the resort. She looked to the north and could see the turquoise gradually turned an indigo blue where she presumed the underwater mountain fell away to the depths. They pushed on until Mads asked AJ to slow down, glancing between her mobile and the shoreline where they were now past the building.

"How deep are we here?" Mads asked.

"Fifty-four feet," AJ replied, looking at the depth finder.

"Okay, come down to idle and turn towards the open water," Mads instructed. "We're going to anchor in sixty-five-feet."

AJ swung the boat to port and called down. "Thomas, can you ready the anchor, please."

Thomas appeared at the bow and AJ watched her depth. "That's sixty-five."

Mads looked around and back at her phone hesitantly. "Sorry, it's a crappy way to do this, from a cellphone GPS; it's bouncing around a bit. Head a bit farther east. Sorry."

"No problem," AJ said and turned the boat, trying to keep it at sixty-five as she idled east.

"Okay. That's good," Mads said, and AJ nodded to Thomas who released the anchor, letting the rode play out as AJ put the boat in reverse to stop its forward motion. Once the anchor bit into the sand and the line came taught and held, AJ shut down the motors and everyone gathered on the deck.

"Okay," Mads started, "the coolest way to do this is to tell you nothing, and let's get in the water. When we come back up, I'll explain everything."

AJ looked at Reg and Jackson sharing a knowing glance, both grinning.

"Those two may have to stay on the boat," AJ said, pointing to them. "This secret boy's club crap is pissing me off."

Reg roared with laughter. "Keep your knickers on, Bailey, not our fault if we're smart enough to look at a website."

AJ stuck her tongue out and started gearing up. Mads grinned and shook her head and after a few minutes, they were all standing near the swim step at the stern.

"Might take me a minute to find what we're looking for as I can't guarantee I got us as close as I'd like," Mads explained, "but stay at around forty-feet and don't follow the sea floor as it keeps sloping deeper."

"We ready then?" AJ asked.

"Sure," Mads replied, and AJ shoved Reg off the back of the Newton.

The pale sandy sea floor reflected the light from the bright sun through the clear water, and it felt like AJ could see forever as she hung by the anchor line at forty feet. The group gathered and Mads pointed towards the deep blue to the north and they all followed as she finned that way. The bottom sloped away from them and AJ wondered where on earth they were heading as they finned towards the open ocean. Away from any reef, she saw fewer fish, but a stingray kicked up sand below them as it used its broad, grey wings to dig down in search of molluscs and crustaceans.

AJ looked up from the stingray and stared into the dark blue ahead. Something darker than the water caught her eye, but she couldn't make out what it was. As they finned farther, a large, unnaturally rectangular outline became clearer, floating in the middle of the ocean. With the lens effect of the water enlarging everything they could see, it appeared like a freight container suspended in the Caribbean Sea. And then she noticed there were more.

The divers all looked at each other with wide eyes through their masks as Mads continued towards the strange objects. As they neared, the details came into focus and AJ realised each mass had a hefty line running down towards the sea floor that was now too deep to see. The object was in fact a large platform with eighteen plastic barrels strapped securely on top, three wide and six along the side from which they approached. As she looked left and right AJ could see there were more platforms, all well spaced apart so, presumably, they wouldn't touch when rough seas swung them around.

Mads waved a hand and got everyone's attention, then tapped on one of the opaque plastic barrels. She took a slate hanging from her BCD and drew a quick sketch of the barrel, then drew another, smaller barrel inside and wrote the word "rum" on it. AJ gave her an okay sign, showing she understood the message. Reg was looking at her and she could tell he was grinning behind his regulator. She gave him a two-finger salute and a stream of bubbles shot out of his reg as he laughed.

Mads made a swaying motion with her hands, indicating the platforms all moved with the surge of the ocean, then pointed to the rum barrel she had drawn. Then she wrote '5 years' on the slate. AJ couldn't imagine these platforms had been down there for five whole years; they had a mild coating of algae growth and seemed far too clean. Mads extended two fingers and wiggled them to show a diver in the water, then rubbed a barrel with her hand, sending a light cloud of algae and sediment wafting around her. AJ guessed she meant they regularly sent a cleaning team down.

As Mads led them away from the barrels, AJ looked back at the ghostly platforms floating in the water. It was an eerie sight, but quite impressive. She looked at her dive computer, which showed they were at forty-two feet. Exactly seven fathoms.

13

SATURDAY

As the group popped their heads above water and could finally converse, they all babbled excitedly about the dive. Mads smiled and waited until everyone was back aboard before attempting to answer the barrage of questions. Once AJ and Thomas had slipped out of their gear, they retrieved towels from the cabin and handed them out.

Mads unzipped her wetsuit and pulled it down to her waist, releasing her vibrant curls from the ponytail she had used to control her locks during the dive.

"Okay," she started, trying to recall all the questions. "Yes, some of those barrels have been down there for five years now, ever since we produced our first batch. At seven years we'll bring them up and bottle them as our second production of aged rum. Some will stay down until they reach eleven years, and we slated a small quantity to remain in the water for twenty-one years."

"You said second run of aged rum?" Reg queried.

"Because the early production was lower quantities as they got the distillery up and running," Mads replied, "and we needed most of it for our regular production runs, they decided to wait, and pull three-year aged batches later, once we hit full output.

We're going to be bottling the first batch for next month's shipment."

"But why are they in the water in the first place?" Pearl asked, drying her hair with a towel. "That has to be a lot of work to set up and maintain."

"It is," Mads agreed, "But it's worth it. The platforms are tethered to the sea floor at around 300 feet. You saw the line from each one. The movement in the water promotes the ageing process and helps bring out even more flavour from the barrels. The rum itself is in smaller charred-oak barrels inside the bigger plastic ones. The rum draws colour and flavour from those barrels, but the agitation in the water column greatly enhances that process compared to sitting stationary in a rack while maturing. A racked barrel is rotated and moved every once in a while, but doesn't compare to our process."

"And of course, they're suspended at exactly seven fathoms," AJ said, giving Reg a punch on the arm.

"Finally, you're getting up to speed," Reg laughed.

"What about storms and hurricanes?" Jackson asked.

"That was certainly a concern," Mads replied, "but so far we've never had a problem. It's why they're tethered at 300 feet though. Deep enough that the anchorage is below the surge and the platforms at 42 feet tend to sway rather than getting thrown around from the wave action. We have them spaced well apart so they can't hit each other."

"And the air in the plastic barrels is what keeps the platforms afloat I assume," Jackson said.

"Partially," Mads replied. "The wooden barrels are a snug fit inside the plastic ones, so there's not enough air in them to keep the platform buoyant, so there's another flotation bladder that provides more lift. We set the pressure in the barrels above atmospheric before we put them in the water," Mads replied.

"Alright, love, you lost me there," Pearl said, wriggling out of her wetsuit.

"They had to explain it to me a few times too," Mads smiled.

"You put some pressure in them beforehand, right?" Reg said. "So they're equalised to the increased water pressure at seven fathoms."

"I figured you dive instructors would understand it better than I do," Mads laughed. "And then the bladder is used to control the descent until the platform is tethered; then it's pumped with air from the surface to make them buoyant. If they broke free, they'd float. Walker, our distiller, and really the brains behind this whole process, experimented for years with this method of ageing before he and the owner met. It's a big part of why Little Cayman was chosen, so we could put the platforms away from where divers might stumble across them."

AJ started up the ladder to the fly-bridge. "We should head back if we're going to clean-up before our tour, yeah?"

Thomas headed to the bow without a word spoken between him and AJ. After working together for so long, they each knew the other's moves, needs and procedures. They worked with perfect synchronisation like a finely tuned Swiss timepiece. Within a few minutes, the anchor was stowed, and they were on their way back to the resort.

The shower felt good, and AJ wished they had more time as she watched Jackson shower while she dried herself off. But they didn't. It was already 10:40am, and she had left her sunglasses on the boat. She threw on denim shorts and a Mermaid Divers tank top, slipped her flip-flops on her feet, and headed for the dock. Hazel's Odyssey bobbed in the calm waters on the lee side of the pier, and she stepped aboard to begin searching. She had spun the boat around this time, before they docked, so the bow faced the open water. She tried to remember when she last wore them and guessed it was on the way out to the dive site as she didn't recall having them on her face for the return. That meant she likely took them off once she had come down from the fly-bridge. She looked on the shelf by the front windows under the fly-bridge, but they weren't there. She looked in the racks behind the bench seats and found them on the port side. She inspected the lenses to see if they were scratched, as they must have slid off the shelf on the ride back. They looked okay.

"Hola hermosa mujer," came a voice from the dock, and AJ turned to see the younger crewman from the Rum Chaser.

He had one hand on the fly-bridge, a foot on the gunwale, and casually leaned in and stared at her with a leering grin. He wore bright green cargo shorts and a hooded tee-shirt with the sleeves cut off, revealing his tanned and muscular arms. Her first thought was 'Why do you need a hood when you don't want sleeves?'

"Hey," AJ replied, "you made me jump."

Apart from 'hola', she wasn't sure what he had said, but by the look on his face he wasn't asking about dive trips.

"Sorry about that, but I wanted to meet you," the young man said with a slight Hispanic accent. "My name is Alejandro, but everyone calls me Jay-P."

AJ managed a polite smile. "I saw you on the boat yesterday," she replied, more interested in leaving than conversing with the man. She had seen him three times now, and this was the second time he'd given her the creeps.

"So what should I call you?" Jay-P asked. "Or is beautiful lady okay?"

AJ put her sunglasses on to hide her eyes. She was certain her expression betrayed her disdain for the fellow and she didn't want to appear rude to someone who worked for the resort. But this bloke was setting off alarm bells. "I'm AJ," she said, "and I'm late for our tour of the distillery so I had better get going."

The man didn't move. "AJ, huh? Jay-P and AJ has a nice ring, don't you think?"

"Jackson and AJ has a better sound, as he's my boyfriend and he's currently waiting on me," AJ blurted, her diplomacy filter failing to engage in time.

Jay-P stepped back and held up his hands. "No problem there, AJ," he said, "I was just being friendly and saying hi, I don't mean to hold you up."

AJ stepped to the dock and forced another pleasant smile as she passed him. "Well, nice to meet you."

She kept walking and heard his footfalls behind her. Her whole body tensed, but she didn't look back.

"Enjoy the tour, but let me know if you have any questions," Jay-P persisted. "My family owns this place, you know."

"Okay," AJ said over her shoulder.

"I'm just saying, the tour is good and all, but if you want the real inside scoop on things around here, I'm the man to hook you up," he bragged. "And Jay-P would be happy to do that for a pretty lady like you."

AJ felt herself shiver. In her experience, people who referred to themselves in the third person tended to be as much use as hooded garments without sleeves. She really wished the pier wasn't 300 feet long, but if she walked any faster they'd be jogging.

"I'll keep that in mind, thank you," she said, and looked up to see Jackson and Thomas stepping out the door of the cottage. She waved, but they were both looking the other way toward where Reg and Pearl were walking away down the path.

"Until later," Jay-P said, his voice sounding farther away. "Maybe we'll have a drink."

AJ turned and just caught the man disappearing behind the first cottage. She ran to catch up with Jackson and grabbed his hand.

"There you are," he said softly, "I thought you'd gone ahead without us."

"I left my sunnies on the boat," AJ replied, catching her breath, "and I met one of the crew from the Rum Chaser."

Jackson looked back at Hazel's Odyssey resting against the long pier. "By the boat?" he asked, "What was he doing there?"

"Good question," she whispered, and wondered what else she should say. On one hand, she shared everything with Jackson and that was one of the things she loved about their relationship. The feeling of being able to talk about anything and everything. On the other hand, he would naturally feel protective and she didn't want to start any trouble when the guy had done nothing more than crudely come on to her. Being creepy might make her uncomfortable, but it wasn't a crime. "He was just saying hello."

She looked up at Jackson, who was staring back at her as they walked. She couldn't see his beautiful hazel eyes as he was wearing sunglasses too, but the tight expression on his face told her he wasn't buying it.

She squeezed his hand. "I'm excited to take the tour now that we've seen the trouble they go to in ageing their rum," she said, quickly changing the subject. "I hope we get to taste some."

The edges of his mouth slowly curled into a smile. "Well, I'm not sure they have any aged rum for us to try yet, but I can tell you their regular pour we had yesterday is smooth enough."

They caught up to Reg and Pearl as they followed the pathway behind the restaurant building towards the distillery.

"This won't be much of a tasting for you, Thomas," Pearl said, looking over her shoulder, "but I'm sure the tour will be interesting anyway."

Thomas looked serious. "It'll be fascinating, no doubt," he said, nodding, "but I hope they have some snacks, 'cos I'm starving."

AJ threw an arm around him and patted his perfectly flat stomach. "Look at you, practically starving to death, you poor fella. I reckon you have a worm in there that steals all the food," she said, laughing. "I heard the resort has had to order in more supplies after you went through the breakfast buffet."

Thomas howled with laughter, causing everyone else to chuckle along. "Dey said 'all you can eat' and I ain't too shy to take on a challenge."

Mads met them at the entrance to the distillery, shaking her head at the group still laughing and ribbing each other. "Are you sure you guys didn't take the tasting tour already?" she joked.

"Nice to see you again, Miss Reed," Thomas said, in the poshest voice he could muster, beaming at the redhead with a toothy smile.

They all died laughing again.

14

SATURDAY

The reception area for the distillery was an impressive array of art, displays and information relating to the production of rum. Mads gave them a brief overview while they waited to meet the man behind the science. AJ wasn't sure what she was expecting an innovative rum distiller to look like, but it wasn't the person that entered the room.

"I'm sorry to keep you waiting," the handsome man, who she guessed to be in his thirties, said. "We're having trouble with our bottle labelling system. I'm Walker," he finished, extending a hand to the first person he came to, which happened to be Jackson.

Walker was dressed in neatly pressed black trousers and a pale blue button-down shirt. As he greeted everyone in turn, AJ laughed to herself that a normal-looking fellow didn't fit her idea of a rum maker. Perhaps his lab coat was hanging in his office, or he had cleaned up his act since his mountain man days running a still in the backwoods of Virginia. She felt like a goofy, grinning schoolgirl when he shook her hand.

"Nice to meet you, Mr. Walker," she said, trying to push the comical visuals from her mind.

"Pleasure is mine," he replied in a firm but pleasant tone with a soft American accent. "But please, just call me Walker, it's my first name."

Before she could apologise, he turned, and instead of taking the glass doors marked 'Tour Entry', he led them through a door off to the side, signed 'Employees Only'. They entered a long, plain hallway with several offices to their right, which Walker explained belonged to the production manager and himself. At the end of the hall he opened another door, and they entered the production area. A huge, shiny, copper still towered over them and a series of other tanks, plumbing and machinery filled the space. Looking towards the front of the building, AJ saw the area behind a railing which the usual tour participants were restricted to.

"Here is where we start the production of Seven Fathoms rum," Walker explained, "and although perfecting the fermentation and distilling process is a science, it's not what makes our rum unique."

He looked over the group. "I understand you had an opportunity to dive and observe our ageing process?"

"We did," Reg replied, "and thank you for the opportunity to do that – we hear it's not usually part of the tour."

Walker smiled and glanced at Mads. "No, in fact it's not something we usually allow for anyone outside of the company, but this young lady was quite persuasive on your behalf."

Walker detailed the production process as they slowly circled the room, before ending up in an expansive warehouse section in the back. There, the bottling machinery lined one side, while a large area was filled with racks containing wooden barrels. The totes of molasses they had seen being unloaded from the boat were also arranged in a neat row near the racks. He led them to a long table, lined with bar stools and an array of rum bottles, most with handwritten labels.

"Please have a seat and if you'd like we can sample some rum?"

"Best part of the day," Reg grinned and waited for Pearl to sit before taking a stool.

"Feel free to have a cracker or two," Walker said, pointing to baskets on the table. "Clear the palate before we begin. I'd suggest a sip or two of water as well."

Thomas devoured a dozen of the dry biscuits before AJ slapped his hand and frowned his way. They both grinned and swigged water from the bottles provided.

"Who has tried our rum before?" Walker asked, and everyone raised their hands except Thomas.

"I don't drink alcohol, I'm afraid," Thomas said.

"And I'm not the one to convert you," Walker replied with a chuckle. "But I'll place a small sample of each before you, and if you'd care to take in the aroma, you'll be surprised how well you'll still relate to the discussion."

Reg looked down the table towards Thomas. "And once you've given it a good sniff, pass it along."

Pearl gave her husband a slap on the arm.

Walker laughed and poured from a bottle AJ recognised as the Seven Fathoms she had seen on the shelves back home and in all the posters and displays.

"This is our current production rum that you can buy at most liquor stores, bars and restaurants in the Cayman Islands. Also across Florida and many parts of the United States. Our boat, the Rum Chaser, transports our export product to Miami and we use the regular barge to distribute amongst the islands."

"We toured the Rum Chaser this morning," AJ said. "Connery was kind enough to show us around."

Walker looked surprised. "Really? You guys truly are VIPs. I've only seen the boat from the dock – he's rather possessive about his baby."

"They're also usually in dock for only a night at most," Mads said. "Sometimes they turn around and ship out the same day."

"That's true," Walker replied. "Okay, so take in the aroma of the rum, let the flavour fill your senses and then take a sip."

They all followed his instructions, except Thomas, who smelled the liquor before sliding his glass down the table where everyone passed it on to Reg.

"It's really smooth," Pearl commented, taking a second sip to finish the sample.

"We had it over ice last night," Reg said, finishing his glass and happily taking Thomas's. "It's nice slightly chilled, but neat like this gives you a real appreciation of the flavour."

Walker nodded. "That's true, and thank you," he said. "I enjoy the rum over ice as well, but as the ice melts, it dilutes the flavours a little." He slid the bottle to one side and picked up another.

The second bottle had a handwritten label that AJ couldn't quite make out. She ate a couple of biscuits and took a swig of water, wondering how many samples they would be trying. Her thoughts of diving later in the day would be out the window with too many more tastings.

Walker poured a small amount of the next rum into their glasses and AJ noticed the liquid had a slightly deeper, caramel tone.

"Try this one and let me know what you think," he said and placed the bottle down, keeping the label facing him.

"That's even smoother," Jackson grinned. "The flavour is fuller, but it has less burn as it goes down. Is that normal as we try more samples?"

"Certainly your taste buds become acclimatised," Walker acknowledged, "but I'd be disappointed if you didn't find this one gentler on the palate."

He looked over at Thomas. "And our man here with a perfectly clear palate, how does the aroma strike you?"

"Dis one burns my nose less than da first one," Thomas said, taking another sniff. "For sure der's a difference."

Thomas slid his glass down once again, but this time Jackson didn't pass it on. He looked at Reg and grinned. "Conveyor broke down, Reg, looks like this one's stuck with me."

They all laughed and took another sip.

"What you're tasting there, you saw floating in the water earlier this morning," Walker announced. "Well, technically, you didn't, as we pulled these barrels a few days ago, but this is our first batch of three-year barrel-aged Seven Fathoms. A portion of what you saw down there will be brought up and bottled over the next few weeks for our initial production run. This is the test sample. You are visiting us at a momentous time for Bloody Bay Rum."

"Blimey," Reg chortled. "This tastes more like rum I've had that's been aged for donkey's years."

"Thank you, that means a lot to us to hear you say that," Walker replied. "We're incredibly pleased with the results so far, I must say, but the process was already proven so our confidence was high."

"And it's the movement in the water that does this?" AJ asked.

"Exactly," Walker replied enthusiastically as he grabbed a third bottle. "That constant agitation promotes the interaction with the wood of the barrels which hold the embedded flavour of the bourbon for which they were originally used. Over time, every drop of rum comes into repeated contact with the barrel, pulling tannins and texture from the white oak." He pointed to the racks of barrels. "Barrels stored like these get moved, rotated and agitated on a regular schedule, but that can't compare to the constant movement in the water. Even on the calmest day, the simple ebb and flow of the tides, a passing boat, even a large fish swimming by, adds movement which we can't replicate on land."

"Your production rum has an amazing taste," Jackson queried. "Does it ever spend time in the water or is it stored on the racks?"

"Good question," Walker replied, nudging the baskets of biscuits towards them. "Here, cleanse your palates, we have one more to try. To carry the Seven Fathoms label, every bottle must contain at least some rum that has spent time at forty-two feet underwater. Our standard schedule is to visit the dive site once a week when we'll take that week's production out and bring in the batch with four weeks of time in the water. As a general rule, the barrels then spend around another four to six weeks on the racks before being bottled."

Walker carefully poured a very small amount of the next rum into each glass.

"Sorry this is a stingy pour, but our supply is extremely limited," he apologised.

Reg looked down at Jackson. "My turn again."

Jackson laughed. "Well played," he replied and held up his glass.

AJ ran the glass under her nose and took in the rich smell of the amber liquid. She took her sip, and the rum rolled keenly down her throat, setting her taste buds tingling on the way without a hint of burn.

"Bloody hell," she said. "I have no idea what I'm talking about, but this stuff is yummy."

Walker laughed. "Good to hear – yummy is something we aim for."

"That is incredible," Reg agreed and eyed Thomas's glass, making its way down the line.

Pearl took it from AJ and instead of passing it on, took a long easy sip and finished it off. Reg's jaw fell open.

Everyone, except Reg, roared with laughter and Pearl winked at her husband. "Never trust the quiet ones," she said, and he leaned over and kissed her cheek.

"That, ladies and gentlemen," Walker explained, "is our seven-year-aged rum."

"Hold up," AJ said with a hand in the air. "I thought this place was built five years ago. How do you have seven-year rum?"

"I've been experimenting with the process for many years," Walker replied. "I met Mr. Castillo and introduced him to my idea six years ago, and I was able to present three-year-aged rums to him at that time. We have a small batch of that vintage we continued to age and bottled at seven years. In two more years we'll bottle samples at eleven."

"Thank you, sir," Jackson said. "We're privileged to be able to taste this, I feel quite honoured."

Walker smiled broadly but before he could reply a raised voice echoed around the voluminous warehouse.

"I can't help it if the damned thing chose to break down now!" a man's voice shouted as he burst through a doorway from the offices. "Our labeller doesn't give a shit about your schedule."

Connery followed the man into the warehouse and replied in a calm but firm tone. "Don't get all worked up, I'm simply asking for a time estimate so I can plan our departure."

"That's what I'm trying to tell you," the man said, throwing his arms up. "I don't have a crystal ball, so I don't know if we can fix it ourselves or if we have to fly a technician here."

Connery looked over and saw a table full of people staring at him and the other man, who he took by the arm. "We have guests, let's discuss this later."

The man swung around and pulled his arm away, appearing even more flustered when he spotted the table full of people. He stomped back out of the door they had entered through, letting it swing close behind him with a thud. Connery smiled, shook his head and walked over to the table.

"Sorry about all that," he said and leaned on the end of the table.

"I think you've all met Connery, our boat captain," Walker declared. "The other gentleman is our production manager. I'm afraid he's under some pressure at the moment."

"I don't know the first thing about labelling machines," Reg said, "but I've worked on various pieces of machinery all my life. If I can be of any help, I'd be glad to lend a hand."

"Same here," Jackson added. "We're happy to get dirty and help in any way we can."

"That's incredibly kind of you," Mads interjected. "But how about we get some lunch first – don't forget you are our guests here at the resort."

Connery nodded. "I for one wouldn't argue with the lady."

Thomas was on his feet in a heartbeat.

15

SATURDAY

After thanking Walker for the personal tour, the group left the distillery building and walked towards the restaurant. Connery saw Mads was waiting for him, and they continued together.

"What was all that about?"

"Storm in a teacup really," Connery replied, veiling his annoyance at the production manager. "You know how dramatic he gets. I was reminding him the boat has a schedule to keep, and needless to say his priorities aren't necessarily aligned with mine."

He fell in step with her pace, which appeared to be casual, letting the guests walk on ahead.

"They don't have enough bottled for your trip back?" she asked.

"No, the labelling system broke down and they haven't managed to fix it yet," he replied. "We're about a third short of the full load."

"Maybe you'll have to squeeze in an extra trip," she said, and he noticed the statement was thrown out like a question and she seemed to be hanging on an answer.

He laughed. "I wouldn't mind that," he replied, glancing her way, "but the boss won't be happy. The margins are already tight, so adding an additional boat run will up the costs a bunch. Once the three-year comes on line, the margins will increase, so I guess this problem should have happened next month, and then I could justify coming back in a few weeks."

He sensed she was holding back a response as they walked in silence around the restaurant to the outdoor bar area, and by then she appeared to have let it drop.

"What happened to your other crew guy this trip?" she asked, taking him off guard.

"How do you mean?" he replied tentatively.

"Mason, right?" she said. "I thought he was your first mate, so I was just curious how you manage without him."

He realised she was just making small talk and relaxed. "Dunno covered okay for him, he has plenty of experience. Mason cancelled last minute, so I have to sort out what's going on with him when we get back. Hopefully he's okay."

Mads laughed. "Why do you call him Dunno?"

Connery smiled, "The lads nicknamed him that as it seemed like every time they asked him something, he'd shrug his shoulders or say 'I dunno'," he explained. "He's sharp as a tack, but he's figured out playing dumb keeps him out of trouble."

"That's funny," she chuckled.

He saw AJ's group had taken a long table overlooking the water and started towards them, but Mads placed a hand on his arm and stopped.

"How about we have lunch by ourselves," she said. "I have something I wanted to talk to you about."

Connery smiled and nodded. "Sure," he replied, and wondered what she had to discuss. Regardless, he was happy to spend more time with her, especially alone.

They continued to the table where Reg and AJ were already joking around with each other about something, much to the others' entertainment.

"We're going to leave you in peace for lunch," Mads announced. "We have some boring business to discuss."

Connery thought he saw AJ wink at Mads, but he couldn't be sure.

"How about a dive this afternoon?" AJ asked. "We were going to wait to let lunch and the rum settle for a while, then nip out to the wall."

Mads looked at Connery with a questioning expression. He had learnt to dive in the military and had taken to diving in the Keys when he was home, but had only had a chance to go out one time on Little Cayman.

"I wouldn't mind," he said, realising he had replied before he thought about what Mads might want.

She turned back to the group. "Great, I'll see if I can get away too. That sounds fun."

"We'll chat after lunch," AJ said, grinning, "and make a plan."

Mads steered Connery towards a table for two, away from the other diners, and he pulled her chair out for her. Once seated, he returned to wondering about the need to talk privately and hoped she wouldn't ask him anything he would be forced to lie about.

"So, what's this business we need to discuss," he asked, figuring his answer was only a question away, and direct had always been his nature.

Mads paused and fiddled nervously with her napkin, and Connery once again wondered what could be so difficult to talk about. The waiter arrived before she could reply and they both ordered non-alcoholic drinks and food without looking at the menu they both knew by heart. When the man left, she looked him in the eyes and again he noted her uncertainty.

"I just thought it would be nice for the two of us to spend some time together," she said.

Connery wasn't sure what to say. His first reaction was 'great, I like being around you', but he didn't tell her that. Instead, he sat in awkward silence while he tried to read the intention behind her words. Did she mean a break from the guests? He figured not. He had seen Mads when she was playing the role of resort host, and that's not how she was around this group. She was genuinely enjoying them, and it was obvious. So, she really wanted to be alone with him? They had flirted around each other for a long time, and he thought about her more than he was comfortable admitting to himself. But neither of them had made the next move. He certainly wasn't shy around women, but the consequences of over-stepping the mark with Mads had kept him from risking an advance. Every time he pulled away from the Little Cayman dock for the past few months, he had kicked himself for not testing the fire behind the spark. But he valued their friendship, and some lines were hard, or often impossible, to step back across.

His love life over the years had been limited to women that tended to sit on his lap and make their intentions clear, including their absence by daybreak. Relationships had never fitted into his lifestyle, or often locations. That had been fine, but Mads had him rethinking things, and now he didn't know if this was her stepping over the friendship line or not.

"Maybe I was being presumptuous," she said, and he looked up.

"Shit, no," he blurted. "I'm really sorry, I'm glad you asked," he said, realising he'd been lost in his thoughts and left her sitting in silence. "I was busy overthinking things."

Mads smiled, her eyes glistening. "And what exactly are you trying to overthink?"

Connery laughed. "No way," he said, shaking his head, "This is your little gathering, you have to pull your pants down first."

Shit, he thought, I spend way too much time around other blokes.

Mads about choked on the water she had just sipped and laughed out loud. "I wasn't intending on anyone pulling their pants down at the lunch table."

"I'm sorry," he started. "Too many years in the army I'm afraid, I forgot my manners."

She waved a hand towards him. "I grew up with two older brothers; believe me, you'll struggle to shock me. But please don't take that as a challenge," she added.

"I'll try and filter my crass ways," he promised. "So, let's get back to you and me spending time together."

He saw her take a deep breath, and before she could speak, the waiter returned with their drinks. They thanked him but he loitered to chat with Mads about nothing important and Connery wished he would leave. He pushed visions of various ways he could eject the poor man from his mind. Military moves designed to incapacitate and launch other humans across a room weren't welcome during what he hoped would be a romantic discussion. The man finally wandered off towards another table and Connery sipped his drink while Mads summoned up her courage again.

"I've just been thinking, you know, for a while now," she started awkwardly, "we always spend time together when you're here, and I enjoy that. In fact, I look forward to it," she said, her eyes flicking up briefly to meet his. "And you seem to like that too, but I don't know if that's what you're happy with or if you've considered, maybe, you know..." she tapered off and caught his gaze again.

Not for the first time, he noted what pretty eyes she had. Considered what? He asked himself. Is she asking me for friends with benefits, or something more? Benefits would be fantastic. He had certainly thought about that aspect of a relationship with her a lot, but it was almost a guaranteed way to end a good friendship. Someone always got left behind at some point. One of the two would find someone they wanted more from than an occasional roll in the hay and good company. But perhaps she meant more than that? Had he considered more than that? Hell yes, he thought, but how can that work when he showed up for a day or two a month?

"All of a sudden you're not very good at this conversation thing," she said, and her nervous expression was back.

He let out a long breath and shook his head. "I'll tell you straight up, I'm not much good at conversing about relationship stuff, I think that's fair to say," he laughed, but her countenance remained the same.

Shit, he thought, don't screw this up completely. "If you're asking if I'm interested in seeing you in a more serious manner," he said, hardly believing these were the words leaving his lips, "then the answer is most definitely yes. It's something I've considered at great length, because, you know, when you spend days upon days at sea you get to ponder such things at great length." He quickly held up a hand. "But, if that's not what you meant, then I just bollocksed up the whole thing, and let's forget I opened my mouth at all."

Her whole body relaxed and a huge smile swept across her face. "It is what I meant," she replied.

Connery slumped in his chair. "Thank the fu..." he started and just stopped himself in time. "I mean, I'm grateful that's the case."

Mads reached across the table and took his hand. "Why has this taken us so long?"

Connery leaned forward and squeezed her hand. "Because it won't be an easy thing with the lives we lead."

She nodded slowly. "That's true, but my gut tells me this could be worth it."

"You might want to keep your expectations low," he said with a smile. "I'm just an old soldier with more than a few years on you, and I've never been much on relationships, so I can't claim to know what I'm doing. But you're the first woman that's had me in a mind to try, so I'll do my damnedest."

She grinned back at him. "Well, you silver-tongued devil, a girl would never know you weren't a regular Casanova with a love in every port."

He frowned. "You're kidding, right?"

"Yes," she said, "I'm kidding. You're terrible at the speeches part, but luckily I'm okay with the strong, almost silent type, so you won't have to tell me you care, you just have to show me you do."

He laughed. "Fair enough. How about I start by taking you out on a date?"

She wriggled excitedly in her chair, "Cool, look at you already planning things for us."

"This afternoon I'm surprising you with a scuba diving trip," he said, trying to keep a straight face, "and tonight I know a lovely restaurant by the water I thought we'd try."

She laughed, and her red locks cascaded around her shoulders with happiness radiating from her beautiful face. Connery felt something he wasn't sure he'd ever experienced before. A warmth and joy that filled him in a way he couldn't remember. Even as a child, unrestrained elation wasn't an emotion he had ever been afforded. As the glow swelled throughout his being, a wave of fear washed it away like a violent surf. The immensity of his violent past and camouflaged present couldn't remain hidden forever. But if she knew, this would be over before it began, and if he continued to live a lie, it would always be a mask that mocked his pretence of a life shared with another. Mason, stepping from the stern of the boat, flashed through his mind. The three of them had shared many meals together, right here on the patio overlooking the pristine water. How could she possibly understand that he, despite his affection for the young man, could sentence him to death and watch while he walked into the open ocean? The idea was insurmountable.

Their food arrived and Connery forced his negative thoughts aside, losing himself in her presence. The more she smiled, laughed, and bantered with him, the more his reservations and fears slipped back into the deep well where they hid themselves, festering and conspiring.

16

SATURDAY

The resort's pontoon boat sat on the east side of the pier, having been out during the morning with divers and snorkellers. Hazel's Odyssey bobbed serenely opposite the smaller vessel as AJ stepped aboard. Jackson and Thomas followed, carrying a bag of ice and a jug of water, with Reg bringing up the rear, a bag of snacks in his hand. Pearl had decided to sit this one out as they wouldn't be back for a few hours and she wanted to be ready for her gig. The boat rocked as they all stepped to the deck, but Reg stopped and stared across the back of the boat.

"Wait up, you lot," he said, his deep voice resonating. "Stay where you are a minute."

AJ was halfway up the ladder to the fly-bridge. "What's up?"

"Look," Reg replied, pointing to the deck and swim step at the stern. "Someone's been on here."

Jackson scanned the pier and the pathway leading to the cottages and restaurant. "Must have been recently if there are still wet footprints. I don't see anyone."

Thomas looked along the coastline. "I'd be surprised if any locals would mess wit anyting here, dey know nuttin' good can come from dat."

"They came from the water," Reg noted, "'cos they dripped all over the deck and I don't see any wet prints on the pier, so they must have left the same way."

AJ continued up the ladder and checked the fly-bridge. "No water up here," she called down.

Reg shrugged his shoulders. "Probably a curious kid or something, but check your gear. Computers and torches would be easy pickings."

AJ started the diesels and came back down to look over her gear with the others. No one had anything missing.

"Afternoon, guys," came Mads's voice from the pier. "Okay if we come aboard?"

"Of course," AJ replied, going over to help Connery with his gear.

"You don't need to help," Connery laughed. "You're on holiday, remember?"

"Sorry," AJ replied. "It's a habit," she said, pointing across the boat. "Mads's gear is over there on the starboard side from this morning if you want to set up next to hers. Those nitrox tanks are all full."

AJ grinned at Mads, who smiled back. AJ mouthed 'Well?' to her friend who smiled even wider. AJ pointed to the fly-bridge, and they both scurried up the ladder.

"Can you get the..." she started to call down until she saw Thomas already at the bow and looked back to see Jackson at the stern.

They cast off the lines and AJ eased away from the dock, carefully checking the shallow water ahead before nudging Mads.

"So what happened?" she whispered. "You had quite the cosy lunch date."

Mads leaned in close. "He said he's wanted to ask me out on a real date for ages, but didn't know if I felt the same way. Looks like we're giving it a try."

"That's brilliant," AJ enthused, giving the coastline behind her one more check as she pointed the Newton straight out towards the wall. "I hope it's great for both of you."

Something caught AJ's eye, and she looked back again. On the point of land, parallel to the pier where the restaurant overlooked the ocean, a figure emerged from the water.

"Is that...?" She pointed and turned to see if Mads had seen them too, but by the time she looked back they were gone.

"What did you see?" Mads asked.

"A bloke coming out of the water over there," AJ said, still pointing. "Did you see them?"

"I didn't," Mads replied, "but we have a ladder to the water over there for snorkellers, so it would have been a guest."

AJ turned her focus back to where she was going, but couldn't shake the brief view of the figure that had seemed familiar.

"Why?" Mads asked. "Were they doing something wrong?"

"I'm sure it was nothing," AJ admitted. "Like you say, it was probably just a guest."

She figured it was best to let it go. She didn't want to cause any trouble over something she wasn't certain of. But, as they motored over the reef, she couldn't put the thought aside.

"Do you know Connery's crew?" she asked.

"I've met them, but they usually keep to themselves," Mads replied. "Except Mason, he joined us for dinner a few times. He's a nice young guy from California."

"Oh, he should meet Jackson," AJ said, forgetting the intruder for a moment. "He grew up in northern California."

"He didn't come on this trip, I guess," Mads replied. "It's just the other two."

AJ looked at Mads and tried to think how best to phrase an awkward question. "One of them, the younger guy, I think he's called JT or something like that?"

Mads rolled her eyes. "He goes by Jay-P – he's related to the owner in some way. He only joined them a few months back."

"He seems a little bit..." AJ hesitated, searching for the words.

"Creepy?" Mads offered.

"Yes!" AJ blurted, relieved she wasn't alone in her assessment. "And when I say a little bit, I mean he's a double-decker bus full of creepy."

Mads laughed. "He winks at me when he sees me, like I'd have any interest in him." She put a hand on AJ's arm and her voice turned serious. "Wait, has he bothered you?"

AJ shook her head. "No." Then she paused. "Well, yes, but nothing happened. He came down to the boat when I was alone earlier today and tried his Rico Suave moves. I told him I was here with my boyfriend and he finally gave up."

"I'm so sorry, I'll ask Connery to talk to him," Mads offered. "He'll want to know if his crew are harassing people."

"Don't say anything," AJ pleaded. "I don't want to start any bother, and I wouldn't have even mentioned it, but I'm pretty sure it was him getting out of the water as we were pulling out."

"Jay-P?" Mads replied. "He was the one going for a swim?"

AJ looked at her again. "Yeah, but someone was on the boat just before we got here. There was water dripped over the deck and whoever it was came from the water and went back the same way. There were no wet prints on the pier."

"Shit, was anything disturbed or missing?" Mads asked, clearly upset.

"No, no, we had a good look around," AJ assured her. "Nothing is missing as far as we could tell." She threw her hands up. "I have no way of knowing it was him, could have been a curious kid swimming around and came aboard to take a look at the new boat."

Mads shook her head. "There aren't any homes around here, apart from Castillo's villa, and as we're a rum distillery, our resort is adults only. If you saw Jay-P getting out of the water, my guess is it was him snooping about."

AJ eased back on the throttles and let the Newton coast towards a mooring ball directly out from the resort, just short of the wall. "Is this the right one?" AJ asked.

Mads looked back at the resort less than a quarter of a mile away, then back and forth across the water to the east and west.

"Yup, this is it," she said, and pointed west. "That's Lea Lea's Lookout." Swinging around to point east, she continued, "And that way is Great Wall where you dived yesterday."

Thomas hooked the mooring line and AJ reversed the boat gently away from the mooring ball before shutting down the motors, letting it gently take tension on the line.

As they headed for the ladder, AJ grabbed Mads's arm. "Let's not say anything about Jay-P, okay? I mean, I can't even be sure it was him I saw."

Mads thought for a moment before replying. "Okay. For now. But, if anything else weird happens, I need to tell Connery."

"Yeah, fair enough," AJ grinned. "You and your new boyfriend will have far better things to talk about anyway, or not talk about..."

Mads blushed and laughed as she started down the ladder. "Shush, let's get underwater where you can't embarrass me anymore."

As the group geared up, AJ kept an eye on Connery, paying attention to how he prepared for the dive. Another habit from running dive boats. She could tell a lot by a diver's gear, the way they checked it over, and their demeanour before ever leaving the boat. In this case, his gear was all resort rental stuff, which he made a point of diligently looking over. He played with the BCD inflater and release controls, made sure his back-up regulator breathed smoothly and was stowed securely. He checked his primary regulator, then sat on the bench and went through the settings of the unfamiliar dive computer.

"All the tanks were analysed before we left," AJ said, looking at Connery, "but I have an analyser in the cabin if you'd like to check it?"

He looked up and smiled. "I'm sure I can trust you. Thirty-two percent?"

"Yup," she replied. "Everything we brought is thirty-two, if we refill any here, we'll double check them before we use them."

Connery nodded and set the nitrox gas mix percentage on his computer. AJ could tell he knew what he was doing. He was relaxed, proficient with gear he didn't know, and showed all the signs of an experienced diver. She had looked up his certification through the online system on her mobile, as he didn't have a cert card with him, and it showed he was advanced trained. He had told her he had been taught to dive in the military and regularly dived in the Keys in recent years. Her final pre-dive assessment would be weight.

A living human is buoyant. A neoprene wetsuit adds to that buoyancy, and an aluminium dive tank starts negatively buoyant when full, but as the compressed gas is breathed away, it becomes positive. To compensate for all that, a diver carries ballast weights on a belt around their waist, or with modern BCDs, in special removable pockets. Most recreational divers carry more weight than they should, mainly as they may be nervous or anxious as they don't dive very often. When they're anxious, they hold more air in their lungs when they breathe shallowly, which makes them more buoyant, which makes them more nervous, and so on. AJ had noticed Mads, who dived for fun occasionally and wore a 3mm wetsuit to stay warm, had asked for 10 pounds of weight that morning. A little too much for her slender body size, but not unreasonable. AJ dived heavy with 6 pounds, and could give two pounds away underwater if someone felt too light.

"How much weight can I get you?" AJ asked, standing next to the crate of lead weights.

Connery thought for a second. "I'm not wearing a wetsuit, but I don't know this gear, so I'll take 6 pounds please."

AJ passed him two 3-pound weights, which he fitted into his BCD removable pockets. He passed that test comfortably.

"Okay, everyone ready?" AJ asked, slipping into her BCD and standing up.

"Waiting on you," Reg replied, already at the swim step.

"Is everyone that's not a grumpy old bugger ready?" AJ asked, and they all laughed and replied they were.

"Alright, Mads tells me this is a newer site called 'Bloody Bay Rum Club', which is pretty cool," AJ declared. "Wall dive so we'll max at 100 foot, check out the drop-off, then wind back up and finish on top at 25 to 30 feet near the boat. Let me know if you get to 1000psi; otherwise, everyone's an experienced diver so you all know what to do. Let's have a fun, relaxing dive."

Reg led the way off the stern of Hazel's Odyssey, stepping into the gin clear water of Little Cayman's Bloody Bay.

17

SATURDAY

The group descended to the reef below the boat, to the disinterest of a myriad of colourful fish. Critters were busy going about their day, searching for food, and avoiding being someone else's meal. The noisy, bubble blowing beasts that invaded their world didn't resemble any predator they knew of in the protected marine park they called home. AJ finned towards the drop-off with everyone in tow and watched the sea fans and willowy soft corals for signs of current. Barely noticeable at 25 feet, the surface swells swayed the taller fans back and forth, but otherwise the waters were calm as they approached the top of the wall.

With a quick glance around the divers to make sure everyone looked comfortable, AJ eased over the drop-off, which while still quite abrupt and steep, didn't have the dramatic sharp corner and vertical face of the Great Wall sites to their east. Dropping through sixty feet, AJ put a little air into her BCD to slow her descent as the increasing water pressure crushed the buoyant air pockets in her wetsuit. She looked up and noticed Thomas had paused by a small overhang, and Reg and Jackson joined him to peer at whatever interesting find he had discovered. Connery appeared to be the smooth, proficient diver she had expected, his arms folded across his chest, relaxed and balanced, with rhythmic and well-spaced exhales streaming bubbles from his regulator.

AJ looked down and saw Mads was dropping below them, which she knew was fine. Their plan was to level off at 100 feet. Connery finned down towards her to stay close. Thomas and the other two tore themselves away from their overhang and Jackson signalled to AJ. He swung his arms with his hands clasped as though he were rocking a baby, then put his hands together in prayer. She flashed him the okay sign back, understanding they had seen a juvenile angel fish. AJ checked her depth on her dive computer which showed 85 feet, and she gave another short blast of air into her BCD to compensate for the depth.

Jackson descended beside her, and behind his mask she could see the glee in his eyes. The wall was a spectacular display of coral growth and life. Not as vertical as East and West Great Wall, the drop-off sloped at a slight angle offering the coral more sunlight. Below them it still fell away to inky black and felt like they were hovering over a bottomless well. Mads caught AJ's eye again as she was still well below them and although Connery was close by, she had certainly dropped below 100 feet. AJ unclipped the stainless-steel carabiner from her BCD and tapped it on her tank a couple of times. Mads and Connery both looked up at the sound, and AJ waved for them to come up to where everyone else was gathered. Mads signalled okay and she and Connery smoothly kicked their fins to ascend. But she didn't ascend.

Connery came towards AJ, but Mads was kicking harder and still not ascending. She reached for her inflater line and hit the button. Bubbles immediately shot from the top of her BCD, and AJ knew she was in trouble. AJ pointed at Connery and signalled him to join the group. She finned head first down while looking back up at Reg and brought the index finger of both hands together, asking him to keep the group together. She didn't wait for his okay, as she knew he would read the situation and take over the other divers. There was nothing worse than having to rescue someone who was trying to rescue someone else. It was better if she handled this alone.

Mads was kicking furiously and just about maintaining her depth, but streams of bubbles were pouring from her regulator as she used all her energy to keep from dropping farther towards the depths. AJ reached her and took a firm grip of her BCD, immediately making eye contact. Mads was terrified and began clawing at her integrated weight pocket quick releases but AJ grabbed her hands and made Mads hold on to AJ's BCD straps. Again she made eye contact and let her own calmness wash over Mads. AJ pumped more air into her own BCD and, taking a hand from Mads, she signalled for her to kick slowly now. With AJ's BCD inflated and the two women clutching themselves together as one, they began to ascend, and Mads's thrashing legs settled into a gentler rhythm.

AJ checked her dive computer. They were at 136 feet. Below the recreational limit, well below their plan limit, but heading safely back up. The more they rose, the calmer Mads became and her vice-like grip on AJ softened. They passed the others, who joined them on their way up, and AJ noticed Connery stayed close by. AJ bled off air from her BCD as they ascended, to offset the lessening surrounding pressure, and once they reached the edge of the wall at 30 feet she levelled off and signalled for them to spend a few minutes there. They hadn't gone into deco, but to build in margin, she would perform a safety stop at 30 feet and spend another three minutes at 15 feet. Mads was a lot more comfortable over the shallow reef without the abyss below her, and the others cruised around close by, killing time.

Connery stayed with them and once Mads appeared to be comfortable, he took a look over her BCD while they hung in the shallows. He beckoned to AJ, who was still holding on to Mads, and she peered over her friend's shoulder. Connery pointed to a cut in the fabric of the BCD, right at the top by her neck. Obviously, the cut had gone through the Cordura nylon fabric of the BCD and penetrated the 'U-shaped' laminated nylon bladder beneath. Any air Mads had inflated into the BCD had simply blown right out of the opening. AJ looked at Connery and tapped two fingers on her mask, then thumbed towards the boat above them. He signalled okay in return, understanding they would look more closely once they were back aboard.

Mads dropped heavily onto the bench and made sure her tank was in the rack. She unbuckled her BCD and looked at AJ, who discarded her own gear and came over.

"Thank you so much," Mads said. "I was really scared. I thought I was heading for the bottom."

AJ rubbed her shoulder. "I'm glad you're okay, but that was a bit sketchy."

"I thought I was supposed to ditch my weights if something like that happens?" Mads asked.

AJ sat down next to her. "That's what they teach you, but it should be a last resort," AJ explained. "It trades one problem for another. You would have ascended, but once you made it shallower, breathing like a sprinter, you would have had an uncontrolled ascent and popped up like a cork. The bends are better than plummeting to 1,000 feet, but only if that's the only option. I knew I could bring us both up with my BCD."

Mads leaned over and hugged her. "I'm pretty sure you just saved my life. Thank you so much."

"All in a day's work," AJ laughed, slightly embarrassed.

Connery sat next to Mads and took off his gear. "You sure you're alright?"

She released AJ, nodded and managed a smile. "I'm fine. Mind you, I'll have a stiff drink as soon as we get back."

"I'm sorry I didn't realise what was going on," Connery said, squeezing her hand. "I was too busy enjoying the dive, and not paying attention."

"That's okay," she replied. "It all went to shit pretty quickly. I should have realised something was up with my BCD sooner. I didn't need to put any air in until we were deeper and then it seemed like it didn't do anything. I felt like I was being pulled down."

Connery and AJ both stood and examined the cut in Mads's BCD. The others crowded around and Mads stood up to look for herself.

"I don't know what you could have sliced that on," Connery commented. "It takes some effort to cut through this material. I would have thought you'd notice jamming against something that hard."

"But the gear has been on the boat, sitting right there since yesterday, hasn't it?" Jackson asked.

AJ and Mads looked at each other, and AJ guessed they were thinking the same thing.

"Excuse me," Reg said, stepping over to look closely.

He examined the slice carefully, then checked over the rest of the BCD. He removed the dive knife mounted on the cummerbund of the BCD and held the tip of the blade into the cut. The width of the blade was the exact size of the cut.

"What the…" Connery muttered.

"Be an odd coincidence, wouldn't it?" Reg said, looking at the Irishman.

"I'm not a big believer in coincidences," Connery replied.

"Me neither," Reg agreed.

"Shit," AJ said, and put her arm around Mads. "Remember the wet prints on the deck, Reg?"

"They're on my mind right now," he replied. "Why? What are you thinking?"

"Well," she started hesitantly, "I think I saw someone coming out of the water as we pulled away from the dock. They were over by the restaurant. I guess there's a ladder over there."

"What are you both talking about?" Connery asked. "Was someone on the boat?"

"When we got here earlier, there was water on the deck. Like someone had come out of the ocean and walked around the deck," AJ explained. "It had to be shortly before we arrived, as in this heat the water would have evaporated in no time."

"And you think you saw them?" Reg asked.

"It was a short glance," AJ said. "But yes, someone climbed out over by the restaurant."

"What did they look like?" Connery asked, his eyes focused and his voice stern.

AJ looked at Mads and let out a long breath. She was terrified she'd be getting someone in trouble without being sure it was him. Maybe it was because he had creeped her out, and he really had nothing to do with it.

"Tell him," Mads urged. "If it wasn't him, he can explain where he was and we'll rule him out."

"It was someone you knew?" Reg grunted.

AJ looked at Connery. "I think it was Jay-P, but I can't be a hundred percent sure."

Connery's jaw tensed and his eyes turned steely cold. "Let's get back."

"Wait up," Reg interjected. "Who the hell is Jay-P?"

"He's one of the crew on the Rum Chaser," AJ mumbled, already worried she'd started an avalanche of trouble.

"How do you know him?" Reg asked, and she sensed Jackson close by.

"He came down to the boat this morning before the tour," she replied.

Jackson turned her to face him. "Is that why you were wigged out when you came back? What did he do?"

AJ felt everybody's eyes were on her and knew the words she chose next would decide whether the avalanche caused a harmless mound of snow, or ploughed through a whole village. As she considered what to say, Mads beat her to it.

"He was hitting on her and being all weird like he always is," Mads said. "The guy gives all the girls the creeps."

"Why didn't you tell me?" Jackson begged.

Reg took off for the ladder to the fly-bridge, and Thomas hustled to the bow to free them from the buoy. That's it, AJ thought. The villagers had better run for their lives. She looked at Mads, who shrugged her shoulders.

"If that little shit cut my BCD, I'd like to know why."

AJ couldn't argue with that, but what if he didn't do it? Between the look on Reg and Connery's faces, the kid might not get a chance to argue his case before they lynched him. Even Jackson's expression was not one she'd seen before. Her beautiful pacifist was ready to join the mob. Although that made her love him a little bit more, and she sank into his embrace as the engines started and they headed back towards the dock. A lot faster than they'd left.

18

SATURDAY

Reg pulled the Newton straight in alongside the pier and Thomas and Jackson jumped to the dock before the boat came to a stop. They tied Hazel's Odyssey into the cleats, and Reg shut the engines down before hurrying down the ladder. Connery had been quiet on the short ride in, sitting next to Mads, but now he stepped swiftly to the pier and spoke loudly.

"Listen up, everyone," he began, and all eyes turned to him. "If one of my crew is involved here, then it's my responsibility. The incident, the person, and the consequences are on me."

Reg walked to the rear deck so he could see Connery clearly. "I appreciate you saying that, but I'm coming with you to find this bloke."

Connery leaned over and put his hands on the fly-bridge overhang, looking Reg in the eyes. "I understand you feel that way, Reg, and I certainly respect where you're coming from. But I'll ask you to trust me on this. It's best if I find him and handle this. At least to start with."

AJ looked back and forth between both men and could see Reg was champing at the bit to go with Connery. He wasn't a man to leave things in the hands of others if he felt strongly about an issue, and sabotaging dive gear was serious. Was the victim random, or did they know whose gear they were messing with? She knew everyone had to be asking themselves these questions.

"You haven't known me long," Connery added, as Reg pondered his options, "but I'm telling you this could be complicated, and it's important I handle it."

"It ain't complicated, mate," Reg retorted. "Someone deliberately cut her gear. That's simple in my eyes. We find out who."

A droning sound built as Connery was about to reply, but he paused to see where the noise was coming from. AJ looked to the sky, shielding her eyes from the bright late afternoon sun, and spotted a plane approaching them. It was low and fast.

"Shit," Connery muttered as the plane – a private jet – roared over them.

"Bugger me," Reg growled. "What the hell does he think he's doing?"

As the plane quickly became a speck to the west, banking around the end of the island, Connery shook his head. "He's buzzing his resort to let them know he's here. That's Castillo, the owner, and when I say things are complicated, they just got exponentially more so."

"Doesn't change a damn thing in my eyes," Reg retorted.

"Jay-P is a cousin, or cousin's kid, or some kind of relative of Castillo's," Mads said, frustration rising in her voice. "Who knows what the boss will think if we start making accusations."

Reg took a step towards the pier. "I don't care if he's related to the Queen of England. If he's messed with our gear and endangered people on our dive boat, I'm turning him over to the police."

Connery held up a hand. "Stop just a minute, Reg," he said firmly, but politely. The big man stood eye to eye with him despite Connery being up on the pier. "I'm asking you again, Reg. Please trust me on this. Let me get this started. I'll head back to the boat where he's supposed to be, and see what he has to say for himself. But he'll have seen that plane, same as us, so if I don't hurry,

Castillo will be here and the little shit will try to hide behind his family."

Reg took a deep breath, and AJ couldn't tell whether he was about to bowl Connery out of the way, or back down. He turned to AJ with a questioning look. AJ bit her lip and looked at Connery. She didn't know anything about this man, but her gut told her they should trust him. At least for now.

"Go help Pearl get ready for tonight, Reg," she said, the words sounding more confident than she felt. "Connery can update us as soon as he knows more. Right?"

Connery nodded and pulled his mobile from his pocket. "Give me your numbers."

The group quickly dispersed. Connery left to find a ride to the Rum Chaser, Reg walked up to his room to find Pearl, Mads headed for the office to make sure Castillo's villa – the largest dwelling on the property – was ready for his arrival, and AJ, Thomas and Jackson washed the boat and all their gear down. This time, once everything was cleaned with fresh water, they moved all the dive gear to the bow cabin and locked the door. When they got back to their cottage, AJ told Jackson to shower while she walked over and made sure they had a table for dinner. He was hesitant to let her go anywhere alone, but she assured him she would go straight there and back.

As soon as she had left the cottage, AJ texted Mads and told her she was walking to the patio overlooking the water. By the time AJ reached the railing overlooking the ironshore and the ocean, Mads had joined her and they both looked down at the ladder. It was mounted to the concrete deck that formed the foundation of the raised patio and restaurant building, extending to the jagged shoreline below. The ladder dipped into a small inlet, making a nicely sheltered entry and exit point. Several guests lazily swam not far offshore, their heads down in the water with snorkels sticking up in the air, attached to their masks. It was over 6 feet from the patio down to the concrete and the top of the ladder.

"Can't imagine anyone up here would have noticed, or could even see who came out of the water," AJ commented.

"I was just thinking the same thing," Mads agreed. "Besides, they'd have no reason to remember. There's always people coming and going here."

AJ leaned over the railing and looked at the concrete pad extending beyond the width of the patio to form a pathway along the side towards the resort. "Be easy to slip away without being noticed too."

"The steps down from the patio are on the east side, over there," Mads said, pointing to the far edge from where they stood. "So, yeah, if the person walked along this side no one would notice them."

"I wish I'd had a better look," AJ said quietly. "I'm really worried I've started a mess based on nothing more than a suspicion."

Mads nudged against her. "I appreciate you speaking up," she replied, "and I'm sure Connery will give him a chance to explain himself, or where he was if it wasn't him after all."

"I'm pretty confident Reg was right, your BCD was cut on purpose," AJ whispered. "So I'm eager to find out who did it. I'd just rather be sure before pointing the finger at anyone."

"But then again, Jay-P is massively creepy," Mads chuckled. "So, regardless, a good scare might do him good."

AJ grinned. "That's true," she said, and shivered at the memory of how he had made her feel.

"Okay, I better get back to it," Mads said, turning around. "I have to make sure the restaurant keeps a table reserved for Mr. Castillo."

"I have to make sure we have one as well," AJ replied, taking a last look at the ladder.

"I'll tell them," Mads assured her and started to walk away.

"Hey," AJ stopped her. "I take it you weren't expecting the owner today?"

Mads shook her head. "No, he told us he'd be here next week

when they bottle the three-year-aged rum. He planned a staff gathering to celebrate."

"I wonder why he showed up now?" AJ pondered.

"He brought the technician to work on the labelling system, apparently," Mads explained. "He picked the guy up in Atlanta I think, then flew down here."

"Wow," AJ said, letting out a whistle. "That's a pricey shuttle for a label machine mechanic."

Mads shrugged her shoulders. "I don't think Mr. Castillo does this for the profit, although from everything I see, we do make money. Whatever else he has going makes him his millions. And he seems to have plenty of millions."

"What else is it he does?" AJ asked.

"I know he has a couple of big resorts in Jamaica, with casinos on the property," Mads replied. "But in Florida, I'm really not sure. He has real estate ventures, but honestly, I don't know what else."

AJ waved. "Sorry, you need to get back to work. I'll see you at dinner, we'll be over at 6:30 or so."

Mads looked at her watch. "It's almost six now."

"Bollocks, is it?" AJ blurted. "I better get cleaned up. I should make an effort to look half reasonable as we are on holiday."

Mads laughed. "You're the only person I've seen look gorgeous climbing out of the water after a dive. It's not a glamorous sport for us ladies."

AJ rolled her eyes. "Please. I've usually got snot coming out of my nose, hair everywhere and seaweed hanging off me."

"Yup, and still look incredible," Mads replied with a big smile. "It's like you belong in the ocean, everything seems effortless to you underwater. You're doing exactly what you were put on the planet to do." Mads started walking towards the building but paused and turned, "And I'm here safe and sound because of that. Thank you again."

It was AJ's turn to shrug her shoulders, blushing again. "Don't be silly, you would have figured it out."

Mads looked her squarely in the eyes. "No. I don't think I would have, AJ."

As Mads walked away, AJ knew deep down what she said was probably true. If she'd been alone, she would have either continued to the depths, or dropped her weights and ended up corking to the surface and risking a life-threatening embolism. There was a satisfaction knowing she had made sure the incident hadn't ended in disaster, but her anger overrode any pleasure. Someone had purposely cut the dive gear; whether they knew whose it was or not, it added up to attempted murder. Those words hung in her mind with the weight of their meaning. Someone tried to kill another human on her boat today. As that thought truly sank in, her concern over Jay-P being put in a difficult position, answering accusations he may be innocent of, drifted away.

19

SATURDAY

The golf cart pulled into the tiny commercial dock, and Connery thanked the driver as he hopped off before the man could come to a complete stop. The whirring electric motor of the golf cart faded into the distance and all fell quiet except the lapping of the ocean against the shoreline. Connery stepped to the deck of the Rum Chaser and walked to the pilothouse door. It was unlocked, and he quietly went inside to be met by cool, dry air. He noticed a hint of movement from the base of the port side stairs and tensed. The steady muffled drone of the air conditioner hid any subtle sounds, so he slowly stepped towards the stairs. He paused, allowing his eyes to become accustomed to the unlit passageway below, and sensed as much as saw movement again.

"Dunno, it's me," he said, and relaxed.

The dark-skinned man moved from the shadows below and nodded to his boss.

"Is Jay-P down there?" Connery asked.

The Jamaican shook his head.

"Where is he?"

"Dunno," came the predictable reply, and Connery stifled a grin despite his mood. "Been gone most of da day."

"Did he come back at all?" Connery pressed on, knowing nothing slipped by the man.

Dunno nodded. "He did. Back for about half an hour, den took off after da plane flew over."

Connery ran the timeline over in his head. That put the kid back at the catamaran around the time they were diving, and he would have been gone for twenty minutes or so. He wished he'd kept the golf cart driver here. Maybe he could have caught up if Jay-P was on foot.

"He had a golf cart," Dunno added, as though he read Connery's mind.

The resort owned six golf carts for running guests around, maintenance and landscaping, and while they weren't intended for guests to drive, the keys were always in them. The tiny airport was barely over two miles away, so Jay-P would already be there meeting Castillo, who would want to go straight to the resort. All he could do was clean up and get back to the resort before Reg or Jackson set eyes on Jay-P. Once that happened, he'd lose complete control of the situation – one he hoped to manage, and keep AJ, Reg and especially Mads well clear of. Castillo's answer to most problems was to make the problem go away, meaning the person causing the problem. Jay-P was almost certainly behind this particular problem, but no matter what Castillo had told Connery, blood was thicker than water, so his wrath would likely move to the next person in line.

Connery realised Dunno was still staring up at him from the passageway, waiting. "Text me if you see him, otherwise don't do anything for now."

Dunno nodded and shrank back into the shadows and returned to his berth. Connery walked over to the starboard stairwell and descended the steps, deep in thought. He couldn't figure out why Jay-P would tamper with the dive gear. He could understand if he thought it was Connery's BCD – the kid certainly had ideas of running the Rum Chaser himself – but Mads's gear had pink accents and was clearly a woman's rig. Was he simply getting a kick out of causing harm to someone, uncaring who it was? Or perhaps the choice was deliberate. Connery had no doubt Jay-P was the type who had pulled the legs off harmless creatures when he was a kid. By targeting Mads he was really aiming at Connery, hurting him in any way he could.

He walked through the galley to the stateroom door and rummaged for his key in his pocket. Turning the lock, he froze. The door wasn't locked. He never failed to lock his door. Connery softly stepped back, keeping his eyes on the door all the while. He gently slid a drawer open, wincing as the security catch, which stopped them coming open during transit, clicked loudly. Connery glanced down, ignored the larger blades, and took out a 4-inch paring knife. He would be in close quarters where speed and agility would be crucial. His two specialities.

Returning to the door, he listened carefully, but heard no movement. Unless this was an unknown threat he couldn't think of, the only person currently on the island he had reason to suspect of wishing him harm was Jay-P. The kid wasn't smart, but he wasn't completely dumb either. Despite his muscular build, he had to know he was no match for Connery hand to hand. Which meant he would have a gun. They kept two assault weapons hidden aboard, plus each of them had a handgun. His knife would be no match for a barrage of bullets from a semi-automatic if the assailant positioned himself correctly. A handgun gave Connery better odds. Dunno would have heard if Jay-P had accessed the panel hiding the assault weapons, which narrowed it down.

Connery had spent most of his life gambling his life on decisions such as this. All he could do was consider the variables, stack the odds as best he could in his favour, and be ready for the unexpected. He crouched down by the hinged side of the door. Natural instinct is to aim for where the door starts to open and most people, amped up on adrenaline and fear, will start shooting too soon. He reached over to the handle and gently turned until he felt the deadbolt clear the strike plate. Connery eased the door forward a few inches until he saw a crack of light and then slowly released the handle so it didn't snap back loudly.

His heart rate picked up, and he felt his legs quivering, taut and wound ready for what was to come. He pushed the door open with the back of his hand, letting it swing inward, and readied himself to launch across the floor into the room. The door slowed to a stop, and filtered light from the evening sky dimly lit the stateroom through the thin sun-shielding curtains. Not a sound came from the room. Connery's heart rate picked up a few more notches as he realised he'd either underestimated Jay-P, or he faced a highly trained adversary. He waited.

After another minute that felt like an hour, his legs were aching from his crouched position and he knew he was losing both speed and agility the longer he sat there. Holding the blade out before him, he eased it across the door opening and watched the reflection in the highly polished stainless steel. It was an imperfect mirror, but the best he had at his disposal. Connery tilted the knife around but couldn't see anything out of the ordinary and certainly no person. Were they hiding behind the opened door? Had he forgotten to lock the door after all? He had been distracted with the drama of the trip over, and his thoughts of Mads, so maybe he had made a mistake. The idea he was losing his edge made him grit his teeth and fuelled his focus.

He needed to make his move. Easing into a standing position, he shifted his weight from one foot to the other, getting the circulation back through both. Without further hesitation Connery took a step into the doorway then slammed his back into the open door, sending it crashing against the dinette table while watching the opening in the partition to the berth. He allowed two beats for an assailant to appear in the opening before returning his focus to the door. Spinning around, he pulled the door back and swept his right arm in an arc with the knife held down and the blade facing away; he would lead with a blow, but could easily transition into a cut.

Connery's fist swung through space and he immediately saw

the figure sat in the chair, their head rising from the table. Connery staggered back and stared into the eyes of a ghost.

"Stop! It's me!" came a voice he knew couldn't be speaking to him, and Connery blinked several times, wondering if this was what happened when you passed into the afterlife.

Mason held up his hands. "Connery, it's me, please hear me out before you kill me again."

"Sweet holy mother of Jesus," Connery mumbled, words from his Catholic upbringing spilling from his subconscious.

He slumped in the opposite chair and stared at the Californian, who was either a perfectly clear apparition, or a man raised from the dead.

"Everyting okay down der?" came Dunno's voice from the top of the staircase.

Connery snapped out of his stupor. "Yup, sorry, I knocked over one of my chairs," he shouted back and stepped over to the door and closed it. He realised he still held the knife in his hand, which Mason eyed nervously. Connery sat back down and put the knife on the table, closer to him than the dead man he faced. They both stared at each other for several moments.

"What are you doing here?" Connery finally muttered, full of questions but struggling to find where to start.

"I was sleeping until you came in like John Wick," Mason replied, and Connery frowned. He had no idea who this Wick bloke was.

"What I mean is..." Connery started to ask, but didn't know how to phrase the question.

"How am I alive?" Mason said, helping him.

"Yeah, that would be a good place to start. Unless I'm dead along with you, and this is the other side," Connery replied, still stunned and unsure of himself.

"No, we're both alive," Mason replied, and looked cautiously at his boss, "and I'm hoping we can stay that way. Can I stay that way?"

Connery thought for a moment. This wasn't a scenario he had ever contemplated. "At least until you explain the how part."

"Okay," Mason said, taking a deep breath. "As you know, I grew up in the water pretty much every day when I was a kid, man, so I knew I could float forever, especially as the ocean was calmer than normal. I figured I'd die of hypothermia or dehydration eventually, but until that happened I'd bob along and stick around as long as I could. I just lay on my back and wondered how far the Gulf Stream would take me." He shook his head. "I couldn't believe it. I wasn't in the water more than two or three hours, and this 48-foot Bertram comes rolling by, heading to the Bahamas from Miami. I waved them down, and they picked me up. Captain was Hispanic, lived in Florida his whole life. He didn't want any hassle, so he was happy to let me off in the water before they hit port. His charter was a group of yahoos from New Jersey who didn't know bait from sushi. All they wanted to do was have a big party in Nassau and land a few fish.

"Anyway, I swam in and headed for the bars by the cruise ship docks. Spent the night on the streets, but next day I found a mark that looked close enough to me. It was child's play to lift this drunk guy's wallet. Passport, cash, cards. I took a taxi to the airport and got a flight Thursday night to Miami. Slept in the airport, then next morning I held my breath while they ran the card for the flight to Grand Cayman, but it worked. Couldn't get a seat over here on the puddle jumper until today, but I hoped you hadn't left yet. Then I walked to the dock, sneaked on board and picked your lock."

Connery was astonished. Not only that Mason was still alive, but how he had managed to efficiently move himself around from country to country in a matter of days. The next burning question on his mind was why. The last Connery had seen of Mason was stepping off the stern of Rum Chaser to what they both thought was certain death. Why on earth would he go to all this trouble to run right back to the man who had condemned him to that fate?

"I don't understand," Connery said. "I sentenced you to..."

Mason nodded. "You did. But I know you had to do it. I gave

you no choice. You're the only person who's ever given me a real chance, and I let you down. From the moment I was picked up from the water, all I could think about was making things right. I had to find you and put my life back in your hands. I hope you can forgive me and we can go back to how things were, but if not, give me your gun. I'll finish the sentence for you."

"Bloody hell, lad," Connery replied, trying to process what he was hearing. "Things can't go back to how they were. It never works that way."

Mason leaned over the table. "Sure it could, man, just tell the others you taught me a lesson and I'm on probation or some shit."

"That won't work," Connery said firmly.

Mason hung his head. "Man, I thought you'd want me back. I don't know why we can't figure this out."

"Because I already told Castillo you'd been terminated," Connery replied, and Mason looked up again. "I messaged him from Jamaica. He thinks you're dead."

"Oh shit," Mason murmured.

"And he just landed here," Connery added. "In fact, I'm late getting back to the resort now."

Mason let out a long sigh and his shoulders slumped. "Guess you better get that gun."

"Don't be daft," Connery retorted. "But no one can know you're here. We have to hide you until we can figure out what to do."

20

SATURDAY

AJ wrapped herself in one oversized luxurious towel and rubbed her wet hair with another. Compared to the compact dimensions of the shower in her little cottage at home, the expansive glass-walled version with the fancy rain-style showerhead was hard to leave. But she was pushed for time, so now she would test her ten-minute turnaround performance.

Jackson was already dressed and sat on the bed, leaning against the headboard, looking at her thoughtfully.

"What are you gawking at?" she asked, grinning.

"A beautiful, intelligent woman," he replied, "who chose not to tell her loving boyfriend about an incident that bothered her, and I'm trying to figure out why that is."

"Bloody hell," she said, taken aback but grinning. "I was expecting more of the 'give us a flash' sort of comment. You went for 'let's talk about deep and meaningful stuff'."

He laughed. "A quick flash never hurts, believe me, but I was hoping you'd help me understand the other part."

AJ plonked herself down on the edge of the bed and continued drying her hair, mulling her answer over before she spoke. "I don't know why, really. I wasn't trying to hide anything, it was just weird to explain. I was going to say something, well I did, actually…"

"You said you ran into the guy," Jackson interrupted, "but you didn't say he was hitting on you, and wigged you out."

"Once he was gone, somehow it all seemed silly," she replied. "I didn't feel physically threatened, he just gave me the willies, and I can't say something every time a guy hits on me."

"I'm sure guys hit on you all the time," Jackson said. "You're gorgeous, and you know I'm not the jealous type, I trust you completely. I hope you do know that. But I'd also hope you'd tell me if someone made you feel that uncomfortable."

AJ groaned. "I didn't mean it to sound like 'guys are always hitting on me'," she protested, blushing, "but I didn't want to bother you or worry you over something that didn't seem like a big deal."

"Does it seem like a big deal now?" he asked in a soft, conversational tone.

AJ took a moment. Her first reaction was to defend herself, but she knew he was right and if she had the moment over, she would have said something.

"I get your point," she relented. "Of course, now, I wish I'd handled things differently. I'm sorry, I'll say something next time."

"Thank you," he said, and smiled, looking deep into her eyes until she felt like he could see how much she loved him.

"But you can't go all Rambo if I tell you some bloke looks at me a bit odd," she said, shuffling over the bed towards him.

"Me?" he replied, pointing to himself. "What about me has ever told you I'd go Rambo on anyone?"

She rested her chin on his chest and he put an arm around her. "The look you had on the boat when the whole story came out," she explained. "You were ready to join the mob with the rest of the villagers, pitchforks and all."

Jackson laughed. "I'm a pacifist, not a pushover."

"You looked like you were willing to do anything to protect me," she whispered.

"Of course," he replied, looking at her curiously.

"But, anything?" she asked.

"Yes," he responded without hesitation. "I'll avoid violence and a fight if there's a reasonable way around it, a better solution. But there are lines, and when those lines get crossed, it's unavoidable sometimes. I would do anything in my power to prevent harm coming to you."

"I believe you," AJ said softly, her voice breaking as tears formed in the corners of her eyes. She felt overwhelmed by her total devotion to this man. Reg had once described his love of Pearl by saying he wanted to leave this world one minute before she did, because life wasn't worth anything without her. AJ had called him a 'romantic old buzzard', but had wondered if Jackson might be the one she wanted to die one minute before. In this moment, staring into his captivating hazel eyes, she knew beyond a shadow of doubt.

"I love you an unbelievably large amount," he said.

AJ laughed, and wiped the tears from her eyes. "I'm starting to think this thing with us might work out too."

She nestled up further into his embrace and felt his heart beating against her cheek. A slow, steady rhythm that mirrored the calm strength of his personality.

"Pearl was asking me if we're getting married," AJ said, as nonchalantly as she could muster. To her surprise, his heartbeat stayed exactly the same.

"What did you tell her?" Jackson asked.

AJ shifted to look up at him. "I told her to mind her beeswax and why would we mess with something that was perfectly fine just as it is."

"No you didn't," he replied, laughing.

"Okay," AJ admitted, "I didn't exactly tell her to mind her own beeswax, but I did say the other part."

"That's more like it," he grinned.

"Oh, wait," she yelped. "Were you listening, you cheeky bugger?"

He laughed again. "I wasn't listening, I just happened to not be asleep, so I accidentally heard some things."

"You should've opened your eyes so we knew you were awake," AJ said, frowning.

"But then I wouldn't have heard your answer."

She slapped him playfully on the chest.

"So what is your real answer?" he asked. "I heard what you told Pearl, but is that how you really feel?"

AJ continued looking up at him and searched his face, hunting for clues to what he might want her to say. She frowned, not at him, but at herself for thinking that way. He was asking for an honest answer, and her first thought was to tell him something that would please him. That wasn't her. She had never been afraid to speak her mind and wasn't short on opinions. Her eyes wandered from his as she lost herself in thought, her brow still furrowed.

"That's an interesting and perhaps unexpected look," he said softly.

She quickly focused again. "Oh, right, sorry," she laughed, and then guessed that wasn't the ideal response either. "I'm not very good at this stuff, I'm afraid. But, to answer your question, I don't think about it. I think about you constantly, and all I can see is my life with you in it. Forever. So, no, I don't need to get married, and it's literally something I didn't think about until Pearl brought it up."

She rested her chin back on his chest and squeezed him tightly. "What about you?"

"I would marry you today," he replied without a moment's hesitation, "if that's what you wanted or needed. But otherwise I feel the same way. I'm like chewing gum on the sole of your shoe. I'm never going away."

She chuckled. "You'll be pleased to know I consider you more of a soulmate than an annoying food product you can't eat adhered to the bottom of my shoe, ruining it forever."

"I can't believe you just ripped my romantic analogy apart."

AJ thought for a moment. "So, you probably heard the other bit when you were spying on us, didn't you?"

"I wasn't spying," Jackson replied. "You two were choosing to have a conversation in my presence. I believe, to be considered spying, I would have to covertly and intentionally employ means with which to hear you. My only crime was waking up."

"You've already been found guilty by a jury of your peers," she retorted. "Or in this case, peer. And don't avoid the question," she added, tapping his chest with her finger.

"Yes," he replied.

"You do want to have kids?" she said, pushing herself up again.

"That wasn't the question," he replied with a grin.

She frowned again. "Don't get all smarty pants, you know what I was asking."

He nodded. "Yeah, well, my answer would be the same as the first point of discussion. I don't feel the need to have kids, but if it means a lot to you then sure, no problem."

AJ searched his face again and could still feel his heart steadily thumping away without change. She wasn't sure how lie detectors worked, but figured someone's heart rate ought to pick up if they were uncomfortable about something. She guessed her own heartbeat had bounced around all over the place for the past few minutes.

"It's a big decision, huh?" she asked rhetorically.

He nodded. "It's life giving, life changing, and lifelong."

AJ thought about her own parents. She had grown up in a loving home, an only child. But her mum and dad both held down demanding jobs that were far from nine-to-fivers, so she had been raised by a mixed bag of daycare, babysitters, and parents when possible. It was the childhood she knew, so it didn't bother her or make her feel like she had missed out, but it also wasn't what she pictured for a child of her own.

"Can't really take a baby out on the dive boat every day," she said, verbalising a thought. "Customers might not find a screaming kid conducive to their idyllic Cayman Islands holiday experience."

Jackson chuckled, his chest gently heaving. "Not if he took after me – he'd be chill."

AJ had no problem picturing a baby version of Jackson happy and hanging out wherever they took him, smiling and rolling with any situation.

"Problem would be with my genes involved," AJ added. "I was a pain in the arse, by all accounts. Until I was four or five, then apparently I relaxed and became a quiet kid. Probably all the different people looking after me finally got me used to everything changing all the time."

"Boy or girl or one of each?" he asked, resting his head back and staring at the ceiling.

"Hmmm," she considered. "Do they do an exchange program? You know, like a test drive. If you don't like the one you got, can you trade it in for different model?"

He laughed again. "No, I don't believe they offer exchanges, or money back."

"Our kid would be a water baby, wouldn't he?" she said, picturing a toddler splashing around in the crystal-clear water lapping against the pale yellow sand of Seven Mile Beach.

"They'd be scuba-diving, motorcycle-riding, adventure-seeking, campaigners for Mother Earth," he chuckled. "Our kids would be pretty cool, I think."

In her mind, AJ looked down from the fly-bridge to the deck of the Newton, where a boy and girl leaned on either side of the tank racks, hair blowing in the wind as they sped across the water. Tanned, healthy, happy. She turned back and standing next to her was her friend, Nora. AJ's heart skipped. At nineteen, Nora had endured years of abuse, loneliness and challenges. AJ opened her eyes and blinked, staring up at Jackson.

"There's so much to consider," she whispered. "So many things that can go wrong."

He gently rubbed her back. "We don't have to decide today," he said softly, "The world is already overpopulated for its resources; it doesn't need another human. But I do think our child, or children, would be the kind of citizens the world needs."

AJ sat up. "Let's think about it," she said. "You're right, we don't have to decide today, but it's something we should consider and plan one way or the other. I'm not getting any younger."

Jackson leaned over and kissed her, softly holding her face in his hands. "I promise I'll give it plenty of thought."

She kissed him back before standing up, just missing the towel as it unravelled and fell to the ground.

"You gave me a flash after all," Jackson grinned, moving across the bed towards her.

She laughed and waggled her finger at him. "No way Wrigley's, we're late already," she chided. "Besides, you're supposed to be thinking about the result, not the cause." She turned and winked. "I know you like that part."

21

SATURDAY

Low, scattered cloud on the western horizon gave the setting sun a stage prop for its evening performance. Shades of deep orange and tangerine haloed the cumulus above the seemingly endless expanse of ocean, now tinted with the same hues. AJ and Jackson spotted Reg at a table on the eastern side of the patio, and squeezed through the packed seating to reach him. Thomas and Mads were already there, and Pearl was on stage covering the Foo Fighters' 'Times Like These'.

"You're late," Reg growled, pulling a chair out from the table for AJ.

She gave him a hug and sat down. "Yeah, sorry. Did we miss much?" adding, before he could answer, "Ooh, I love this version. She's playing it like the charity song with all the different singers."

AJ waved to the others at the table and grabbed the nearest glass of water, taking a long cool drink. They had rushed over, and coming from the air-conditioned room, the hot, humid evening had her black Ducati-logoed tee-shirt sticking to her clammy skin.

"Second song, she just started," Reg grunted.

She leaned closer to Reg. "Where's Connery?" she asked quietly.

He shrugged. "Haven't seen him."

AJ caught Mads's eye and mouthed the same question. Mads held up her hands, indicating she didn't know either. The waiter came by and everyone ordered drinks and food, except Reg, who had eaten with Pearl before she went on stage. Thomas had already finished a large appetiser, but eagerly ordered a full meal.

Pearl had moved on to 'Me & Bobby McGee' by Janis Joplin, when Jackson nudged AJ and nodded towards the steps to the patio. Connery, looking like he had hurriedly cleaned up and thrown on a different shirt, spotted their table and walked towards them. He walked around and put a hand on Mads's shoulder as he took a seat next to her.

Reg immediately leaned over. "What'd he say?"

Connery shook his head. "He wasn't there, I couldn't find him."

Reg noticeably tensed. "So he's gone missing?"

Connery held up a hand, "No, no. My guess is he saw the plane, like everyone else did, and went to the airport to meet Castillo."

"Do you think they'll come here?" Jackson asked.

Connery looked from Reg to Jackson and back again. "Almost certainly. I'm surprised they're not here already."

"I'm sure Mr. Castillo stopped by the distillery first," Mads offered. "He brought the technician with him to fix the labelling system."

"Okay," Connery nodded, "then they'll come here next."

"And you'll be leaving tomorrow if they fix the machine," Mads said softly.

AJ noticed Connery squeezed her hand before returning to Reg. "If I'm right, and Jay-P is kissing up to his cousin, it's even more important you let me handle this."

"He'll not hide behind his family, just because they have money," Reg replied. "I don't care if this Castillo bloke is a billionaire, if that kid was the one on AJ's boat, then he needs to answer to the law."

"You know, we haven't talked about that," AJ interjected.

"Shouldn't we involve the police? Maybe he left fingerprints on the knife – then we could prove it was him."

They all looked at Connery.

"We all handed that knife around, so we contaminated the evidence and likely rubbed off or overprinted any prints," Connery pointed out. "Besides, if his hands were wet, he may not have left any prints. Right now, all we know is it appeared someone was on your boat before our dive. The evidence of which is your word as there's no physical trace left. Sure, we think the BCD was deliberately cut, but I'm guessing the police department on this tiny island has zero forensic analysis capabilities, and as no one was injured, they'll have little interest."

"It's beginning to sound like you're defending this kid," Reg said, glaring at Connery.

Connery met his stare. "That's not true at all, Reg," he said, keeping his tone calm. "Maybe you're forgetting it was someone I care deeply about that was the victim here. I want to get the culprit every bit as much as you lot do. I'm just playing devil's advocate. The police aren't gonna do shit about this, but I assure you I am."

Reg sat back, looking thoughtful, and AJ wasn't sure whether the Irishman had convinced him or not. He made a compelling argument in her opinion. If they were back home on the larger Grand Cayman, she would call their friend Detective Whittaker. He would probably tell her the same thing, but it would put the incident on his radar and he might have a suggestion they hadn't thought of. She glanced over towards the restaurant where a smartly dressed Hispanic man spoke with the lady at the hostess stand. Two other men, overdressed for outdoor dining on a tropical island in neatly pressed black trousers, white button-down shirts and black zippered lightweight jackets, flanked the man she guessed to be in his sixties.

"Is that your fella, Castillo?" AJ asked, nodding towards the double doors to the inside restaurant.

Connery and Mads both turned. "Yeah, that's him," Connery confirmed.

Mads got to her feet and made her way over. Castillo's face broke into a warm smile when he saw her approaching, and he shook her hand before placing a discreet kiss on her cheek. She pointed towards the stage before turning and looking back at the table. Castillo followed her gaze and waved to the group.

Connery stood. "He'll probably ask me to join him," he said. "Please have the waiter send my food over when it arrives."

"I see he brings protection with him," Reg commented. "Where's the kid?"

Connery leaned back over so he could talk to Reg without shouting over the music. AJ and Jackson both edged closer to hear as well.

"I see Jay-P, he's behind the henchmen," Connery said, and looked straight at Reg. "Dayán Castillo is not a man you want to know, and it's better if he doesn't know you. I promise you I'll get to the bottom of the BCD incident, okay?"

Reg glanced at the owner of the resort, still talking with Mads as the hostess hovered patiently with menus in hand. Reg looked back at Connery.

"Understood," he replied.

Connery left and met Castillo with a firm handshake. After a short discussion, which appeared amiable, Castillo, Connery and the two men headed towards a reserved table overlooking the water at the front of the patio. Jay-P emerged from the shadows and trailed along behind. Mads returned to the table and sat down.

"We won't be offended if you need to join the boss, Mads," AJ offered.

Mads shook her head. "That's okay," she replied, "Mr. Castillo said they had boring business to discuss, so I should stay with you. He said to say hello and welcome to the resort."

"I see Jay-P was with him," AJ commented with a scowl.

Mads took a deep breath. "Yeah, he made sure I noticed him leering at me."

"Ballsy when he's hiding behind his cousin's security," AJ vented.

"His balls will shrivel up real fast if I get him on his own," Reg muttered.

22

SATURDAY

Connery attempted to gauge Castillo's mood as the hostess led them to their table. He wasn't an easy man to read – he was always polite and courteous in public, and careful to keep to discussions surrounding his 'other business interests' behind closed doors. Connery ignored the two bodyguards, as was customary. Their job was to keep the man secure, staying focused on the surroundings, not socialising. He had met them both and chatted with them in a different setting. One was former US military, the other a product of the streets of Miami. Despite the strict gun laws of the Cayman Islands, he knew they would both be carrying.

Castillo took a seat by the railing and Connery chose the chair opposite, leaving Jay-P, who had slunk along behind, a choice to make. Connery stared coldly at the kid, whose smug grin evaporated now he faced the reality of being in Connery's presence. Jay-P sat next to his cousin and avoided further eye contact for now. One bodyguard stood between Connery and the next table, which had been spaced farther away per Castillo's standing instructions. The other guard took up position at the corner of the patio.

Castillo had never invited Jay-P to dine with them, although the kid had only been around for a few months, so there hadn't been much chance. But he had been clear when he'd placed Jay-P on the crew that the kid either sank or swam on his own merit, and didn't deserve or shouldn't be afforded any special treatment. The rules applied equally to him, kin or not. Why he was at their table remained a mystery.

"I heard you brought a man to fix the labelling system," Connery began, hoping to further test the waters with small talk.

"Yes, we detoured through Atlanta," the man replied in a pleasant tone, his voice firm and sure with only a hint of his native Cuban accent. "He's working on it now. He brought tools and parts, so he was hopeful he would have it working tonight."

Connery nodded. "That's good, if they can finish the production run in the morning, we can load and be on our way by early afternoon."

The waiter brought Castillo a drink, a rum over one large ice cube, which Connery guessed was from a batch he wouldn't be invited to try. He turned to Connery. "A drink for you, sir?"

"Rum over ice, please," Connery replied, ordering what he was expected to drink in the owner's presence. His pour would be from the regular bottle behind the bar, but he happened to enjoy Seven Fathoms, so he didn't mind.

"And for you, sir?" the waiter asked Jay-P.

Jay-P slouched in his chair and rubbed his left arm with his right hand, pushing the sleeve of his multi-coloured collared shirt above his muscled bicep. "A Painkiller," he said with a smirk.

The waiter looked confused and glanced at Castillo.

"Bring him a Piña Colada," Castillo interjected.

Jay-P glared at the waiter. "You don't know how to make a Painkiller, or what?"

The local Caymanian waiter took a step back, and pointed to the menus on the table. "I'll be right back with your drinks, gentlemen, and I'll take your dinner order once you've had a chance to look over today's menu."

He turned and scurried away.

"What an idiot," Jay-P grumbled.

Castillo sighed. "A Painkiller is made with Pusser's rum, Alejandro. As we make our own rum here, it may surprise you to know we don't offer the products of our competitors."

Jay-P started to say something, then apparently thought better of it and kept his mouth shut. Connery waited for the kid to glance his way, knowing he wouldn't be able to stop himself. When their eyes met, Connery gave him the best condescending look he could muster before turning back to Castillo. He wanted Jay-P on the back foot where he was far more likely to slip up.

"I have every confidence you'll be casting off by mid-afternoon at the latest," Castillo said, picking up where they had left the conversation.

Both men returned to ignoring Jay-P's existence, but Connery remained puzzled.

"The singer is very good," Castillo commented, as Pearl wrapped up her first set.

"Mads brought her over from Grand Cayman for the weekend," Connery replied. "She's brought quite a few more people in by the look of it."

Castillo nodded in appreciation. "Have you enjoyed the extra time at the resort?" he asked. "The delay must have some positives."

The waiter arrived and placed their drinks on the table. "Have you had a chance to look at the menu, gentlemen?"

"Whatever today's special is," Castillo said with a smile. "Tell the chef to surprise me."

"Certainly, sir," the waiter replied, and looked at Connery.

"I had ordered at the other table, so my apologies for messing up your system, but perhaps you could just bring it over when it comes out?"

"No problem, sir," the man replied. "Do you recall what it was you ordered?"

"It was the fish special," Connery answered.

The waiter looked at Jay-P.

"Burger and fries," he said flatly.

Connery noted Castillo's jaw tensed, a subtle but rare reaction from the man. Whatever the reason for Jay-P's presence, which still eluded Connery, his cousin appeared to be tolerating rather than enjoying his companionship. The waiter thanked them and left.

"I did go diving today," Connery said, returning to Castillo's question, "which isn't something I usually have time for."

Castillo looked out over the water, softly illuminated by the light spilling from the patio. "I don't scuba dive, but I'm told this is one of the best locations in the world. How was your dive?"

Connery stared directly at Jay-P, who was suddenly sitting really still.

"Great, yeah, dive was perfect," Connery lied. "It's incredible here with the sheer wall." He continued looking directly at the kid, whose eyes were focused everywhere but at Connery. "What were you doing on the dive boat today?" he asked, pointedly.

Jay-P finally shot him a puzzled look. "What do you mean?"

"You were seen on our guest's dive boat this afternoon, while it was docked. What were you doing?" Connery asked again and Castillo turned to his cousin, waiting for his answer.

Jay-P shrugged his shoulders. "I went down to the pier and said hi to the hot chick with the tats and purple in her hair, that's all."

Connery shook his head. "That was this morning," Connery continued. "I'm talking about later this afternoon – you were on their boat alone. What were you doing?"

Jay-P fidgeted and looked at Castillo, presumably for help. Castillo said nothing.

"I don't know what you're talking about," Jay-P squirmed. "I wasn't anywhere near here this afternoon."

Connery was about to press harder when the waiter returned. "Here's your fish special, sir. Can I get anyone anything else at the moment?"

They all shook their heads. "I'll be back shortly with your dinners, gentlemen," he added and retreated.

Castillo waved at the food in front of Connery. "Go ahead, don't wait for ours."

Connery nodded, and picked up his knife and fork. His moment had passed to grill Jay-P. Pushing the issue further in front of the boss in the resort's restaurant wasn't a wise plan, and unlikely to reward him with anything more than the lies he'd already heard. He needed to get Jay-P alone. He would talk then, by one means or another. Connery started his meal and Castillo pulled his mobile from his pocket. He unlocked the screen and pressed a few times before placing the mobile on the table and sliding it towards Connery, who finished chewing and placed his cutlery down. He picked up the mobile and looked at the screen.

'Man overboard, miraculous rescue' read the title of an online news article. There was a picture of three men posed on the deck of a fishing boat. A 48-foot Bertram by Connery's best guess. The article went on to explain that the New Jersey natives reported picking up a man from the Gulf Stream on their way to Nassau. The mystery man told them he had fallen overboard from his sailboat during the night, while taking a leak off the stern. He went missing again before they docked in Nassau. The captain of the charter fishing boat refused to comment.

Connery took his time reading the short article, which contained very few facts. He gathered his thoughts and kept his expression blank. Finally, he slid the mobile back to his boss.

"Unlikely that's anyone we know."

"What makes you say that?" Castillo asked, his voice giving away nothing and his face blank.

Connery sipped his rum before replying. "Odds of him surviving long enough in the water to be picked up are slim."

Castillo chuckled quietly. "And you think the odds of two young men falling into the ocean in roughly the same area at the same time is more likely?"

Jay-P sat forward, the smug grin back on his face. "Should have put a cap in his head like I told you, man."

Castillo grabbed him firmly by the arm. "Not another word, understand?"

Jay-P snapped back. "He screwed up, man, that's all I'm saying."

Castillo gritted his teeth, put an arm on the back of Jay-P's chair and leaned in really close. "When I tell you not another word, I'm not asking, is that clear? We're so distantly related I don't even know how to find the branch of the family tree you fell from. You get me? Now go sit at the bar over there and eat your burger and damn fries."

All the colour drained from Jay-P's face and when he stood, he realised the bodyguard from the corner of the patio was now right behind him. Castillo shook his head, and the man returned to his spot as Jay-P pushed and banged his way off people and chairs. Castillo took a few deep breaths.

Connery still wasn't completely sure why Jay-P had been at the table in the first place, but was glad he'd been dismissed. His best guess was he'd been sending reports to Castillo and ran to his side when he landed earlier, squealing about anything he could think of. Maybe Castillo had him there in case Connery had changed his story. Either way, it appeared the boss had decided his presence was superfluous and probably a mistake. Connery just hoped Reg didn't take the opportunity to start his own line of questioning now Jay-P was alone. He dare not look that way. If Reg was grilling the kid, he didn't want to draw Castillo's attention to it.

"I didn't want anything to look suspicious," Connery said quietly. "In case a body was ever found, it's better he drowned."

Castillo held up a hand. "You've worked for me for a long time, I've never had cause to question you," he said, and finished off his drink before continuing, eyeing the empty glass with appreciation. "But this one may have got away from you. Literally. Can I trust you to make this right?"

Connery knew what was being asked of him. It was his duty to make the problem go away. For as long as he could remember, whether the order came from his senior officer, or his boss, he carried out the task without question. Without hesitation. Without remorse. For the first time, as he considered what that entailed, he wasn't sure he could tick any of those boxes.

"Of course," he replied, finding a confident tone that belied his doubts.

23

SATURDAY

AJ watched Castillo and his two bodyguards wind their way between tables, nodding politely to patrons as they left the patio. He paused briefly at the bar to say a few words to Jay-P, who downed his drink, looked around, then also left. But not with his cousin. Connery returned and took his seat next to Mads, giving her a warm smile. Pearl was finishing up for the evening with her stirring version of Dishwalla's 'Give', bringing the crowd to their feet in applause as she said goodnight.

When they all sat back down, Reg immediately turned to Connery.

"What did he have to say for himself?"

"Denied being there, of course," Connery replied. "I pushed as much as I could in front of the boss. I need to get him alone now, which I'll do back at the boat."

Pearl arrived at the table, where they all congratulated her and made a fuss which, as usual, caused her cheeks to blush. Reg gave her a big kiss once they'd sat back down.

"Last round?" Reg asked the table.

Connery looked at Mads, who smiled and shrugged her shoulders. "Up to you."

Thomas stood. "I'm stuffed. I need to call Jacqueline anyway, before she send some family by to check on me."

The waiter came by as they all said goodnight to Thomas, and Reg had drinks ordered before anyone else had a chance to leave.

AJ kicked him under the table. "Some people might want to get back to their rooms," she whispered, flicking her eyes towards Connery and Mads.

Reg's frown turned to surprise as her hint dawned on him. He shrugged his shoulders and grinned. "Fifteen more minutes won't change anything," he grumbled.

Connery enjoyed a drink or three, like any self-respecting Irishman does, but he would have preferred to slip away earlier with Mads. Finally, they left a tip on the table, said their goodnights, and the group dispersed their separate ways. Mads held his hand as they walked down the pathway leading away from the restaurant building. Ahead lay the car park, distillery and lane towards the employee apartments. It was farther than if they'd taken the path by the east side guest cottages, but more discreet.

"How was Mr. Castillo?" Mads asked as they ambled slowly along.

Connery had no idea how to answer that simple question. He was certain Mads knew nothing of Castillo's other businesses, and so in turn had no suspicions of his own involvement. They had only made the leap into a relationship that day, but with their history as friends, he knew she could be the love he had avoided his whole life. Truths would have to come out.

"He seemed fine," he answered. Preferring brevity and vagueness over falsehoods.

They walked on in silence, the cicadas serenading their stroll down the narrow lane lined with casuarina, sea grape and bitter plum trees. Connery wondered what lay ahead when they reached her door. A kiss goodnight? An invitation to stay? The incident with Jay-P still bothered him, and he needed answers. Reg would also be pushing to know in the morning, and more than anything Mads deserved the truth. He almost laughed aloud at his own thought. Truth. His life had been a string of casual relationships, his only commitment to the job and his fellow soldiers. He had thought about the woman who warmly held his hand for a long time and hoped for this moment. Now, faced with the reality that it could actually happen, the fears and concerns he had easily batted aside when this was nothing more than a fantasy, were walking beside him down the lane. They could be ignored no longer.

Connery's mobile buzzed in his pocket, and he instinctively retrieved it to check the text. It would be work related. The only other person who ever texted him was right beside him. The message was from Dunno and read, simply, 'He's back.'

"Everything okay?" Mads asked, and he realised they had reached her apartment, the first unit of the row of four.

They stood in the short, sloping driveway and he put the mobile away. *If Jay-P is back at the boat, he'll be there for the night,* he thought.

"Yeah, everything's fine," he replied. "I asked Dunno to let me know when Jay-P came back. That was him."

"Does that mean you're done with work for the day?" Mads said softly and moved closer.

He welcomed her into his embrace and wondered if she wore flats for his benefit as they met eye to eye. "I intended to interrogate Jay-P some more. I think I can get the truth out of him away from his cousin."

She squeezed him a little tighter. "He'll be there in the morning, I'm guessing."

Connery leaned forward and kissed her softly. Mads reacted in kind and they shared a long first kiss, rising in intensity as their passion, which had built over months, was finally released. She broke away and took his hand, leading him to her door. Once inside, they kissed again, and her hands pulled him firmly against her. When they parted lips, he dipped his head, resting his forehead to hers.

"There are things," he gasped, breathlessly, "things you don't know, Mads."

"Of course there are," she whispered, "and we'll learn all about each other over time. Lord knows, we'll have time apart when all we can do is talk over the phone."

He was in uncharted territory and for a moment his desire almost won, casting aside his doubts to lose himself in her touch. He eased back and in the dimly lit room could see the confusion on her face.

He managed a smile. "You mean too much to me, Mads," he began. "Too much to take the next step without sharing a few things that you need to know. Things that will change your world, and maybe your feelings about me."

She grinned nervously. "I was hoping you were going to change my world," she said. "I've been sorta thinking about this for a while."

Connery laughed. "And believe me, I'm more than keen to give it my best try," he said, before his expression turned serious once again, "but we can't start off this way. I've never wanted anyone more than I want to be with you, Mads, but not just for a night, and not just for a night or two every month. And for this to work out, you have to know what you're getting into."

Her lip quivered and her eyes searched his face as though clues and answers lay hidden for her to find like Easter eggs. He guessed her warm intoxication of rum and sexual desire was dissipating, but he would rather lose her with honesty than have her in deceit.

She pulled back. "Should I make us some coffee?" she asked, her tone echoing her concern.

Connery pulled her back towards him and kissed her softly, but swiftly on the lips. "I think coffee might be a good idea."

She nodded and left his embrace, heading for the small kitchen beyond the living room. While she opened cupboards and drawers, preparing their unexpected late-night caffeine fix, Connery looked around the room. He guessed the place came furnished as he had seen the same sofas and table in the guest cottages. The place was small, with the living area and kitchen on the lower floor, divided by a four-chair dining table, and stairs against the wall leading up to what he presumed was the bedroom and bathroom. Family pictures stood upon a low bookcase whose shelves she had packed with novels, board games and photo albums.

Connery sat at one end of the dark wood-framed sofa and tried to conjure up words that would not leave him standing outside the front door in a matter of minutes. How do you explain to someone that you'd spent your life reducing the world's population? Sure, most of his victims were busy killing others, often innocent people, but not all. Collateral damage was a delightful phrase tossed around in meeting rooms and media interviews to justify the unfortunates who were caught in the crossfire. Or happened to be near the appointed target. Or were incorrectly identified.

Mads walked in with two steaming mugs of coffee and placed one on the table in front of Connery and kept the other in her hand as she sat. He noticed she placed herself farther away than he would have liked, but their legs were touching so she hadn't given up on him before they started. She looked at him expectantly.

Connery took a deep breath. "How much do you know about Castillo?" he asked, still with no real idea how to have this conversation.

Mads shrugged her shoulders. "Not much, I suppose. I mean, I've Googled him and surprisingly little comes up. I know he has the resorts in Jamaica, and someone told me he invests in real estate in Florida. I know he's originally from Cuba and came to America in the Mariel boat lift."

Connery nodded. "And all that is true. He's an interesting man. He left Cuba at the age of twenty-one with nothing to his name and was granted asylum in the US. He was serving a prison sentence in Cuba when they emptied their jails and sanatoriums onto the boats and rafts."

Mads's eyes got wider. "What was he in prison for?"

"Killing a man," Connery replied. "According to him, the man broke into his family home and tried to steal the little food they had, so he killed him. The guy was a relative of someone in the local police, so Dayán was convicted."

"Do you believe him?" she asked.

"I have no reason not to," Connery answered honestly. "He had nothing to gain by lying when he told me."

Mads sipped her coffee, then tilted her head thoughtfully. "Why are we sitting here talking about our boss?"

"Probably because I want you to be disappointed in him, before you're disappointed in me," he replied, surprising himself with his honesty. This woman certainly brought out a side of him he would have sworn didn't exist.

She looked confused and avoided eye contact as she tried to process what he was saying. "Why will I be disappointed?" she uttered under her breath.

"Castillo makes the majority of his money through illicit means," Connery explained, diving in head first. "His resorts, and certainly this distillery, are just fronts. Sure, they make a profit on their own, but that's not the main reason they were chosen. No one in their right mind would put a rum distillery on Little Cayman, it makes no business sense." He paused and gathered his thoughts. The opening admission was the first hurdle, but how he presented the next part was critical in so many ways. Not least of which would be her reaction in the morning when she ran into Castillo again. The man could sense a problem like a shark picked up a drop of blood from miles away. "The only reason the Bloody Bay Rum Club exists is for the boat. The whole resort was built and operates as a ruse for the Rum Chaser to stop in Jamaica and return to Miami. The rum is a cover for what's really going on."

Mads looked at Connery, her eyes dark and intense, a far cry from the dreamy pools of affection they'd been when they entered her apartment. "And you know all this, because you're part of whatever illegal antics are going on."

She phrased it as a statement rather than a question, so he let her think for a moment before he ventured any further. There was so much more than their relationship on the line. He was risking her calling the authorities, confronting Castillo, abruptly quitting and drawing attention to herself, any number of reactions that could trigger a violent outcome. He was gambling on her being reasonable and understanding, even if she ended their relationship before it had even begun.

"How deeply are you involved?" she asked, her voice delicate and unsure.

He knew she was now unknowingly asking questions with answers neither of them wanted to hear. Once the words left his lips, they couldn't be undone. Some things can't be unheard, or forgotten. But spoken they must be, and he knew it, regardless of the outcome.

"I manage the delivery service," he said, "meaning, I run the boat and everything to do with it."

He saw she wanted to speak, with a flicker of hope across her face and a glint in her eyes. He knew she wanted to believe he was innocent in some way, just an employee like her, unaware of the foul deeds going on behind the scenes.

He held up a hand and stopped her. "I knew what I was getting into, and I know what I carry for the man. He also has me run various errands and handle things for him back in Miami. But my main role is to make sure the cargo gets safely from port to port without any problems."

Her shoulders wilted and the glint left her eyes. "Drugs?"

How to answer that question? He thought for a moment. "I don't carry any drugs aboard the boat. In fact, we have a strict policy about that."

"But?" she said, picking her chin up to look at him again.

"But, I'd say the majority of the man's business is drugs."

Mads sighed and her head sank once more. Connery noticed a tear rolling down her cheek, and he wanted to wipe it away but held himself back. He had no idea if she was repulsed by his presence and wished him gone, or whether there was still a chance for them. He couldn't hold himself back and reached out, gently clearing the tear from her soft skin. She didn't flinch, and her hand came up and held his.

"I'm so sorry to burden you with this," he whispered, "but we didn't stand a chance without you knowing."

Her body shivered, and more tears rolled unhindered down her face.

"You're the only woman I've ever wanted to be completely open and honest with," he continued, "and now it means you'll never want to see me again."

Mads sniffled and shifted uncomfortably, wiping her hand across her face. "Damn it," she groaned, letting go of his hand and using both her hands to dry the tears.

"Should I just go?" he asked, praying she would think about it overnight and he might have one more chance to talk to her in the morning.

She flung out an arm and thumped him carelessly in the chest, sobbing again. "You can't leave," she cried, and flung herself towards him, wrapping her arms around him, hiding her face in his neck where her tears ran down his back. "I'm in love with you."

24

SATURDAY

Dayán Castillo sat on a plush sofa in the living room of his villa. By his Miami home's standards, the place was more like a guest house. Two stories, with only three bedrooms, it was adequate in his mind for weekend escapes, and he could bring a friend or two if he chose. The open-plan lower level lent itself to entertaining, and the patio stretched from the all-glass front towards the ocean. With the crystal-clear Caribbean Sea so close, he had forgone a pool in favour of shaded outdoor seating and a bar beneath a palapa, including a large barbecue. In reality, he visited the island once a month and rarely brought many guests.

He sank into the soft cushions and ignored the figure passing across the patio in the shadows cast from the low lights of the house. His bodyguards slept in a bunkroom off the double garage, but one of them would be on vigil at all times, alternating every few hours. Castillo sipped from a glass of rum and considered what was left to accomplish before he turned in. Numerous men and women managed most facets of his varied businesses, but very few had his trust, and none had his complete faith. He was still alive because he trusted no one. Everyone had their price, or their trigger, something that meant more to them in a given moment than their loyalty to him.

It was a lonely existence, despite his wealth and the number of people in his life, but the solitude didn't bother him. He had always been alone. Castillo's father had wandered in and out of his early life, taking work and women wherever he could find them. As the eldest son, he had provided for his mother and siblings, filling in the gaps his father left. His mother took the man back into the house every time he returned. He was rarely sober, and with little of the money he had earned in hand, but she opened the door and allowed him back into their lives. Castillo could never understand why, and her weakness and need for his presence wore away his empathy, until all that remained was pity and contempt.

Castillo was seventeen years old when the stranger broke into their home. Except he didn't break in. He walked in through the door his father had left unlocked after returning from a bar. The intruder was starving, like they all were, and probably thought the drunk he followed home would be an easy target. Maybe the man considered the older Castillo undeserving of anything he had, choosing to waste what little money there was on booze. But the young son in the house, the one who had really been providing for the family by working long hours each day since he was twelve, was not undeserving. Dayán Castillo stabbed the stranger to death in the kitchen of their small home. He gave the man no warning, no demand to leave, no opportunity to reconsider the theft. Every ounce of anger, frustration and resentment released itself in the thrusting blade that tore into the man's flesh.

Taking the life had been easy. It was simple. Someone was trying to take something from him, and he wouldn't allow that to happen. His father slept until the police arrived, oblivious. His mother was hysterical, adding nothing but noise to the already chaotic situation. No one thanked him. No one said 'Well done, Dayán, you protected your family and your home.' The last words he heard from his mother, as the police dragged him away, were 'What will I do now?'

Four years in prison was plenty of time to contemplate her question. But it didn't take him four years to find his answer. As the police car left the only home he had ever known, he already knew. Never again would he rely, trust, or depend on anyone else.

Castillo placed his glass down on the end table and picked up his mobile. It was late, but by the nature of his businesses, no one he employed or dealt with was in bed before the early hours. He himself usually slept five to six hours a night, turning in around one and up by seven in the morning. He called a number he had saved on speed dial. A man answered in Spanish.

"Hey Boss, how's the island?"

"Should be back on track by morning. I got a text earlier to say the technician had fixed the problem," he said calmly. "They're working through the night to have the shipment ready to load first thing. As he was successful, I'll drop the guy off in Atlanta on my way back."

The man grunted amusedly on the other end of line. Both men knew an unsuccessful attempt at correcting most problems meant the individual would be removed from further service. Permanently. In this case, being an employee of a vendor for one of the legitimate concerns they did business with, the fellow would simply be left to find his own way home. He would no doubt feel annoyed and slighted, and blissfully unaware of their leniency.

"What more do you have on the kid, Chico?" Castillo asked.

The man's voice was muffled as he held his hand over the receiver, but Castillo could make out he was telling people to leave the room. After a few moments he came back to the call. "Sorry, Boss. Too many ears."

Castillo heard a door close through the phone line.

"We found the boat captain. He said he didn't believe a word the kid told him. Some story about taking a piss and falling overboard in the night," the man explained. "Showed him a picture, and he said he was pretty sure it was him."

"Pretty sure?" Castillo questioned.

"Yeah, you know, the picture is a few years old I'm guessing,"

Chico replied. "He don't have a Facebook or nothing with photos on it, so all I had was one I grabbed from his apartment."

"Had he been there?" Castillo asked. "To the apartment?"

"Maybe," Chico said. "Bed wasn't made but he could've left it that way before. There's a camera out front of the apartments, but it's busted, so no recording, I checked."

"What do you think, Chico?"

"I think it's him, no doubt, Boss."

"That's what I think too," Castillo said quietly. "Keep on it, I want him found. If he's pissed off about being tossed overboard, he can make trouble we don't need."

"You got it, Boss," Chico replied. "What's the Irishman have to say about it? Never known him to slip up. Shit, that guy could make my balls disappear without me noticing."

"Said he didn't want it to look suspicious if a body ever washed up somewhere up north," Castillo said, thoughtfully.

"The odds have to be stacked against anyone surviving, man," Chico chuckled. "Getting tossed over the side in the frigging Gulf Stream."

"That's the thing about odds," Castillo retorted. "The odds of anything happening are zero until it happens once; from then on there's always a chance. Two in the skull is a guarantee. I'd take the gamble on the body not showing up again, and a sure thing on the kid never talking."

"Shouldn't O'Brien be making this right, Boss?"

Castillo paused and considered his answer for a moment. "He will," he replied firmly. "I'm worried he's going soft in his old age. From what I hear, he's got himself involved with my resort manager, here. A beautiful creature, which someone should be enjoying on their visits, but I'm surprised Connery is succumbing to her charms. If you find Mason, keep him alive for me, Chico. We'll see if the Irishman is still with us or not. As you said, he needs to make this right."

"Sure thing, Boss," Chico replied and Castillo ended the call, placing his mobile on the table and retrieving his drink.

He sighed and ran through his mental checklist of items requiring his attention. He hadn't bothered bringing one of his usual escorts with him on this trip, and now he wished he had. Someone to relax his body and distract his mind before the end of the day. The island was too small to find local talent. Everybody knew everybody with a residential population under 300 people. Opening his resort had raised the number by several percent.

Damn it, he thought, recalling another item he would need to address. That stupid cousin of mine. First cousin once removed, to be accurate. His cousin's son. A cousin who had also escaped Cuba many years ago and somehow found Castillo in Miami. The family had been a pain in his ass ever since, always wanting or needing something, usually money. He had thought Alejandro could be useful as a set of eyes and ears on the boat, a double check on what was happening. But something told him the kid was a liability, a loose cannon trying too hard to undermine O'Brien. He didn't have the smarts. Castillo needed to reassign the idiot before he caused him trouble.

25

SUNDAY

Connery strode briskly down the coastal road towards the diminutive commercial dock and the Rum Chaser. It was 5:30am and an envelope of darkness shrouded the island with a hint of approaching sunrise nothing more than a faint glow along the eastern sky behind him. His ever-reliable internal clock had woken him at five, and leaving Mads sleeping peacefully in bed had tested his resolve. He wasn't a man taken to wishing for different circumstances; he believed it to be a waste of time. If you wanted something different, then you had to make that change. Dreaming of an alternate situation was like hoping you'd win the lottery without buying a ticket. But lying next to her, feeling the warmth of her body beside him, he wanted nothing more than to close his eyes and let the blissful night last a little longer.

By the time he reached the narrow lane leading to the dock, sweat glistened on his brow in the humid, balmy night air, and his focus was back on the here and now. If all had gone well at the distillery, the truck would begin bringing pallets loaded with boxes of rum to the boat not long after sunrise. There was much to resolve before then.

He quietly slipped aboard and opened the pilothouse door,

easing inside. Many of the gauges glowed from the helm as the boat was connected to shore power, and he noticed a light was on in the galley, down the stairs to his right. Dunno looked up at him and held up a coffee cup with a questioning look. Connery nodded, pointed two fingers to his eyes and then the other stairwell. Dunno ducked back into the galley to continue making coffee for them both, understanding something was going on with the other crew member that didn't involve him, until the boss said it did.

Connery descended the metal stairs on the port side and stepped lightly down the dark passageway. The entry to the crew berths consisted of sliding pocket doors, and each had a lock on the inside. He hoped Jay-P had been consistent with his usual lack of attention to detail and not locked his door last night. He undoubtedly overindulged at the bar after being unceremoniously dismissed from the table, further fuelling his sloppiness. Connery pictured the simple layout of the berth in his mind, letting his breathing settle to a steady calm and his eyes adjust to the darkness.

Before Jay-P could open his eyes, Connery slid the door open, stepped inside, and dragged his surprised victim to the deck, still wrapped in his bed sheet like a mummy. With Jay-P's face pressed into the cold, metal floor, Connery pinned him with a knee across the back of his neck. Jay-P yelped, gasped and cussed, wriggling violently, but was cocooned and held firmly down. Connery waited, and finally the kid quit fighting in favour of trying to catch his breath.

"Time for us to have a little chat," Connery said calmly.

Jay-P struggled again for a moment, hearing the Irishman's voice, but quickly stopped when Connery pushed down with his knee a little harder.

"Keep squirming and I'll keep shoving," he said, his voice betraying no signs of physical effort. "Eventually I'll snap your neck and neither of us will get what we want." Connery leaned down closer. "And to be clear, what you should be hoping for from our time together here is to leave alive."

"My cousin will kill you for this, comemierda," Jay-P wheezed, and Connery jerked his knee, scraping the kid's face on the metal floor, making him groan in a mixture of pain and fear.

"Dayán Castillo doesn't care whether you live or die," Connery continued. "What he cares about is that all the cogs in his wheels of business keep moving smoothly, without any interruptions or distractions. So your amateur efforts at screwing with me are nothing but an annoyance to him."

"I don't know what you're talking about," Jay-P spluttered.

Connery applied a touch more pressure and received more groans. "Come on, you stupid little shit," he laughed, "you know how this works. You can lie and make up shit, but I already know what you've done, I just want to hear you admit it. The question is how much pain you choose to endure before you do."

With his cheek crushed against the floor, Jay-P could look up and see Connery from his right eye in the dim light of the room. The sun was edging above the horizon and light seeped in through the porthole curtain.

"I could take your eye, for example," Connery said and put his thumb over Jay-P's eye socket. The kid wriggled and tried to roll but was perfectly constrained by a simple, polyester bed sheet.

"No, man, no, not my eyes," Jay-P squealed.

Connery took his thumb away and could make out the pure fear on the kid's face, blinking and staring up at him in terror. He knew he had him now, which was good, as his lean, diminutive size had applied almost all the pressure his body weight could manage to Jay-P's thick, muscled neck.

"Why were you on the dive boat?" Connery asked.

"Okay, I was on there, but I was just looking around," Jay-P admitted.

"So, you're telling me, at the cost of your right eye if you're lying, that you didn't cut a hole in the dive gear?"

The only thing Jay-P could move was his eyeball, which darted and flicked around as though some form of escape he hadn't seen eluded his vision. Connery reached down with his thumb.

"I did, I did, I cut a hole in the BCD," Jay-P yelped, closing his eye tightly.

"Did you know whose it was?" Connery asked, keeping his voice calm and even.

"Yeah, yeah," Jay-P mumbled, daring to open his eyes again. "It has all that pink shit on it. I was just screwing around, I figured she'd realise as soon as she got in the water. But I watched from the shore, and you guys went straight down, and so then I thought maybe I had messed with the wrong one. I wasn't trying to hurt her, I was just screwing with you."

Connery sighed to himself. He had already put Mads in danger within hours of them deciding to see each other seriously. How did he think he could shelter her from this life he had led for so long? There would always be an ambitious fool like Jay-P who wanted to stake some territory or muscle in on a good thing. He wanted to squeeze the life from the kid, add him to the many souls he had sent to the other side without remorse. Jay-P certainly fell into that category. Connery could think of nothing redeeming he had seen from the young man in the time he had known him. The world wouldn't miss him.

"When we get back to Miami, you're off the boat," Connery growled, unveiling his contempt. "Castillo can decide what he wants to do with you from there, but I've given you more chance than you deserve."

Jay-P blinked up at him, but Connery kept his knee hard against the back of his neck.

"Help load, do as you're told, and don't make trouble before we leave," he added. "Understand?"

Jay-P couldn't nod so he was forced to speak. "Yeah, I get it," he spat back.

Connery was outside and closed the sliding door before Jay-P could free himself from the sheet. He waited a minute in the dark passageway, listening to the kid shuffle around inside. If the hothead was about to reappear with his handgun, hell bent on instant, rage-fuelled revenge, Connery would stop him in his tracks and there would be no more discussion. Fortunately for Jay-P, he stayed in his berth, and Connery quietly slipped away.

People were unpredictable, especially angry ones without much sense, but Connery hoped Jay-P would fall in line for a few days until they returned to Miami. Or at least until they left port. On the open sea, his tolerance for the kid's bullshit would be zero. It dawned on Connery: the dichotomy between the tenderness and love of the previous night, and the return to his world of distrust, deceit and violence. One foot couldn't remain on each side of that chasmic divide for long.

He walked slowly across the pilothouse, lost in thought. What would he say to Reg and AJ? Or Mads for that matter. Don't worry, he'll get what's coming to him back in Florida? Reg and AJ would rather involve the police, and Connery couldn't blame them. He also couldn't allow that to happen. Coming clean with Mads was a monumental commitment and risk, one he wasn't about to repeat with virtual strangers, regardless of how much he liked the two of them.

Last night, he had made a promise to Mads. He would find a way to remove himself from Castillo's employment, and once he had, they would leave together. Maybe travel for a while. They both had savings, places they would like to see, and it would give them the time to see where their relationship could go. It all sounded wonderful, but Connery knew Castillo didn't take kindly to anyone stepping away from the inner workings of his business. It wasn't like he could hand in his two-week notice and they would throw him a party with a good luck cake. Somehow he would have to convince the Cuban that he offered no threat. He almost laughed. Offer no threat? While he breathed, he was a loose end in Castillo's mind, and he knew it. People stepping away from a life of crime at the level he had been involved at for years now was unheard of. The fruitful income revenue stops, but the lifestyle and spend rarely does. It doesn't take long for a nice pile of savings to whittle down into a small jar of pennies. The retiree is back knocking on the door of his employer, or his employer's rival, or worse still, caves to the Feds begging for information in exchange for a new identity and a steady income. Very few slide away into anonymity and frugally live out their days in peace. Of course, very few in his line of work lived until the time they desired retirement. It was a self-retiring business.

He descended the steps to the galley, where Dunno handed him a cup of coffee without saying a word.

"Thanks," Connery said, taking the mug and leaning against the wall in the narrow kitchen area. "I'm expecting the truck somewhere around 0700 to 0800. If all goes well, we'll be on our way after lunch."

Dunno nodded. "Breakfast?"

Connery glanced at his watch. It was 6:05am. "Give me thirty minutes to clean up," he replied, then stepped towards his door at the far end of the galley. "Are we good on provisions for the run back?" he asked as he turned his key in the lock and looked back over his shoulder.

"I got fresh eggs and a few udder tings yesterday," Dunno replied.

Connery nodded and entered his stateroom, swinging the door closed behind him. He walked across the tiny living space towards the bedroom, ignoring Mason, who sat silently watching him. Connery continued to the bathroom where he turned on the shower, then pushed the foot pedal on the unflushed head. He beckoned for Mason to join him, who quietly approached and leaned against the opening into the bathroom.

"Get some sleep?" Connery whispered.

"Yeah, you?" Mason replied with a grin.

"Cheeky bastard," Connery retorted. "I'll get you some breakfast in a while."

Mason nodded. "Cool, thanks," he said in a hushed voice. "Got a plan?"

Connery took a deep breath and let it out slowly. "Well, Castillo suspects you got picked up – those idiots on the charter blabbed to a newspaper," Connery explained. "So hiding you through to

Miami is less appealing than it was. There's someone I need to talk to, and things may happen pretty fast this morning as we'll be leaving around midday."

"Who can you talk to?" Mason asked cautiously. "I'm not sure we can trust anyone around here."

"I know someone with a boat. Now piss off out of here while I take a shower."

Mason returned to the living area and Connery stripped off his clothes, stepping into the hot shower. As the water cascaded over his body, refreshing and cleansing, he thought about stacking the odds in his favour before entering a hostile environment. Well, he considered with growing concern; they seem to be stacking the wrong way, from a multitude of different angles. He wondered what new twists awaited him.

26

SUNDAY

AJ begrudgingly trudged along the path towards the restaurant. She paused a moment, turned around to face east, took out her mobile and snapped a photo of the sunrise. The sky had a pale-yellow glow, silhouetting the cottages and trees as the sun peaked above the woods. She had woken at 6:15am, remembered she was on holiday and was about to roll over and go back to sleep when something urged her to look at her mobile. Sure enough, a text message from Mads had silently arrived a few minutes earlier. She had squinted through sleepy eyes to read the message: 'If for some crazy reason you're up early, join me for breakfast in 10.'

She had wrestled with the invitation for a minute or two. Jackson was fast asleep, and AJ loved to sleep in when she could. But her curiosity won over, and she was dying to hear what happened after they all left the restaurant the night before. She was proud of herself for not making Jackson come along and suffer the early start with her, a fact she would make him aware of later. Of course, secretly she knew that had more to do with wanting gossip than being selfless.

Walking up the steps to the covered outside patio, she spotted

Mads at a table for four near the outer corner where she was taking in the sunrise. Mads looked as perfectly put together as always and AJ felt like a slob in her well-worn Mermaid Divers sweatshirt and unbrushed hair.

"You're up," Mads greeted her excitedly. "I didn't wake you with my text did I?" she added, her expression turning to worry.

AJ plonked down in the seat beside her. "No, I had my mobile on silent, I just happened to look at it and saw your message."

Mads looked at her with a grin, her eyes sparkling in the soft hues of dawn.

"Oh, somebody had a good night," AJ beamed back. "I want to hear all about it, but unless I have some coffee, you'll just have to tell me everything all over again after I do," she said, looking around.

Mads stood up. "I need a bucket full of coffee this morning too," she said leading AJ towards the buffet the staff were setting up. "They don't officially open until seven, but we can help ourselves."

They loaded up with two mugs of coffee each and a couple of pastries, then made their way back to the table. AJ burnt her tongue in her eagerness for the hot Cuban roast, but immediately felt a step closer to facing the day.

"Okay, give me the scoop," she begged, and took a bite of the sugary pastry.

Mads took a deep breath. "So, it was wonderful, and then he got really serious, and told me some difficult stuff," she explained. "And then it was really wonderful," she finished, her cheeks blushing.

AJ thought for a moment. She hadn't known any of them very long, but Connery didn't strike her as the deep, soul-searching conversation type. "Serious, like I've been married twelve times? Or serious, like a steamy Italian Romeo type thing?"

Mads didn't laugh. "A different serious," she replied. "Stuff I can't repeat, but it was intense and there were tears."

"Connery cried?" AJ asked in surprise.

"No, silly," Mads laughed this time, "I cried. But I think it made the next part even more intense."

AJ was intrigued about their serious conversation, but reluctantly avoided prying any further. If Mads was sworn to secrecy, she didn't want her to betray that trust. Despite her imagination and curiosity running rampant.

"So how were things this morning?" AJ asked instead.

Mads sighed. "He had to get back to the boat early. He wanted to catch Jay-P and get to the bottom of yesterday's mess," she replied, "and thank you again for saving my butt so I could enjoy last night."

AJ sipped her coffee and shrugged her shoulders.

"But he left me a note," Mads said, and fished a piece of paper from her pocket and slid it across the table.

AJ unfolded the note and read, 'Just the beginning, CO'B.'

"How about Connery?" AJ smiled. "Quite the romantic tucked away in that military man exterior."

Mads beamed again, but her brow furrowed and her expression turned to a frown. AJ turned to see what had caught her friend's eye and saw Castillo walking out onto the patio. He waved to the two women and AJ smiled and waved back.

"Do you need to go have breakfast with the boss?" AJ asked, not wanting to get in the way of Mads's work.

Mads placed her hand on AJ's arm and squeezed tightly. "No," she whispered sharply. "Don't leave me."

They both stood as the resort owner approached their table.

"Good morning ladies," he greeted them politely. "I am Dayán Castillo," he said, extending a hand to AJ.

She shook his firm grasp. "Nice to meet you, I'm AJ Bailey," she replied. "I'm with Pearl Moore, the singer who's been entertaining here this weekend."

Castillo pecked Mads on the cheek and said good morning before turning back to AJ. "Yes, she is wonderful, I heard her last night. Thank you all for coming over – this is your dive boat at the pier?" he asked, pointing to the Newton.

"Yes, that's mine," AJ replied. "Pearl's husband Reg has three just like that too. They're not really intended for open ocean trips, but they do fine in the calm seas. Thank you for your hospitality, the resort is brilliant and of course your rum is to die for."

He bowed his head modestly. "Thank you. Madison deserves all the credit for the resort," he said, smiling at Mads who looked uncomfortable with the praise. "She keeps this place running like a fine timepiece. Bringing your friend Pearl to play here is a perfect example. Would I be intruding if I joined you two for breakfast?"

"Of course not," Mads said after a brief pause, but AJ noticed her demeanour had changed.

Castillo took a seat against the railing with his back to the morning sun.

"Can I get you coffee?" Mads offered, still standing. "Something to eat?"

"I'll eat once they open for the guests," he replied, "but a coffee would be nice, thank you."

Mads walked away, leaving AJ to drum up conversation with the man she had just met.

"Has your technician fellow been able to fix your labelling machine?" she asked, recalling the issue from the day before.

Castillo nodded. "Fortunately, yes. It required a small part he brought with him, and the usual computer programming update. I think these companies tell you they're always updating something, so you believe their ludicrous service contracts are valuable. Or at least essential," he laughed. "Imagine if your boat stopped running unless a spotty-faced child just out of school sent some new code from a laptop every few days. I prefer mechanical systems to all this computer technology, but perhaps I'm showing my age."

AJ laughed politely. "Well your untraditional style of ageing your rum works really well, and that's as mechanical as it gets. Nothing like harnessing the energy of the ocean."

"I heard you were able to dive the platforms, yes?" he asked.

"We did," AJ replied. "It was incredible, and thank you for

letting us do that. I'm told very few people outside the company get to, so we felt very honoured."

Mads arrived back with a mug of coffee, which she set down in front of Castillo before taking her seat.

"Please, that was this lovely lady once again," he said. "I trust her with all matters concerning this place."

Mads smiled, but looked down and sipped her coffee. AJ hadn't seen her around the boss before, but she certainly appeared tense and uncomfortable. The man was charming and very complementary, so she couldn't help but wonder if he changed when not around guests. Mads certainly hadn't mentioned anything and had seemed nothing but happy with her job.

"When are you returning to Grand Cayman, Miss Bailey?" Castillo asked.

"After Pearl performs later this morning," AJ replied. "I think you have a brunch, or lunch thingy? So once she's done we'll load up and head back."

"We do a brunch on Sundays that starts at 10:30 and runs through the normal lunch hour until one o'clock," Mads clarified.

"How long is the trip?" Castillo asked.

"Took us five hours, give or take, on the way out," AJ replied. "Should be about the same back if the seas are still laid down."

"The forecast is good for the next few days," Castillo said confidently. "I check because of our own boat, the Rum Chaser, has to return to Florida."

"That's a beautiful boat," AJ grinned. "Connery showed us around yesterday morning before they unloaded. Impressive how everything is perfectly tailored for what you need."

Castillo paused, and his eyes flicked between the two women. After a moment, he relaxed again and smiled. "Another perk not many get to experience," he said, "I think Madison is hoping to lure you all back again sometime."

"Well, I for one volunteer Pearl to come back," AJ enthused, "just so we can tag along again."

Castillo smiled broadly and stood, offering his hand to AJ again. "I will leave you two in peace. It was a pleasure to meet you and if I don't see you before you leave, have a safe and pleasant journey home."

AJ stood and shook his hand. "Thanks again for your hospitality, I hope we get to see you again when we come back."

Castillo nodded, smiled politely to Mads, and walked towards the restaurant. Once he was gone, Mads almost slumped onto the table.

"Are you okay?" AJ asked. "What was going on there? You were like the kid caught copying off her mate in class."

Mads groaned. "Was I that obvious?"

AJ shook her head. "Not that bad I suppose," she said, then thought a little more. "No, actually you were. It was sort of awkward," she added, laughing.

Mads groaned again and buried her face in her hands. "Shit, shit, shit."

"Blimey," AJ said and rubbed her shoulder. "What's the problem?"

Mads slowly sat up, looking tired and frazzled. "It's all part of what Connery told me, about which I'm sworn to secrecy," she said. "And it's for good reason, too."

AJ was bubbling over with curiosity now but leaning more towards concern than entertainment.

"Let's just say," Mads started carefully, whispering, "there's a lot going on with this place that I had no idea about." She fiddled with her wristwatch and stared at it.

"Really?" AJ replied. "Was that a gift?"

Mads looked up and realised AJ was referring to the watch. "Yeah. A thank you after two years here. Mr. Castillo gave it to me himself," She replied, but didn't look happy about it.

"That's a pretty nice bonus," AJ commented and managed to stop herself asking another question as Mads fell quiet. If her curiosity was bubbling before, it was boiling now, but she respected her friend's need to keep her promise. "Well, if there's anything I can help with just ask, okay?"

Mads looked at AJ, then surprised her by throwing her arms around her in a big hug. "You've already saved my life once this trip, hopefully that's enough."

AJ squeezed her back and laughed. "I hope so too."

27

SUNDAY

The flatbed lorry backed down the narrow access lane to the dock and parked parallel to the Rum Chaser. Dunno was already manning the crane and swung the boom across the dock, extending the arm until the pallet lifter hung over the bed of the lorry. The lorry driver, and another man from the distillery, both locals, wrestled the pallet lifter under the first stack of boxes loaded with rum. Connery watched from the deck of the boat, keeping an eye on Jay-P, who waited to guide each pallet into place. They had a precise system of arranging the cargo, and if the first piece aboard was out of place, they may only discover the error when the final pieces wouldn't fit.

The first pallet dangled from the arm of the crane and Dunno deftly lowered it perfectly on the marks with minimal guidance from Jay-P. Connery double checked the position as the boom swung back towards the lorry. Jay-P stood back and avoided eye contact with his boss, but Connery could sense the lingering anger and resentment from five paces away. The kid's left cheek bore inflamed red scratches from the metal floor in his berth.

"Looks good," Connery said, throwing an olive branch Jay-P's way. He didn't much care how the young Cuban American reacted once they left the dock – he could feed him to the fish if he made trouble – but stirring up more problems before they set sail was a much bigger concern.

Jay-P ignored the comment and watched the crane swing the second pallet over, so Connery left him be. Down in the galley, Connery poured himself more coffee and went back up the steps to the pilothouse from where he could see the men were continuing the load without any issues. Comfortable that everyone was busy and occupied, he walked over to the helm and stared out of the front window. He drummed his fingers on the dash, deep in thought.

An idea hit him, and he went down the port side stairs, turning right into the crew shower and head. Mounted in the ceiling was an escape hatch, one of four in the hulls, two on each side, one fore, one aft. Connery reached up and turned the handle, releasing the latch, and pushed the hatch open. A rush of balmy, humid air swept inside, a stark contrast to the dry, air-conditioned room. Connery looked around for something to stand on to avoid pulling down the emergency ladder snugly fixed and hinged on the ceiling. With one foot on the head, he could poke through the hatch far enough to look around. The pilothouse obscured the activity on deck and the entire dock. Looking straight back, he could see the side of the pallets stacked in a neat row, but once the first line was all aboard, the hatch would be safely out of view.

Connery used his strong arms to lever himself higher in the opening until he could sit on the edge. He peered over the side of the catamaran below the railing to the clear blue water lapping gently against the aluminium hull. He could easily see the sand and turtle grass on the bottom. For once, he wished the island waters were green and murky, but this would have to do. He dropped back inside, landing lightly on his feet, and re-secured the hatch.

Leaving the head, Connery quietly closed the door and went to climb the stairs to the pilothouse, but stopped when something caught his eye. He bent down and picked up a countersunk Allen head bolt lying on the floor under the first metal step. He instantly recognised the 1/4-inch fine threaded bolt and turned his attention to the panels in the ceiling of the passageway. All told, there were probably over a thousand of these fasteners used throughout the boat. They were relatively small, easy to drop and lose, so they carried spares with them in the storage cupboard. The one he had just found could have been mislaid months ago and happened to roll back into view by chance. Or, as Connery stared at the single, empty hole in the panel above him, it could be more recent.

He thought back to Friday evening when they had stowed the bags and was confident all the bolts had been tightened securely. AJ had even surprised him by commenting on the bolts during their tour on Saturday morning. All the bolts had been there then. These were fine thread bolts that didn't fall out on their own while the boat rested at the dock. Sure, over time, if they didn't tighten the fastener all the way, one might back itself out after days being tossed about by the seas, but someone had removed this. The question burning through his mind was who.

Both crew members on the boat knew where the bags were stashed, and of the two, Jay-P was the obvious suspect. He was pissed off, shunned by his boss and his cousin, and had been told he was out on his ear when they returned home. He was also short sighted enough to risk stealing from Castillo. Perhaps he believed his cousin would overlook an indiscretion, or more likely he planned to set someone up. In that case, his target wasn't hard to guess. Connery stared at the bolt in his hand. It would be like Jay-P to be careless and drop a bolt, thinking no one would notice. Or maybe the culprit had been hurried by someone else arriving. The thought occurred to him, with a sinking feeling in his stomach, he was forgetting about another crew member. Mason was back on the boat and had been since sometime Saturday. Surely he wouldn't be that stupid?

Connery looked at his watch, it was 08:25. He wanted to pull the rest of the bolts and see what was missing, but that would take far too much time. It was unlikely the perpetrator had removed all, or any, of the bags, so going through the contents of each one and taking stock would be a lengthy process. Shit, he thought, what new twists would today bring? This one was the mother of all problems. He pondered whether to put the bolt back in place. If he knew he'd be present the next time the culprit entered the passageway, possibly to replace the bolt themselves, it would be ideal to gauge their reaction. But the timing was unlikely. Connery placed the bolt back on the floor by the step in a slightly more visible spot than where he had found it. If it found its way back into the threaded hole in the panel, that might tell him something too, he decided.

From the pilothouse, Connery could see the load was going swiftly. They were working on the last pallet of the third row, which put them halfway through the job. He stepped outside and Dunno nodded without taking his eyes from the boom he now swung back over the dock. Jay-P glanced towards Connery, then quickly looked away, pretending to stay focused on the job. Why did Mason have to sneak the cocaine aboard, he thought, why couldn't it have been that fool? He would have gladly put a bullet in Jay-P's head and watched him fall into the Gulf Stream. For the first time, Connery realised beyond a doubt, he had indeed chosen to give Mason a chance. The notion had nagged and clawed at the back of his mind, where he had buried the idea and evaded the truth. But facing the fact he would have guaranteed Jay-P's demise in the same circumstances left no ambiguity.

He stepped back inside the pilothouse and trotted down the steps to the galley. His even temperament was being tested, not only by the wave of problems caused by Jay-P, and further confused by his emotions for Mads, but questions he now raised over his judgement. If Mason was playing him, there would be no more chances.

Connery opened the door to his stateroom and closed and locked it behind him. Mason looked up from the chair and smiled. Connery didn't smile back. Gauging someone's response to a question was an art form. Phrasing, timing and delivery were all critical to eliciting a reaction that could be accurately measured, visually.

"I'm going to ask you a question," Connery said quietly, "and if you lie to me, we're going to have a serious problem."

Mason tensed and frowned. A natural reaction to the question whether he was guilty or not. No one likes being accused of anything. The key was to follow up swiftly, without giving him time to formulate a story if he was hiding something.

"Have you touched the bags we hid since you've been here on the island?" Connery asked, and watched carefully.

Mason looked puzzled, as though he was computing the words and what they meant. "The bags in the overhead?" he said, and Connery noted the young man's shoulders relaxed slightly.

It takes an incredibly confident and well-trained person to relax when a question hits the nail on the head. Innocent people are initially relieved if the accusation is misplaced, often followed shortly by stress or anger.

"I haven't left this room since I got here," Mason added, his tone becoming defensive.

"Good," Connery replied. "Well get ready, you're leaving now."

Three minutes later, Connery stood on the deck, next to the crane, and watched the men continue loading, now working on the fourth row. The diesel motor powering the hydraulic system droned on, its note rising and falling slightly from the demand of the pumps feeding the rams on the crane. Barely above the sound of the operations, Connery heard a dull thud and kept an eye on Dunno, who thankfully appeared oblivious. Jay-P now had earbuds in, no doubt listening to the obnoxious music he liked. He'd been told several times not to listen to music while working, as he couldn't hear instructions, but now was not the time to reprimand him. This time the earbuds worked in Connery's favour. He made a mental reminder to make sure he latched the emergency exit in the crew head before the guys were finished and went below.

28

SUNDAY

Connery took the inventory paperwork from one of the delivery men on the lorry. It listed all the rum by pallet number. They produced Seven Fathoms in bottles deliberately designed a little under three inches in diameter to allow a dozen to fit snugly in a 12-inch x 9-inch divided box. At 13 inches tall, the slimmer shape kept the desired volume, but twenty boxes nestled neatly on the 4-foot square pallets. Loaded five layers high, each pallet contained 1200 bottles. Loaded to capacity, the Rum Chaser carried 102 pallets, which added up to 122,400 bottles with a retail value of $3,672,000. It also sat a lot lower in the water with the added weight.

He was about to step back aboard to verify the count, when a golf cart pulled up, driven by one of Castillo's bodyguards. The man himself sat next to the driver and the second guard rode on the back seat. Connery looked at a pallet hanging from the boom of the crane, swinging gently as the arm was lowered into place on the deck. They had two more to load before they were done, and he hadn't made it down to secure the emergency hatch yet. He wondered what on earth the boss wanted. He walked over to the golf cart as the two guards stepped away, taking positions close by with a clear view of everyone present. Castillo stayed seated and patted the driver's seat next to him.

"Morning, Boss," Connery said as he sat down. "As you can see, we're almost done."

Castillo stared off across the ocean. "When do you plan to leave?"

"Should be on our way by noon," Connery replied. "Make sure we have everything strapped down, get the lads some grub, and then we'll shove off."

The Cuban sat in silence, and Connery wondered again what the impromptu visit was all about. He looked over at the boat and saw the final pallet was being lifted from the bed of the lorry. There would be no good explanation for the emergency hatch being unlocked, and unless Castillo got to the point pretty soon, whoever was next to use the head would discover it. That in itself wasn't the end of the world, but it would raise questions, and more doubts and suspicions were not what he needed.

"It's been a while since I looked over the Rum Chaser," Castillo said. "Mind if I take a look around?"

Connery was stunned and for a moment floundered over an answer. "It's your boat, Boss, you can come aboard anytime you choose."

Castillo got out of the golf cart and walked towards the opening in the railing of the catamaran without another word. Connery noticed he nodded to the two guards, who followed them aboard. Dunno had shut down the diesel motor, the crane now resting with the pallet lifter under the final pallet brought over. He could hear straps being tightened towards the stern and presumed both men were securing the cargo. Castillo squeezed past the rear of the crane and entered the pilothouse.

"Anything in particular you'd like to see?" Connery asked, following behind and trying to assure himself that his boss's curiosity was purely coincidental.

Castillo looked at one of his guards, pointing to the stairs leading down to the galley. "Wait there," he ordered, and walked to the opposite steps leading down to the crew quarters. He glanced back at Connery, his expression hard to read, but his eyes were steely cold. Purposeful.

Connery knew there was always a reason for the man's actions, and his lack of explanation meant he himself must be under suspicion. Castillo descended the stairs and Connery reluctantly followed, dreading what the observant man might notice. The guard followed closely and remained on the steps as Castillo paused and tried the door to the crew's head. It was locked. Castillo turned to Connery, a hint of a grin on his face, then stepped back, allowing room for Connery and the guard to enter the passageway. The guard knocked loudly on the door.

Unsure, and extremely concerned what, or more accurately who, was behind the door, Connery shifted his thoughts to how he might leave the passageway alive. He wasn't armed, and both men before him certainly were, but the confined space of the passageway was in his favour. Castillo would be his shield, taking away the guard's opportunity for an immediate shot, and allow him a narrow opportunity to relieve his boss of his weapon. The passageway was quiet beyond the low hum of forced air through the ceiling vents, and the guard turned to Castillo for his next instruction. The man's eyes flicked towards Connery for a moment, no doubt making the same assessments the Irishman had just run through.

A flushing sound came from the head and a moment later the door unlocked. The guard stepped back and tensed with his hand inside his jacket, ready to pull his weapon. The door opened and Dunno peered out from the head, his eyes widening as he saw the huddle of people in the passageway. Dunno nodded to the crowd and nervously edged his way out and started up the stairs. The guard looked around inside the empty room and Connery peeked past Castillo and saw the emergency hatch was closed and locked. Connery backed out of the way as Castillo and his bodyguard moved down the passageway, opening the sliding doors to each berth.

Connery stole a glance up at the ceiling and noticed all the bolts were securely in place on the first panel. Castillo and his guard continued down the hall, checking all four berths. While they were busy, Connery turned and looked around inside the head. All looked to be in place. And then he noticed a cordless drill with an Allen bit in the chuck was tucked behind the toilet. Connery pulled the door closed.

When they moved over to the starboard hull, Connery waited in the pilothouse. Castillo didn't say a word. His boss had always treated him with respect, and over time included him more often in the inner workings of the business. But today, something had changed. Castillo didn't ask if it was okay to look in Connery's stateroom. He breezed through the galley and tried the handle to Connery's quarters. Connery held his breath. He had stayed up top, opening up his options for an escape if the door was still locked. He heard the door open.

Two minutes later, the three men returned to the pilothouse, where Connery waited, leaning against the helm.

Castillo nodded towards the door. "Wait by the golf cart, I'll be right there," he said to his men, and they both left, closing the door behind them.

"What's all this about, Dayán?" Connery asked, trying to bring the situation back to a personal level.

Castillo looked at him, and by the way the man's eyes searched his face, he guessed he was deciding whether to trust him again, or not.

"A day after the mysterious survivor who was pulled from the water arrived in Nassau," Castillo began, "the passport of a young American man was stolen, along with his wallet and credit cards."

Damn it, Connery thought, knowing what was coming next.

"The passport was used to fly back to Miami, and the next day to Grand Cayman," Castillo said, and Connery knew his face was being studied for a reaction.

"Shit, it's got to be him, right?" Connery replied, playing along and hoping his expression showed surprise.

"The passport was then used to fly here, to Little Cayman. Yesterday," Castillo finished.

Connery frowned and looked at his boss. "He's here? Why the hell would he come back to the people that just threw him off a boat in the middle of the Atlantic?"

Castillo shrugged. "What would you do? I know what I'd do."

"I'd want to kill the bastard," Connery acknowledged. "But Mason's no trained soldier, he's more the path of least resistance type of bloke. He's a California beach bum with some street smarts."

"Blind rage is a powerful motivation," Castillo said. "I think perhaps you underestimate the young man. He was thrown to the sharks and lived. He avoided the authorities in the Bahamas and procured paperwork and money to facilitate his escape. He's managed to travel all the way here without being detected, and now has us watching our backs. Or at least you should be watching yours."

Connery thought for a moment. If Castillo truly believed Mason was here for revenge, then Connery would be the target and his boss would keep him under watch, hoping to lure the kid into a trap. He needed the freedom to move about for the next few hours before they left, which meant shifting the focus.

"Or he's here because he knows where to find an easy score," Connery said. "As you've pointed out, he's not stupid. He must know he has to disappear, and vanishing doesn't come cheap. What if he came here knowing he could fund the rest of his life?"

Castillo mulled the suggestion over as Connery stayed quiet, giving the man time to digest the concept.

"What are your plans before you leave today?" Castillo asked.

"I told the guests from Grand Cayman, the ones I went diving with, I would have an early lunch with them before we left," Connery replied. "But obviously I can blow that off, we need to focus on finding Mason and protecting the boat."

Castillo held up a hand. "No, no, do as you planned," he said. "I will leave one of my men here at the boat, and you continue as usual. We'll see if we can draw him out. I'll be at the resort. My second guard can stay with you."

"I appreciate the gesture," Connery replied, "but your protection is more important than mine. Keep your guard with you. I'll be coming to the resort shortly, anyway. Besides, if Mason's after me he'll know something's up if I have a guard all of a sudden."

Castillo walked towards the door and paused before opening it. "I wasn't thinking of your protection," he said, without humour. "I want to make sure the problem goes away completely this time."

Connery looked suitably offended. "I don't make the same mistake twice."

Castillo opened the door. "See that you don't."

As he watched his boss leave the boat and join his men at the golf cart, Connery took a deep breath and tried to adjust his plan for the new developments. The situation was spiralling out of control. Or at least out of his control. He watched the golf cart turn around and head down the lane towards the road with Castillo in the passenger seat and one of his men driving. The other guard was looking at the boat, no doubt evaluating his best vantage point. The answer to that question would be the pilothouse, and Connery knew he would soon come to that conclusion. He stepped out of the door as Dunno and Jay-P rounded the corner, coming from the stern.

"All tied down?" Connery asked.

Jay-P ignored him and Dunno nodded.

"Alright," he said, looking at his watch, "it's 10:05, and we'll leave at 1200. Grab some food and check everything inside is ready to go."

Jay-P walked by and entered the pilothouse, avoiding eye contact, and Connery nodded to Dunno, directing him to return to the stern. As they made their way aft, the guard stepped aboard.

"There's probably coffee left in the galley," Connery said, turning to the man. The guard made a minimal acknowledgement and continued to the pilothouse.

Once they reached the stern, Connery stood close to Dunno and spoke quietly. "Who's been in the ceiling panel, you?"

The Jamaican shook his head. "Dunno, man. Wasn't me."

"Did you put the screw back in?" Connery asked pointedly, and Dunno nodded. "How did you know about it then?"

"I went down to take a leak when Mr. Castillo showed up," Dunno explained. "I saw the bolt on the floor under the steps and figured that be bad if the boss sees it. So I screwed it back in. I thought it were you that been in there."

"Me?" Connery said in surprise. "Why did you think it was me?"

"'Cos you were down here while we were unloading," he replied.

Damn, Connery thought, Dunno was brilliant at playing dumb, but he never missed a trick.

"What else did you see?" Connery asked, hoping he could trust the man's reply.

"Nothing," Dunno said, and shrugged his shoulders.

"Why did you lock the emergency hatch in the head?"

"Because it was unlocked," Dunno replied.

Connery nearly laughed. That was a perfectly good reason, he had to admit. From where Dunno operated the crane it would be impossible for him to see down the stairs to the crew head, so the only time he might have spotted anyone would be when they crossed the pilothouse, if they hadn't stayed low and crawled.

He slapped Dunno on the arm. "Thanks, we'll figure out the panel later when we're under way. I think we know who it must have been. I have to go to the resort for a bit. I'll be back by noon to leave."

Dunno nodded, and Connery took out his mobile to call for a golf cart ride. For what was coming next, he wished he possessed the Jamaican's ability to be invisible. Too many eyes would be watching him closely, and one slip would bring disaster down upon him, and others. Mads being one of them. That thought left a lump in his throat.

29

SUNDAY

AJ knelt over the diesel engines with the bay doors open on the deck of the Newton, and checked the oil level on the dipstick for the starboard motor. Wiping the long metal strip clean with a rag, she dipped it again to double check. Seeing the same result, she replaced the dipstick and stood up, made sure her hands were clean, then swung the heavy bay doors closed and checked they latched.

"Everything alright?" Reg asked, sitting on the bench in the shade below the fly-bridge.

"Yup, right as rain," she replied, throwing the rag in a tote of tools which she carried to the bow cabin.

When she came back up the steps, she turned and looked out of the front windows facing the shore.

"Here's Connery," she said, seeing the man approaching them down the pier.

Reg held up his coffee mug. "Good, I want to know what happened about that little prick on his crew."

AJ frowned at Reg. "Don't go all grumpy old sea salt on him first thing," she admonished him. "Remember, we are guests here."

Reg shook his head and mumbled something she couldn't hear.

"Morning," she said, turning towards the pier as Connery arrived.

"Morning," Connery replied. "Good, you're both here. I wanted a word if you have a minute?"

"Of course," AJ said. "Come aboard, we were just checking over the boat, getting ready for the trip back," she looked at Reg who hadn't said a word. "Well, one of us was anyway." Reg scowled back at her.

Connery stepped over the gunwale and nodded to Reg. "Morning, Reg."

Reg lifted his coffee mug again in greeting. Connery sat on the opposite bench and AJ moved over by Reg, both looking at their visitor expectantly.

"Let me start with Jay-P," Connery began. "I confronted him one on one last night and, with some persuasion, he admitted it was him that was on this boat yesterday."

"Bloody hell," AJ blurted, "that little wanker. Did he confess to cutting Mads's BCD as well?"

She wasn't sure if it felt better or worse knowing she was right, and it was Jay-P. On one hand, she had accurately thrown suspicion on the culprit and didn't need to feel guilty about that anymore. But now, knowing the person responsible for endangering a diver on her boat gave her a sick feeling in her stomach. Reg leaned forward and AJ sensed his whole body tensing.

"He did," Connery replied. "Says he didn't intend to hurt anyone, he was just messing with me."

Reg couldn't stay seated any longer. "Where is he now?" he growled. "In police custody would be the right answer to that question," he added, glaring at Connery.

AJ put a hand on Reg's arm. "Sit down, Reg, Connery's on our side."

Reg grunted, but sat back down.

"I hope you believe what AJ just said is the truth," Connery said, calmly. "Related to the boss or not, it makes no odds to me. Doing the right thing here is what matters."

"And doing the right thing means that bastard should be behind bars," Reg replied, with slightly less venom to AJ's relief.

"That isn't happening, is it?" AJ said bluntly.

"What do the police have to go on?" Connery replied. "If there was any evidence beyond my saying he confessed, and you saying you think you saw him a quarter mile away, there's no proof."

"And he'll deny everything to the police," AJ agreed.

"Let me talk to him," Reg said.

Connery laughed. "I'm guessing that would give the police some evidence. But against you for assault."

"I'll wring his bloody neck," Reg mumbled.

"Best I keep him under my watch," Connery said. "I've told him he's off the boat when we get home, and I doubt Castillo will come to his aid, so he's lost his cushy gig. He'll end up in the Miami-Dade County morgue one day when he crosses the wrong people."

"I guess we can hope," Reg said, and the three sat in silence for a few moments.

AJ wasn't sure what to think. Jay-P deserved punishment for what he did, but Connery was right, the police had nothing to charge him with. Reg trying to knock some sense into the kid wouldn't accomplish anything positive. She guessed there was no place for good sense in Jay-P's brain, and Reg could find himself in the jail cell instead. She looked off the side of the boat towards the restaurant, where Pearl would be setting up for her brunch gig.

"Who the bloody hell is this?" she said, seeing a swimmer heading towards Hazel's Odyssey. "If it's Jay-P coming for another go, he's gonna get more than he bargained for."

The two men stood and looked at the figure in the water, swimming effortlessly their way. Whoever it was used smooth, even strokes, and breathed from alternating sides at regular intervals, occasionally tipping their head to sight the boat.

"So, that's the other thing I wanted to discuss with you," Connery said, and Reg and AJ both turned to him. "He's with me."

"Who is it?" AJ asked.

"A missing person I could do with staying missing a little longer," Connery replied.

"What the hell do you have going on?" Reg asked. "There's starting to be too many odd things happening around here, and they all seem to lead to you, mate."

AJ noticed Connery's jaw clench and for a moment she wondered if the much smaller man was about to bite back at Reg. She presumed he could handle himself with his military background, and he was twenty years or so younger, but he ought to think twice about challenging the big man. His face relaxed.

"I understand," Connery replied, maintaining an even tone. "You're right. I'll leave you in peace. I enjoyed meeting all of you and I wish you nothing but the best." He moved to the swim step and waited for the approaching figure.

AJ smacked Reg on the arm. "So much for 'don't be a grumpy old sea salt'," she whispered.

"I'm just calling it as I see it," Reg retorted, not as quietly as he intended.

AJ stepped in front of him and looked up, tapping her finger on his beefy chest. "Do you trust Mads?"

He shrugged. "Yeah, she's a sweetheart."

"Well, she's known Connery for a while and she trusts him," AJ hissed. "So why shouldn't we at least hear what he has to say?"

Reg rolled his eyes. "Doesn't it seem like there's something fishy about all this?" he replied, lowering his voice this time. "Castillo, the resort, their boat, all of it? He can say what he wants, but with the price of diesel, there's no way sending that boat to make laps around the Caribbean is the most cost-effective way of doing business. I'm telling you, something doesn't add up."

"I have to admit," AJ relented, "seeing Castillo show up with two bodyguards was a bit odd. I get it, he's a gazillionaire or whatever, but who needs protection on Little Cayman?"

"Someone who's used to trouble elsewhere," Reg answered. "Trouble that might follow him."

"I suppose," she said thoughtfully. "Mads was weird around

Castillo at breakfast this morning too. Almost like something had changed. Still," AJ continued, "my point is, we all like Connery, and he seems like a good bloke. Mads is in love with the man for goodness' sake. I think we should hear him out."

They both looked to the stern, where Connery was subtly directing the swimmer to the side of the boat next to the pier where he'd be hidden from view.

"Connery," Reg called, and the man turned towards them. Reg waved him over.

Connery said something quietly to the swimmer, then walked over and they all sat down again on the benches in the shade.

"Tell us what's going on," Reg said firmly. "And no bullshit, tell us the real deal."

Connery sighed and looked back and forth between them both. "Okay," he started carefully, "Everything I tell you will be the truth. If I say I can't tell you something, it'll be for your own protection, understand? There's certain stuff it's important you don't hear."

AJ sensed Reg's 'I told you so' stare bouncing off the side of her head and ignored him. "Alright, let's hear it," she replied to Connery.

"The resort, the distillery and the Rum Chaser are all a front for what's going on behind the scenes," he said in a low voice, surprising AJ with his openness right out of the gate.

Reg elbowed her, and she smacked him back. "Hush up, grumps," she groaned. "Let the man tell his story."

"The what's behind the scenes is the part you don't want to know," Connery continued, "or it's best you don't know, put it that way. What you need to know is that I'm working on getting out of this deal, and I'd like to make that happen and keep everyone safe."

"So who's the bloke in the water?" AJ asked, feeling uncomfortable talking about the fellow who was hanging on the boat, just out of her view.

"He's our fourth crew member, who made a mistake, and I'm

trying to give him a second chance," Connery said, "but if my boss finds out, he'll insist on other plans for him."

"So I'm guessing you want us to hide him for you?" Reg asked.

"It's a huge favour to ask," Connery replied, "but yes."

"And take him to Grand, I figure?" Reg added.

"I don't want to sound too dramatic," Connery answered, "but if you could, you'd probably be saving his life."

"And in doing so, risking ours, right?" Reg added.

Connery thought for a moment. "I don't believe it would go down like that, Reg," he said. "I wouldn't ask this of you if I thought I was putting you in harm's way. If Castillo or his men find out, hand him over and say I asked you for the favour. Tell him you have no idea who this guy is. Don't put yourselves between Mason and Castillo."

"That's his name?" AJ asked. "Mason?"

Connery nodded as he stood up and moved to the gunwale, beckoning to the young man in the water. Mason pulled himself over the side and, staying low, moved under the cover of the flybridge out of sight of the resort. He sat down, dripping water from his shorts and tee-shirt, and nervously smiled at AJ and Reg.

"Hi, I'm Mason," he said quietly.

"Where did you swim from?" AJ asked, unsure what to say and wanting to start the conversation before Reg began interrogating the young man.

"The Rum Chaser, it's moored at the dock up the coast," he replied.

"Blimey, we know where that is. Has to be a mile away," AJ commented.

Mason shrugged. "Probably, it's not too far. But I swam out deeper past the restaurant over there. So hopefully no one noticed me."

"Did you arrive on the island with Connery?" Reg asked in a friendly tone, to AJ's relief.

Mason glanced over at Connery, who nodded, so Mason turned back to them. "I flew here, but I can't leave that way."

Reg was about to ask something more, but Connery stepped in. "He used a fake ID to fly here, but that won't work anymore."

"Where's your passport?" Reg asked.

"On the Rum Chaser," Mason replied, "but Castillo will find me if I use that."

"How come you flew here when your passport was on the boat?" AJ asked, confused. "Weren't you supposed to be on the boat?"

"He became separated from his paperwork," Connery said, and Mason grinned.

AJ figured there was more to that story, but it probably wasn't important right now. They had to make a decision. The guy looked pretty forlorn, sitting before them like a drowned rat. He certainly didn't come across as a threat or a creep, like Jay-P, but there again he was embroiled in something illegal, so she doubted he was an angel either. She defaulted to Mads, or at least her gut feeling about her. Mads trusted Connery, and Connery needed a favour. That favour now sat in front of her.

"Okay," she said, "go below and stay down there. It's hotter than hell in the bow cabin, but you'll live for a few hours until we leave. I'll give you plenty of water."

"Are you okay with this, Reg?" Connery asked.

Reg scratched his beard. "Ain't my boat," he replied, tipping his head towards AJ.

"True enough," Connery replied, "but you lot are a family, and I don't want to cause any rift between you."

Reg thought for a moment before responding. "You're right, we are a family," he finally said, "so if miss 'save the world' here thinks we should do this, then I'll back her all the way."

Reg stood up and Connery offered him his hand. Reg shook firmly and held on for a moment longer. "But if this goes sideways for any reason, you gotta understand it's my family who come first."

Connery nodded. "Understood, Reg."

Mason thanked them and stepped down into the bow cabin

where AJ handed him a jug of water. "I'm sure you know how to use a marine head, it's in there if you need it," she said, pointing to the narrow door to the port side. "Otherwise, we'll be back in a few hours. I'll leave the door unlocked but don't come out unless one of us tells you to or the boats on fire."

Mason chuckled. "No problem, dude."

AJ frowned at him. "I'm a woman, not a dude."

"Sorry," he smiled, "I'm from California, we call everyone dude."

"My boyfriend's from California," she replied. "You'll meet him later. He doesn't call me dude."

"Is he from Southern California?" Mason asked.

"No, he grew up in San Francisco," AJ replied as she pulled the cantilever door closed and held the top hatch open.

"That's why," Mason said with a big grin.

AJ closed the hatch and wondered where the 'dude line' cut the state in half.

"Alright, Pearl will be playing soon," Reg announced. "I'm going over to the bar."

"Mind if I join you?" Connery asked. "You can say if you've had enough of me, I'll not be offended," he added.

Reg laughed. "Don't worry, I'd tell you." He slapped the Irishman on the back. "Let's go."

Feeling her mobile buzz in her pocket, AJ checked the text.

"You two go ahead," she said, reading the message. "Mads wants me to run over to her apartment, we'll join you in a bit."

Reg shrugged his shoulders, stepped off the Newton, and walked up the pier with Connery.

AJ read the message again, then shouted after Connery, "How do I get to her apartment?"

30

SUNDAY

Pearl's gear was already set up on the stage and she was sitting at a table with Jackson and Thomas enjoying a drink when Reg and Connery arrived. Reg gave her a peck on the cheek before he sat down by her side.

"Everything ready, love?" he asked. "Sorry I was gone longer than I planned."

"I'm all set," she replied. "I haven't seen Mads, but I presume I just start playing at eleven."

Reg looked at his watch. It was 10:55am. "AJ said something about going to see her. I suppose they'll be over shortly."

He looked around the outdoor patio and spotted one of Castillo's bodyguards before he saw the man himself. Reg wondered where the other guard could be. Castillo was seated at the same table he had used the night before, and appeared to be alone. Reg noticed Connery had made the same observations.

"I'd better check in with him," Connery said quietly, and left the table.

Reg kept an eye on him as he made his way across the patio. Castillo pointed to the chair opposite, and the Irishman sat down. That's good, Reg thought, keep him entertained and busy for a few hours and they'd be on their way back to Grand Cayman. He had been enjoying their trip away, but now all he could think about was getting home. He ordered a rum neat over ice from the waiter who came by. At least he could enjoy their rum. He doubted Walker had anything to do with whatever else was going on around the place, so it seemed a shame to boycott the fine liquor.

Pearl stood and pecked Reg on the cheek. "Alright, it's eleven, I better go to work."

"Best part of the trip," Reg said with a smile. "I'll text AJ and tell her to hurry her arse up and get over."

Pearl waved him off as she walked away towards the stage. "She's heard me play plenty. I'm sure she's got something more important going on."

Jackson looked at Reg. "Where did she say she was going?"

Reg typed a message on his mobile while he replied, "Mads's apartment, I guess. She asked Connery where it was." Reg finished typing and looked up. "I just told her there's an Italian girl sitting on your lap whispering something in your ear. That should bring her over."

Jackson laughed. "I doubt it."

AJ followed the pathway beyond the guest cottages, through the trees and brush until she came to a narrow road. To her left she saw the apartments, just as Connery had described. Her mobile buzzed in her hand and she read the new text from Reg. She grinned and typed back, 'Ask her to order me a rum when she's done with my boyfriend.'

She walked down the quiet road to the sounds of cicadas and birds chirping in the bushes and low trees. The brush was tall enough to block all the other buildings except the roof of the distillery behind her. It felt like a tranquil walk in the park, and if it wasn't for the faint sound of water against the ironshore, it would be easy to forget the ocean was close by. The trees also sheltered the coastal breeze and sweat beaded on AJ's brow as she approached the first apartment.

They were more like two-storey versions of the guest cottages in slightly subdued and plainer trim. Four of the identical dwellings stood in line, spaced twenty feet apart, with a short concrete driveway leading from the road to their doors. Enough room for a small car, which no one bothered owning on the tiny island with resort vehicles available. One of the BBRC golf carts sat in Mads's driveway, facing the road, ready to leave. The fan from an air-conditioning condenser whirred from the side of the small building, dispelling the isolated feeling of the surrounding woods. AJ knocked on the door. From inside, she heard what sounded like Mads's voice, but couldn't make out what she said. Guessing it had something to do with coming in, AJ tried the handle and the door opened inward.

"Hello, it's me," she called out, then abruptly stopped with one foot inside.

The room was dimly lit and her eyes struggled to adjust from the bright sunlight outside, but she couldn't miss the handgun pointed directly at her.

"Come in," Jay-P grinned. "Now the party can start."

AJ's legs felt weak, but she stumbled forward and Jay-P swung the door closed behind her, bolting the lock. Mads was on the couch, duct taped around her ankles and wrists with more tape over her mouth. AJ realised the muffled voice she had heard was her friend's attempt at warning her. Mads's cheek sported a rosy red mark where she had either been struck or bashed up against something. She wore white capri pants and a flowery blouse that was ruffled but thankfully still mostly buttoned. She stared at AJ with wide eyes, full of terror. A rucksack rested on the coffee table next to a roll of duct tape.

"What do you think you're doing?" AJ asked, struggling to keep her voice from trembling.

Jay-P laughed and shoved her further into the room. "What does it look like I'm doing?"

AJ knew right away she'd blown her best chance. She should have run as soon as she saw the gun. Unless he was already squeezing the trigger, it would have been tough for him to get a shot off around the door. After that, he'd be trying to hit a moving target and the gunshots alone would have brought people rushing to the scene, hopefully saving Mads, even if AJ was hit. Now, they were both at their captor's mercy.

The sudden rush of adrenaline and fear caused her hands and knees to shake, and she gritted her teeth. She needed to think. What were his intentions? Her whole body shook even more. It was obvious what his intentions were, she realised. The bigger question was, what then? The thoughts raced through her mind and she wondered if she could succumb to the sexual attack if it meant they would ultimately live. She felt nauseous with fear and disgust.

Jay-P didn't strike AJ as someone making decisions with much thought. When he was done with whatever revolting plan he had in mind, surely he'd realise they were a loose end that he couldn't let live. She decided their fate was sealed, regardless of whatever took place between now and then. She gritted her teeth again.

She may have blown her best chance, but she wasn't about to go down without a fight. Jay-P wasn't tall, but he was stocky and muscular. It was obvious he would easily overpower her in a straight fight, so her only chance now was finding an opportunity to even the odds. The main thing was to buy time. Time expanded the chances for opportunity.

"Apparently you're tired of living, 'cos what you're doing here is pure suicide," AJ said with more confidence than she felt.

He slapped the back of her head. "I ain't the one with a gun pointed at 'em, bitch," he retorted and picked up the roll of duct tape from the coffee table, dropping it to the floor beside her.

"How do you think you're getting off this tiny island?" AJ persisted. "There's three real men that'll never let you get away."

He slapped her head, harder this time, and she blinked to clear her vision. He grabbed her by the hair and put the gun to her ear. "You're about to find out what a real man can do to you."

"Think you can waltz into the airport and fly away?" she spluttered.

"Look around you, stupid," he laughed. "We're surrounded by nothing but ocean. They'll be looking for a needle in a haystack."

Okay, AJ thought, now we know his getaway plan. He'll steal the Rum Chaser and head for who knows where.

AJ's mobile buzzed inside her pocket and Jay-P released her hair and shoved his hand in the back pocket of her shorts. She squirmed at his rough hand touching her backside. Retrieving the mobile, he looked at the screen and laughed, shoving the phone in front of her face.

"Check that out," he cackled. "Your buddy Reg sending you three laughing emojis. Now that's damn funny considering the situation, don't you think?"

He dropped the mobile to the floor and smashed the heel of his tennis shoe through the screen. AJ winced. The cell company would never give her another phone – that had to be the fifth or sixth one she'd lost, drowned or destroyed. Probably not the biggest problem on her current agenda. She noticed Mads's mobile lay in pieces on the tile floor as well. She guessed he destroyed hers once he had seen AJ coming.

"Sit down," he barked, and shoved her head down.

AJ dropped to the floor with the gun still pressed against her ear.

"Tape your ankles up," he ordered. "And make it tight, I'm watching," he added and pushed the gun against the side of her head again for emphasis.

Bugger, AJ thought, this way he doesn't have to put the gun down, at least to get my ankles secured. She picked up the roll of tape and deliberately made a meal of trying to pick the end of the strip off the roll with her fingernail.

"You know Connery won't rest until he finds you," she said, stalling. "And you don't know Reg, but he's the one you should really be worried about."

"You don't know shit about O'Brien, either of you," Jay-P

snarled, taking the gun away from AJ's head and waving it towards Mads. "Nothing about him, or this place, is what you think it is."

AJ tensed and tried to will herself to swing at Jay-P's gun hand while her hands were still free. Her brain told her to take the opportunity, but her limbs refused to comply. She felt the gun barrel against her temple and knew the narrow window had passed. She cursed herself. Inaction and hesitancy, she knew from experience, played into the hands of her captor. The disbelief that what was taking place couldn't possibly happen to the individual, combined with the blind hope of rescue, caused most captives to comply. AJ's hands shook again as she weighed up the likely outcomes. Raped or tortured for fun, or both, and then shot, versus probably shot while trying to escape. In theory, she would take the latter, but getting her mind and body to cooperate was a different story.

"If you don't stop screwing around with that tape, I'm going to shoot her," Jay-P growled, firmly tapping the gun against AJ's head, but not aiming it away.

AJ picked the end of the tape and stretched out enough to stretch across her ankles, moving slowly but deliberately. She wanted him to take the gun away from the side of her head. She breathed deeply and convinced herself it was the only opportunity they had. Before he could aim at Mads, but was clear of her temple, she would swing back with her arm, knocking his gun hand away and then turn and whale on him with all she had. The adrenaline surged and her whole body quivered like a coiled spring ready to be released. All the while she steadily wrapped the tape around her ankles, taking too much time, hoping to provoke him into pointing the gun away.

After three wraps around her ankles, the gun barrel remained at her temple. A wave of disappointment replaced the fear and nervous anticipation. The feeling of inadequacy and failure made her want to curl up and cry. AJ hated crying, nearly as much as she hated guns.

"That's good. Tear off the tape," Jay-P grunted.

AJ did as ordered and he stepped back, taking the gun from her head, but she couldn't tell where it was aimed now. It didn't matter. Wildly swinging her arms on the chance of hitting him, with no way to follow up with the attack, was a sure way of getting shot. Now that her feet were bound, she was immobile. Maybe that would be okay, she thought morosely. Push him into shooting her now and not facing what lay ahead before the inevitable bullet in the brain. And then a thought occurred to her. If he intended to have his way with them, strapping their ankles together was not going to work. She looked at Mads. Her ankles were taped and her wrists were restrained in front of her. She couldn't have taped her own wrists, so why did he choose to tie them in front of her body. Surely he would have taped their hands behind their backs? The victim would feel far more vulnerable with their hands behind their backs. Nothing was happening to them here, she realised. He was taking them to the boat, using the golf cart in the driveway.

31

SUNDAY

Pearl's daytime set featured a mellower background feel for the diners in the heat of the late morning. She was already on her fourth song, Bill Withers' 'Ain't No Sunshine', when Reg checked his mobile again, and not seeing any sign of AJ and Mads either on the patio or via text, he typed another message. 'Get over here.'

He thought for a moment. AJ loved hearing Pearl play, so there had to be a good reason she was late. Maybe Mads needed to talk about something in private, he considered. What he really wanted was the whole crew in one place where he could watch over them like a lion protecting his pride. With all they had learnt recently, his protective instincts were in overdrive, and he'd rather keep the group together and be on their way as soon as possible. He erased what he had previously written and typed. 'Everything OK?' He hit send and put his mobile down on the table, joining the applause as Pearl finished her song. He noticed Jackson checking his watch and looking around too.

Castillo was as difficult to read as ever. He had chit-chatted about the new three-year-aged rum, Pearl Moore's singing, and diesel prices in Jamaica, where they regularly refilled the Rum Chaser's tanks. He had avoided any conversation about Mason, and Connery was yet to bring up his issue and suspicions about Jay-P. Connery needed to check behind the panel and see what was missing, if anything, before they left Little Cayman. He strongly doubted the nine heavy duffel bags had been removed, knowing the few people who had access, but someone had been in there, so the chance of something missing was high. If he told Castillo about it, they'd be marching down to the boat immediately, an inventory done, the crew lined up and the whole boat searched. It would be much better if he called Castillo later today and told him the whole situation had been resolved. At least with one of the guards at the boat, he felt the Rum Chaser was secure.

"When are you planning to leave?" Connery asked, curious.

Castillo wiped the corner of his mouth with his napkin and pushed his plate away. "It was to be after lunch, but now I'm not certain," he replied, leaving the obvious reason unsaid.

"I'm surprised he hasn't revealed his intentions by now," Connery said quietly, "if it is indeed him. He knows neither of us stay on the island long."

Castillo's expression remained impassive. "It's him," he replied. "Perhaps he got cold feet. Or it's possible his intentions have already been made clear to someone I'm unaware of."

Connery knew better than to bite on the hook. Castillo suspected everyone of everything, so his thinly veiled accusation was nothing more than a shiny lure.

"It's a small island without many options to leave," Connery countered, ignoring the bait. "If the authorities are aware of the stolen passport, that rules out the airport. Leaves him with the option of hiding out here, or hiding on our boat. I guarantee he won't be on the Rum Chaser when we leave at noon."

Castillo looked around the patio, and then across the view he had of the guest cottages and the pier to the east. His eyes remained in that direction for longer than Connery would have liked.

. . .

After her epiphany, AJ's immediate reaction was one of hope. If Jay-P intended to take them to the boat, they may live a lot longer than she had initially guessed their fate to hold. Time could bring them opportunity. Then it dawned on her. Time would simply extend the misery between now and the same final outcome. He could abuse them at will while he sailed across the ocean. They would have no chance of escaping, and their bodies would ultimately be dumped over the side. If he got them to the boat, they were doomed.

"Lie down and hold your hands up, wrists together," Jay-P demanded.

AJ looked over at Mads, slumped on the sofa, breathing hard through her nose with her mouth taped over. Her eyes stared back, and through the terror, AJ sensed her friend's tenuous thread of hope. Their last chance lay in the unrestrained hands of AJ. Once her hands were taped, their fate rested in the unlikely chance of rescue. They both knew it. AJ wanted to wink at Mads. Let her know it would be okay – but she had very little confidence that anything would be okay. An impatient tennis shoe kicked her in the backside, and AJ lay down on her back, raising her hands in the air. She stole a glance at Mads as her head rested on the tile. Her friend's eyes slowly closed as her last vestige of hope drained away.

Jay-P picked up the roll of tape and stood over AJ's midriff, looking down at her. He held the roll in his right hand, along with the handgun, and used his left to pull out a length of tape.

"Move, and I'll beat the living shit out of you," he grinned. "Understand me?"

The grin was a telling sign. It felt like he was daring her to challenge him, giving him an excuse to hit her. Once they were aboard the boat and out to sea, he wouldn't be tethered by such thin restraints as excuses. He would abuse them both at will, she was certain of it. This guy pulled the wings off butterflies when he was a kid. Maybe still did. AJ willed herself to relax, and half closed her eyes, passively.

"Good girl," he whispered, and reached down to her wrists with the strip of tape.

AJ swung her legs upwards with all her might, kicking Jay-P in the rear end. Bent over, he began to topple forward as she drew back and threw a punch aimed squarely on his nose. Reg had always told her, if it's for your life, don't fight fair. Stack the odds in your favour with whatever you have available. Hit the painful, soft bits and avoid the solid, hard parts of the human. His stocky frame falling forward met her best thrown punch in a collision that momentarily halted his tumble and caused a grim crunching sound as his nose shattered. Jay-P groaned and everything clattered to the tile floor next to AJ, including Jay-P, the tape, and the gun. AJ rolled to her side and reached for the gun as Jay-P sat up. He clutched his face, blood running around his fingers and spraying from his mouth as he spluttered curse words in Spanish. Her hand found the gun as he regained enough focus to take a swing. She whipped her hand towards his face and the gun smashed him in the temple as he brought his fist forward. His punch sailed wildly across the air above her head as he wobbled and roared in pain and anger.

AJ realised she had the gun held awkwardly across the top of the barrel and had hit him with the bottom of the grip. She tried turning the gun around in her hand before he could recover, but he was already lurching towards her. He swatted at the gun with his left hand, knocking her arm away, and wound up for another swing with his right. This time she was defenceless and brought her left hand up to try and soften the inevitable blow. If he started pounding on her, she knew he would beat her to a pulp and there'd be nothing she could do. AJ closed her eyes and prayed she could deflect the first blow and stay conscious.

She heard a loud grunt and opened her eyes to a blur of colour and bodies. Flipping the gun around in her hand, she sat herself upright and aimed towards Jay-P, who was half covered by Mads's sprawled body. Somehow, she had hopped over and bowled him out of the way. Jay-P elbowed out from under Mads and glared at the gun pointed his way. Their eyes met, and she saw his rage, guessing he was about to charge her. She had never fired a gun in her life and now faced a crazed man who undoubtedly intended to kill her. She released a guttural, primal scream and pulled the trigger. The noise was deafening and echoed around the small apartment. She had been in close proximity to gunfire several unfortunate times before, but couldn't imagine becoming accustomed to it. Jay-P lurched towards the door and she realised she must have missed and he'd, not surprisingly, chosen flight over fight as she now had the firearm.

It was hard to believe she had missed a full-grown man just six feet away, but she was sure she had closed her eyes and the gun had leapt in her hand when she fired. Jay-P struggled with the lock and Mads moaned from the floor next to her.

"Stop!" she yelled across the room, and Jay-P turned her way. "Stay there, don't move."

Jay-P's face was smeared with blood and his nose was buckled at an odd angle. More blood had dripped down his shirt and the whole scene was rather macabre, at least by AJ's standards. The door handle was splattered red from his hands. He paused a moment, and she guessed he was deciding whether to rush her, try to run, or give up. Based on her lousy aim at six feet, he had to fancy his odds at fifteen. Sure enough, he wrenched the front door open and lurched out. The bright sunlight streamed into the room, blinding AJ's aim, but she fired anyway and heard glass shattering.

As the echoes of the second shot died down, the room fell strangely quiet and AJ set the gun beside her and tore at the tape around her ankles. Once free, she shuffled over to Mads and began pulling the tape from her limbs, then paused when it came to the piece over her mouth.

"I'm sorry," she said, "this will probably hurt a bit."

AJ yanked the tape away in one swift motion and felt the resistance from strands of hair being pulled from Mads's head.

Mads hugged her, breathing deeply through her mouth. "You saved us. My God, that shit was going to kill us both."

AJ pulled away and jumped to her feet. "We have to stop him," she said and ran to the door.

The golf cart sat in the driveway, and the narrow road was still. Birds chirped as though nothing had happened.

"Shit, he's gone," she muttered and stepped back to examine the door.

One of the glass panes in the upper half of the door was smashed and next to it was a splatter of blood. She must have hit him with the second shot. She felt a touch less useless.

Mads joined her at the doorway. "Are you sure he's not lurking out there somewhere, waiting for us?"

"I don't think so," AJ replied. "He's heading for the boat is my guess. I'm pretty sure he intended to take us there on this golf cart, then steal the boat."

Mads nervously surveyed outside her apartment. "If he's on foot we should be able to catch him on the way."

"We need help," AJ said, looking around the living room. "Do you have a phone?"

"Not a landline, no," Mads replied. "We all use our cells."

"Come on then," AJ said, pointing to the golf cart. "Let's take this impressive getaway vehicle and recruit the cavalry."

32

SUNDAY

AJ barrelled the golf cart around the corner towards the main car park and reception office, where several staff members were outside looking around. Apparently her gunshots had indeed stirred up a fuss. She spotted Reg leading a crowd, coming down the footpath from the restaurant towards them. She skidded the golf cart to a stop as everyone gathered round.

"Call the police," Mads shouted to one of the office staff. "Tell them to meet us at the commercial dock."

"And come armed if they can," AJ added. "There's been an attempted murder and kidnapping," she trailed off, wondering if she fell under the attempted murderer category, having shot at Jay-P and probably winging him. "And some other things…"

"What the bloody hell happened?" Reg growled, arriving by their side with Jackson and Thomas in tow.

"Jay-P," AJ explained. "He had Mads tied up in her apartment and then me too, but we managed to get away."

Connery arrived beside Reg amongst a wave of questions from everyone at the same time. AJ couldn't figure out who to answer, so she let Jackson hug her and held him close.

"Hush the hell up, all of you!" Reg bellowed.

"Where is he now?" Connery asked firmly.

AJ reluctantly pulled from Jackson's grasp. "He ran away, but I think I hit him."

"You shot him?" Jackson asked. "He had a gun?"

AJ nodded. "Yeah, but I got it from him, and then I missed, but I think I hit him the second time. He can't be hurt too badly 'cos he ran off and disappeared."

"Mads, you said for the police to go to the dock," Reg asked. "You think that's where he went?"

"We guess so," Mads replied. "We think he was going to take us to the boat and steal it."

"What's happened here?" came Castillo's voice as he pushed people aside to reach the golf cart.

"It's Jay-P," Connery answered. "He attacked these two and they think he's headed for the Rum Chaser."

Castillo glared at Connery. "What the hell is he doing?"

"We can ask him when we find him," Connery replied coldly. "If he can get the words out before I kill the little bastard."

Connery nodded to the two women. "Get in the back."

AJ and Mads moved to the back seats and Connery jumped in the driver's side, quickly followed by Reg into the passenger seat.

Reg turned to Thomas. "Stay with Pearl, make sure she's safe, mate."

Thomas nodded as Jackson squeezed between AJ and Mads on the back seat. An employee brought another golf cart around, which Castillo and his guard immediately commandeered. The two vehicles set off at their full speed, which was a frustrating and unimpressive 15mph.

"What do they have for police on the island?" Reg turned and asked Mads.

"We have two officers," she replied. "There's more on Brac who come over if needed, which is almost never, but they have a boat over there."

Reg grunted and turned back to Connery. "You armed?"

Connery shook his head. "No. It's on the boat."

Reg swung around again. "Where's the gun Jay-P had?"

AJ rolled her eyes. "I left it in Mads's apartment."

"What did you leave it there for?" Reg complained.

"I thought it was evidence and what have you," she replied meekly. "You know I hate bloody guns. I'd already been shooting it off like a Wild West movie – I thought everyone would be safer if I left it behind."

"My intention is not to keep that bastard safe," Reg growled.

"At least he doesn't have one now," Mads said, coming to AJ's defence.

"Well," Connery commented, "until he gets to the Rum Chaser." He looked over at Reg with a frown. "He'll have access to some firepower once he gets there."

Reg let out a long breath as they trundled along the road towards the dock with the ocean lapping serenely against the ironshore on their right. In the distance, AJ heard a siren wailing. She looked behind them. The second golf cart was right on their tail, running at exactly the same speed with both vehicles up against their speed governors. Castillo's guard was driving and his boss sat stern faced next to him, speaking into his mobile phone. Whoever he was calling appeared not to answer as he put the phone away without speaking. Castillo waved to AJ, indicating he wanted to come up alongside.

"Connery, your boss wants to pull up next to us, I think."

She looked ahead and saw they were approaching the tiny side road leading to the dock. Connery eased off the throttle and let the second golf cart pull alongside. He then sped up again to stay even with the other cart. Castillo leaned forward and pointed to his guard. AJ noticed Connery nodded and eased off once more, allowing the other golf cart to go ahead of them, both still travelling at an excruciatingly slow pace. Better than running, AJ thought, but not by much. The two vehicles turned into the short lane to the dock and AJ's jaw dropped open. They pulled up to the edge of the concrete dock and everyone tumbled out and surveyed the empty ocean. The Rum Chaser was gone.

Mads screamed and pointed at the water below them. AJ looked down and saw Castillo's second guard floating face down in the water with a tint of red surrounding his corpse. The man was being unceremoniously bumped up against the dock by the gentle surge, and a crowd of fish already circled in the water around him. Behind them the siren grew louder, and as Jackson jumped into the water to pull the body ashore, a police car pulled in with lights blazing.

Mads knew both the police constables, so she tried to explain what had happened at her apartment and led them all to the dock. The constables, a man and a woman, were both wide eyed and quick to radio for support from the sister island, four and a half miles east of Little Cayman. AJ knew that it would take time to gather the people required and come over by boat. Castillo stood by the golf carts talking into his mobile in Spanish, keeping his voice low, and she noticed his guard, the one still breathing, kept his distance from the police. They wouldn't take kindly to the handgun he had hidden under his lightweight jacket.

She quietly stepped away from Mads and the police, and beckoned Reg over. Connery came with him.

"Jay-P is still here somewhere," she whispered. "No way did he have enough time to get back here, murder that poor bloke, and get clear out of view on your boat. I know it's pretty fast, but not that fast."

"I agree," Connery nodded. "The guard had his throat cut. There's no way Jay-P showed up here and jumped that guy. He was left here to watch for..." Connery paused and double checked no one was close enough to hear them, "our guy we have tucked away."

"Tucked away on a boat," Reg said, trying to keep his booming voice low. "You say Jay-P was taking you to a boat, AJ – you sure it was this boat?"

"Shit," AJ exclaimed, "maybe not. He could have had a different boat in mind."

"Like your boat?" Reg groaned.

"Then who the hell stole the Rum Chaser?" AJ asked, no longer keeping quiet.

"I think I know the answer to that," Connery sighed. "My whole damn crew have gone rogue on me."

"We have to get back to the resort," Reg growled. "How we gonna do that? These coppers won't want us going anywhere."

AJ strode over to where Mads was still talking to the constables, who were furiously writing in their notebooks.

"We have to get back to the resort," AJ blurted. "One of you stay here and secure the scene, the other one come with us in the car. He's not on the Rum Chaser," she explained. "He's still here on the island and we're pretty sure he's back near the resort."

"Our orders are to keep everybody right here," the male constable said firmly. "Nobody is going anywhere."

"There's a crazy bugger running around, possibly armed, and definitely looking for a boat to steal," Reg barked. "One of you stay here and the other come with us, 'cos we're gonna stop the bastard. It's that or you both stay here and yell at us to stop leaving, which we'll ignore."

The two constables looked at each other and AJ felt sorry for them. Only a handful of the Cayman Islands police force were armed, and guns were issued only when absolutely required, which was rare. She doubted the two on Little Cayman even had access to a firearm.

"Macy, take them to the resort," the constable relented. "But the boat owner, Mads and the fellow who pulled the body gotta stay here with me. You three can go with her. And for God's sake, don't nobody get themselves hurt. Just try to delay or hold this guy till they get over from da Brac."

Connery and Reg headed straight for the police car and AJ looked over at Jackson. He was sitting on the golf cart, where the constable had told him to stay after he had dragged the body from the water when they arrived. He looked at her, water dripping from his hair and shirt, a questioning expression on his face.

"You have to stay with him," she said, pointing to the male policeman. "We're going back to the resort, I'll see you in a bit."

"I'm not sitting around here if you're going off chasing that guy," Jackson shouted back. "I'd like to get my hands on him."

AJ couldn't help but smile. She could tell by the look on his face Jackson was angry and desperate to be part of catching Jay-P. "You can't my love," she replied. "He's only letting the three of us go with the lady constable. I swear I'll be careful, and Reg is with me, I promise I'll stay behind him."

The constable pointed to Jackson. "You need to stay here, sir."

Jackson looked deflated, but Mads put her hand on his arm. "We'll follow them as soon as we're done here."

"Okay," Jackson relented. "Please be careful. Try not to do anything..." he paused, trying to find the words, "you know... too AJ-like..."

"What's going on now?" Castillo shouted. He held his mobile away from his face and marched towards the constable.

AJ quickly waved to Jackson and gave him an okay sign as she dived into the passenger seat of the police car. Macy reversed down the lane, and AJ could just hear Castillo yelling something about his plane and hunting for his stolen boat. Looking back out of the windshield as dust began enveloping the car, AJ watched the constable shaking his head and wagging a finger at Castillo. She guessed that wouldn't go over well with the owner of the missing boat.

33

SUNDAY

Macy screeched to a stop by the reception building, back at the resort, and everyone piled out of the police car. Several office staff ran out to see what was going on, but AJ didn't have time to stop and chat. She sprinted down the path towards the restaurant, then cut right to the path heading east in front of the staggered guest cottages, and eventually the pier. Once the ocean came into view, she could see her Newton was still moored at the pier and felt a wave of relief. She slowed her pace and heard the others' footsteps catching up to her.

"It's still here," she said, breathing hard from the sprint.

Her relief gave way to confusion as she wondered where Jay-P could possibly have headed. Maybe she did more than wing him? He could be holed up somewhere close, wounded, or worse. The idea that she had taken a life, even the life of a scumbag, was disturbing. She had been party to the death of a human once before, but technically a stingray had killed the man in that case. This would be different. She had fired the gun.

"The resort boat's gone," Connery noted, jogging beside her.

They both came to a stop and Macy caught them. Reg wasn't with her.

"Where's Reg?" AJ asked.

"He ran into the restaurant," Connery replied.

"So where dis fella go, you tink?" Macy gasped, her generous figure clearly not used to running anywhere.

"He may have taken the boat that belongs to the resort," Connery replied, "or it could simply be out on the water with guests. We'd better ask."

They jogged back to the patio where people watched from the railing and AJ noticed no music played. Their little scene had brought the resort to a standstill. Macy reported in to her partner using her handheld radio, and AJ spotted the crowd splitting as Reg bowled his way through.

"Pearl thinks he took the other boat," Reg shouted, descending the steps to meet them. "She saw two blokes on the Newton, then they jumped on the pontoon and it left."

"How long ago?" Connery asked.

"She said just a few minutes, five at most."

"Two blokes?" AJ questioned, somewhat relieved she hadn't killed anyone so far, but quickly guessing who the second person had to be.

"Shit," Connery groaned.

"Exactly," AJ replied as they took off running for the pier, Macy and Reg lumbering along behind.

AJ leapt aboard Hazel's Odyssey, saw the door to the bow cabin was open, and headed straight up the ladder to the fly-bridge, not bothering to confirm what she'd already assumed.

"Mason?" she heard Connery shout from below, but she knew he was gone.

From the fly-bridge she could see the pontoon in the distance, heading east. She guessed the Newton could easily outpace the twin 130hp outboards on the pontoon boat, but Jay-P had a healthy head start.

"Why didn't he take this boat?" Connery yelled up.

AJ started the diesels. "Guess he doesn't know how to hot-wire the ignition," she called down. "Keys were in my pocket."

"Bow line clear," Reg shouted, releasing the line from the dock and throwing it over the railing.

Connery ran to the stern and released the second line, throwing that one to the dock where it was tethered to a cleat. Reg stepped over the gunwale and everyone looked at Macy. She stood on the dock, panting and obviously unsure what to do.

"Come aboard, quick," AJ yelled.

"We should probably be staying here and waiting on da back-up from Brac," she huffed.

"Macy," Reg barked, "get on the bloody boat." He held a big paw her way and after a brief hesitation, she grabbed his hand and stepped over the gunwale. Reg and Connery pushed the Newton away from the wooden pier, and AJ reversed faster than she preferred in the shallow water.

"Clear!" Reg shouted once the bow was beyond the end of the pier, and AJ spun the wheel to the right and put the starboard motor in forward. The Newton pirouetted almost within its own length, and she spun the wheel back to centre and brought the port motor into forward drive once the bow pointed east. Easing into both throttles, she winced as she checked behind at the brown froth of water churning in her wake. The props were stirring up the sand on the bottom.

Once up on plane, the ride smoothed out, the wake cleared and AJ pressed the throttles to the stops, pushing the Newton to its top speed of 26 knots. The others joined her on the fly-bridge.

"Can we catch him?" Connery asked, shouting over the drone of the hard-working diesels and wind rushing by.

"Eventually, in theory," AJ replied. "I don't know exactly how fast that pontoon can go, but I'd guess it's under 20 knots."

"We can't run like this for too long though," Reg added.

"That's the bigger problem," AJ agreed, "if we get into a prolonged chase. Running wide open, we're sucking down diesel."

"Of course, we don't know how much petrol he has," Reg said optimistically.

"I'm betting he doesn't know either," AJ grinned. "Probably

have to dip the tank to find out and I'm thinking that dipstick doesn't know a fuel dipstick from a trim tab."

"What's da plan here?" Macy shouted, hanging on to her cap. "I need to radio in."

The other three looked at each other blankly, and then out ahead where the pontoon was creating a decent-sized wake a mile or so in the distance.

"The trouble with chasing boats with other boats is what to do when you catch up," AJ pointed out. "It's not like you can run them off the road."

"Get us alongside," Reg barked. "We'll jump aboard. He can't drive and fight."

"Nice one, Long John Silver," AJ replied with a grin. "I don't think he'll let us pull up beside him – he'll just steer away."

"Or shoot us," Connery added, and Reg and AJ looked at him.

"AJ took his gun off him," Reg pointed out, "and you said he would have access…" he trailed off and glanced at Macy listening in. "You suggested all was okay in that department, if he didn't reach the Rum Chaser."

"How would he have got Mason to go with him?" Connery replied.

"Bollocks," AJ said, shaking her head. "He went back to the apartment."

"That's my guess," Connery confirmed. "If not, he'd be five miles ahead of us with the time we spent at the commercial dock."

"He went back, got the gun, and then stole the boat," Reg said, adding up the steps.

"Probably planned on stealing this boat, until he realised he couldn't start it," AJ rued. "Stumbled across Mason in the bow cabin while he was hunting for the key, then took the resort boat instead."

"Keys must have been in it," Reg added.

"So, what's da plan?" Macy asked again.

"Catch him and keep him in sight," AJ said, shrugging her

shoulders. "Tell them to send a fast boat, helicopter, plane, whatever they have, but it better have a gun."

"Bigger the better," Connery noted.

"Oh my," Macy mumbled, and shielded her radio from the wind to call in their predicament.

Jackson leaned against one of the golf carts next to Mads, and listened to the radio transmissions coming across the constable's handheld VHF. A boat was on its way from the Brac, and while the policemen on the boat struggled to hear the constable, their stronger marine VHF came across clearly. There was much discussion over which location to head for initially. They had a body and a crime scene at the dock, shots fired and a second crime scene at the resort apartment, two stolen boats, one missing, and one being pursued by civilians with a constable aboard. When Macy made her last report, which apparently the police boat must have heard, they chose the crime in progress.

"I guess they were still between the two islands," Jackson commented to the constable.

He nodded. "Must have been," the man agreed. "They're going to da north of da island. Cut dem off I suppose."

"They would have gone to the north to reach us anyway, wouldn't they?" Mads asked.

"Probably so," the constable agreed. "Depends where da boat was located when dey got da call."

Mads looked at her watch and then at Jackson. He shrugged his shoulders. They both knew whatever was going to happen; they had a long wait ahead until anyone made it back to the dock. He wished he had pushed harder to go along.

Castillo had made several attempts at persuading the constable to allow him to leave, and Jackson had been impressed how the policeman held his ground. The resort owner had stood off to the side and talked in a low voice with his guard for the last few minutes, and now it was the guard who approached instead of Castillo.

"We're leaving," the man said in a flat voice. "It's best for you that you don't interfere."

The constable slipped his radio back in its holster and turned to face the guard, his hand resting on the truncheon hanging from his belt. "That's not possible, sir, as I explained to da udder fellow. You must remain here till my chief gets here."

The guard reached inside his unzipped jacket and paused with his hand hidden. "We're leaving," the guard repeated. "Up to you what happens between now and when we do."

Jackson glanced at the constable, whose expression was a mixture of defiance and fear. The guard almost certainly had his hand on a gun, or was playing a convincing bluff. The penalty for calling that bluff could well be two or three more corpses.

Jackson ushered Mads behind him and heard her mumble, "Where did all these guns come from?"

Jackson placed one hand on the constable's arm and held the other up to the guard. "There's enough chaos going on, no reason to cause any more."

The guard's eyes moved to Jackson, a steely cold glare that left no doubt the man didn't have an issue causing plenty of chaos.

"We're leaving," he repeated, his hand still hidden inside his jacket.

"Fair enough," Jackson said. "No reason for anyone else to get hurt."

Jackson turned to the constable. "I'd say the prudent decision would be to let these two go about whatever they need to do. I'm guessing they'd like to look for their stolen boat."

The constable's arm tensed like a drawn bow under Jackson's hand, and he glanced back and forth between Castillo's remaining bodyguard and Jackson. Finally, his arm relaxed, and he nodded to the guard.

As they watched Castillo and his man disappear down the lane on one of the golf carts, Jackson turned to the constable. "That was the right call."

"He had a gun under der, right?" the constable asked.

"He convinced me he did," Jackson replied. "Enough to not take the risk."

"I was sure he did," Mads added shakily.

"Where do you tink they going?" the constable asked.

"Airport would be my guess," Jackson replied. "He has a private jet sitting there. I assume he'll go searching for his missing boat."

"Da one dat was stolen from here, or da one dat's being chased?"

"I think he's far more interested in the Rum Chaser that was taken from here," Mads verified.

"Do you have anyone at the airport who can stop them?" Jackson asked. "Maybe shut down the airport?"

The constable retrieved his radio. "It's only me and Macy here on da island, and da airport isn't manned unless a flight coming in," he said, his face breaking into a grin, "but I have an idea."

He clicked the button on the VHF and spoke into the microphone. "Dis is Constable James at da dock. Two of da men detained here have left for da airport, I repeat, dey are heading for da airport. At least one of dem is armed and should be considered dangerous. Over."

Next, he pulled his mobile from his pocket and dialled a number. After a moment, Jackson heard a voice answer.

"Dexter, listen up good, now," the constable started, and Jackson smiled as he heard the plan explained.

34

SUNDAY

AJ piloted the Newton past Jackson's Point, which made her think of her boyfriend. He would be worried and frustrated he couldn't go with them. Macy had just told them that Castillo and his guard were heading for their plane, according to her partner's radio transmission. AJ knew that would have only happened through a confrontation and hoped Jackson and Mads were both okay. She figured the constable would have reported otherwise if they weren't, but it didn't stop her fretting. AJ wasn't sure which felt worse, her concern for Jackson, or her guilt at knowing the anxiety she was causing him.

"We're catching him," Reg said, and AJ refocused on the boat in the distance.

"He's got a problem," Connery noted. "Look, the front of the pontoons keep settling and then lifting back up in the water."

AJ kept the throttles pinned as they stared at the boat in the distance, trying to figure out what was going on.

"Could he be running out of petrol?" AJ suggested.

"Wouldn't have thought they'd let their boat be that low on fuel," Reg replied.

"Bloody hell," AJ blurted. "He's stopped."

The pontoon boat had settled in the water and the soft rolling swells were slowly turning her sideways to them.

"He's dead in the water," Connery agreed.

"He will be once we reach him," Reg growled.

"Now, now," Macy intervened. "I'll hear none of dat now. Remember, we're to keep his location in sight until da chief gets here."

AJ didn't touch the throttles, and they continued speeding towards the stricken boat.

"We're tinkin' he got a gun," Macy continued, more urgently. "Let's not go rushing up close. He might be shooting us, or da hostage."

When everyone ignored her, Macy keyed her radio, forgetting her protocols in the heat of the moment. "Dis is Macy on da boat. The suspect has stopped just east of Jackson's Point and we'll reach him in a minute or so. Please tell me you're getting close."

The radio was silent for a few moments before it crackled to life. "Boat in pursuit, this is Brac Marine Unit 1, stand down and observe, I repeat, stand down and observe. Our ETA is fifteen minutes. Over."

"Der you go, now," Macy announced. "They just minutes away. We gotta sit back and observe till they get here."

AJ kept the throttles wide open and Reg turned to Macy. "Your radio broken?"

Macy looked at the handheld. "No, sir. You just hear it working fine."

"I didn't hear nothing," Reg replied over the wind. "You?" he added, looking at Connery.

"Bloody electronics and salt water," Connery grinned. "Always going on the blink."

Macy's shoulders dropped, and her mouth fell open with no idea what to say.

AJ felt sorry for the poor woman. This was probably more excitement than Little Cayman had ever seen on her watch.

"Keep your head down and you can observe, Macy," AJ said. "It'll be alright."

They were 200 yards from the pontoon boat and AJ rolled the throttles back, slowing Hazel's Odyssey as they neared. The Newton came off plane and AJ began arcing around the stationary boat, 50 yards out. Jay-P was a mess. He looked frantic behind the helm, searching for something. His tee-shirt and right arm were streaked in blood below his shoulder, and the arm hung limply at his side. In his left hand was the gun.

AJ cursed herself. "I'm sorry, I shouldn't have left the gun in the apartment. That was stupid."

"How many shots were fired?" Connery asked.

"I fired twice," AJ replied.

"Looks like you hit him too," Reg noted.

Jay-P looked over as they circled and waved the gun at them, before pointing it to his right. Mason sat on the starboard bench that ran the length of the vessel and fidgeted uncomfortably with the barrel facing him. Blood seeped from Mason's nose, so AJ guessed he'd already been the victim of Jay-P's rage.

"That's an M&P 9mm with a standard 10+1 magazine," Connery explained. "We keep one in the chamber, so he has nine left if he hasn't fired since the apartment."

AJ looked at Connery. "That's double Dutch to me, but I think you said he still has nine chances to shoot somebody."

"Aye," Connery replied, "that's the gist of it."

Jay-P continued fussing between the helm and the two outboard motors hung off the back, occasionally waving the gun in Mason's direction.

"Is he left handed?" Reg asked.

"Nope," Connery quickly replied.

"Ambidextrous, by any chance?" Macy chirped in.

"Nope," Connery said. "That kid can barely walk and chew gum at the same time."

"But he still has a gun with nine bullets," Macy pointed out.

"Yes he does," Connery agreed.

AJ shut the motors down and let the Newton drift, still 50 yards off the pontoon's bow. Quiet settled over the water, and Connery moved to the starboard side of the fly-bridge. He turned to the group and spoke softly. "Get down."

They all hunched down low while Connery yelled, "It's over. Throw the gun in the water and give yourself up."

AJ peeked around the fibreglass side of the fly-bridge where it became an open railing towards the back. Jay-P was staring over at them, shuffling from one foot to the other. He raised the gun and fired. AJ covered her ears as three loud shots rang out over the open ocean. She looked up at Connery, who didn't flinch or move.

"Get down, man," Macy urged.

"If he hits me with a handgun from a bobbing boat at 50 yards with his left hand," Connery replied calmly, "he's the luckiest bastard in the world, and I deserve to get shot."

He turned and looked at AJ on the floor. "But I'm sorry if he hit your nice dive boat."

"Six," AJ replied.

Connery stared across the water. "Exactly."

AJ shuffled to the port side as the Newton lazily swung around with the bow pointing west towards the pontoon boat. She looked over at the shoreline and saw a beige two-storey waterfront building with a white metal roof. She hauled herself into the helm seat and turned the ignition on.

"Get your head down," Connery said. "I'm gambling with my luck, not yours."

"Keep him busy," AJ replied, looking at the depth finder which read 240 feet. "I have an idea."

"What the hell are you up to?" Reg asked, shuffling next to the seat.

"Why do you think that pontoon boat stopped running?" AJ asked.

"Could be a million things," Reg replied. "Something that cut the two engines though, so it must be common to both."

"Like running out of petrol?" AJ suggested.

Connery looked down. "Yeah, but like Reg said, I doubt they'd leave the boat almost empty."

"What if it has two tanks," AJ grinned.

Connery nodded. "That could be," he said thoughtfully. "It just ran out on the first tank."

"And that plonker has no idea where the switch is," Reg chuckled, "or even if there is one."

"Mason would figure that out in a heartbeat," Connery said, "but he's not telling."

All three looked over the helm towards the pontoon and watched Jay-P smack Mason over the head with back of his hand.

"That bastard," Connery muttered.

"He might beat it out of him," Reg said sullenly.

"Connery," AJ said, dropping out of the seat, "keep us pointing towards them so he can't see our stern, okay?"

Connery looked at her quizzically. "Sure, what are you thinking?"

"I'm gonna make sure he doesn't leave even if he gets the motors started," she replied and slid across the floor to the ladder.

"Oh no," Macy groaned. "Please stay on the boat, they'll be here soon."

AJ smiled as she descended the ladder. "Don't worry, I'll be safer where I'm going."

"I doubt that," Macy mumbled as Reg shuffled past her and descended the ladder behind AJ.

Under the fly-bridge, AJ opened the cantilever door to the bow cabin and jumped down the two steps.

"What have you got in mind?" Reg asked, holding the door open.

AJ reappeared with her dive gear and a coil of rope with a carabiner attached to one end. "Recognise the building on the shore?"

Reg gazed out of the window towards the island. "Is that the Central Caribbean Marine Institute building?"

"Yup," AJ replied and threw the coil down on the deck near a dive tank.

Reg scratched his beard and she could see he was mulling things over as she quickly readied her BCD and made sure she had plenty of air.

"I'll go with you," he said after a few moments.

AJ slipped her arms through the shoulder straps and cinched the cummerbund and chest clasp. "No you won't," she scolded, "you'll stay here with Connery. If Jay-P notices everyone else is gone, he'll spook and the only one he has to take it out on is Mason. Make sure he sees you're still here."

Reg groaned. "Damn it, be careful then."

"I'll be safer underwater than anywhere up here," AJ said, standing up with the heavy tank hanging from her back. "He can't shoot at me."

The diesel engines started, and Connery used the starboard motor in reverse to rotate the boat, keeping the bow pointed towards Jay-P on the pontoon boat. Reg and AJ both checked to make sure they were hidden from view, then AJ waddled to the swim step where Reg helped her sit on the edge and slither into the water. She swung around as she dropped so the tank didn't hit the swim step. It was an awkward entry, but better than making a loud, suspicious splash. Reg grabbed the coil of rope and handed it down to her. AJ stuffed the coil under her cummerbund and clipped the stainless-steel carabiner to a D-ring on her BCD, so she wouldn't lose the lot if the rope slipped out.

"If you hear his outboards start up, abort the idea, okay?" he said, leaning over her in the water. "He might not be able to shoot you, but he can make a hell of a bloody mess with them props."

AJ gave him an okay sign, put her regulator in her mouth, and dropped below the surface into the vast open ocean. She looked down and all she could see was an inky blackness. The pontoon boat was too far away even to spot through the turquoise water. If they were even a hundred feet in the wrong place, she knew this would be a waste of time. Oh well, she thought, only one way to find out. AJ dropped to thirty feet, turned in the direction of the pontoon boat, and began kicking towards it.

35

SUNDAY

Using a compass heading AJ had taken before leaving the boat, she headed in the direction the pontoon boat had been. There was no current, and very little wave action, so she hoped the drifting vessel was still in the same general vicinity. After a few minutes the twin pontoons came into view, slightly right of her heading, and she veered that way. As AJ approached, she noted the props were at the far end, farthest away from her, meaning the bow was now just above her. She considered her options. Looking around in the water, she couldn't see anything around or below except empty, open ocean with the occasional school of fish wandering by. And one curious barracuda hanging under the shadow of the pontoon boat, her only witness.

She eased up to the surface by the port side pontoon and poked her head above the water. She immediately heard Jay-P's voice.

"You know boats and shit," he yelled. "Fix the damn thing or I'll start cutting you apart bit by bit."

"I don't know this boat, man," came Mason's strained and quiet reply. "It could be a hundred things."

AJ winced at his tone. She guessed the young man had taken a further beating already.

"Then start with the first damn thing, and work your way to a hundred," Jay-P retorted.

"Okay, okay," Mason mumbled so quietly AJ could only just hear him. "It sounded like it was starved of gas, so I'll start with the fuel filters."

AJ forced herself to stop worrying about what they were doing and get on with her task. She looked up at the nose of the pontoon where a metal ring was welded, used for towing the boat if needed. She took the stainless-steel carabiner and quietly clipped it to the ring, trying hard not to make the two metal parts clank together. Pulling the large coil of nylon rope from where she had stuffed it beneath her BCD's cummerbund, she put her arm through the middle of the coil to act as a reel and put her reg back in her mouth.

"Wait," she heard Jay-P say from above. "Did we just run out of gas?"

Silence followed, and she surmised Mason was playing dumb.

"Where's the gas gauge on this piece of shit?"

"I doubt it has one," Mason replied.

"That's stupid. How do you know how much gas you have then?"

"They probably dip the tanks," came Mason's response, and AJ groaned to herself.

If Jay-P picked up on the plural use of tanks, he might quickly figure out what she had guessed the problem to be. Her time could well be running out and if they started the motors before the Marine Unit arrived; they'd be back in a boat chase which could give Jay-P enough time to reach international waters. If he used Mason as a shield, preventing the police from firing on him, the three boats would be stuck motoring their way offshore in a stand-off.

AJ ducked back under and let herself descend to twenty feet, scanning the surrounding ocean. When she had checked the depth from Hazel's Odyssey, it had shown 240 feet and she needed deeper water. Taking out her compass, she headed north-north-west and kicked hard, feeding the line out behind her. She tried to allow slack in the rope so it didn't rattle the carabiner on the ring, but it became harder to control the farther away she swam. After a minute, not knowing the exact depth of the sea floor below her, she paused to search the open water. She had lost sight of the pontoons and was hanging at twenty feet below the surface in the open ocean, surrounded by nothing but turquoise water giving way to dark blue and black as she looked down. The isolation was daunting, and her pulse quickened. AJ had been in similar situations before and knew she needed to stay calm and level headed.

After a few deep, soothing breaths, AJ held out her compass and tried to decide which way to head. Assuming she was over the right depth, her choices were left or right, taking a ninety-degree turn either way. She looked both ways, as though the empty ocean would hand her a clue. A sound through the water made her spin around and gasp. It was an engine starting, but just as swiftly it stopped again. Was it Reg and Connery keeping the Newton positioned? Surely they wouldn't run the engines for only a few seconds if they were changing positions. Fighting back the urge to panic, she realised it had to be the pontoon boat. The fuel-starved motors were trying to start on the new petrol supply and would fire up as soon as the system primed. She looked at her compass and made a decision.

Kicking hard east-north-east, AJ gambled on the direction. She was now swinging the line across the water and the drag pulled and tugged on her arm as she frantically kicked in long sweeps of her finned feet. Her thighs burned and she could feel herself being jerked by the rope, ripping her off course. The sound of motors starting reached her again, and she checked how much line was left in the coil. Not much. If the pontoon boat took off, she had to either let go or be dragged through the water like a lure on a fishing line. Except she'd be dragged up once the line went taut, and would pop to the surface like a cork, risking a gas embolism.

AJ kicked for all she was worth and scanned the surrounding water. The motors cut once again, which gave her a burst of hope and energy, but she knew it would be short-lived. Running at all meant some petrol was reaching the motors, and with an electronic fuel injection the pressure would quickly build, purging the air from the lines, and Jay-P would be on his way. To her left, AJ spotted something darker than the surrounding water and turned in that direction. The motors started once again, but this time they kept running. She was out of time. Kicking like a maniac, she let the line run through her hand, viciously rubbing at her flesh as it went. The object became a full silhouette ahead. She had found one of the rum platforms, but it was still sixty feet away and twenty feet deeper. Angling down, AJ kept kicking as her legs screamed with the effort and her calves threatened to cramp at the strain from the long fins.

The note of the motors changed to a deeper tone, and she knew the revs had gone up, meaning the boat was moving. A second set of motors joined the racket now echoing through the water and she figured the Newton was about to give chase. She glanced down at the line and saw the last coil unravelling in her hand. If she let it go, the rope might eventually drag under the pontoon boat and foul one of the props. But only one of them, and he would still be able to run on the second engine. If she held on and they headed away from her position, she'd be dragged along with them. But, if Jay-P took off for deeper water and the international waters mark, 12 nautical miles from the coastline, the boat would be coming towards her and she would have a little more time.

She wound the line around her hand so she wouldn't lose it and continued towards the platform. If the line was yanked tight, she probably wouldn't be able to unwrap it, but gambles are gambles and she just went all in. The platform was now only 15 feet ahead, and what she needed was a place to tether the line. The sound of the engines had melded together in one, raucous noise, making it impossible to tell if one was moving closer or away. She had no clue if she had one second or thirty, but it was certainly seconds available, not minutes. The best option she spotted was the tether below the platform stretching down to the ocean floor, so she angled deeper still.

Almost to the platform and 6 feet from the heavy line, the rope in her hand stopped her dead in the water. AJ spluttered through her regulator as she was wrenched to a stop. She quickly tried to unwrap the line from her hand before she was ripped away behind the boat. She managed to set her hand free and waited for the rope to disappear, but it hung in her hand. She pulled hard on the line, but she moved closer to the rope instead of it coming towards her. What was happening? she puzzled.

The sound of engines grew louder and looking up, AJ saw two aluminium pontoons slicing through the water towards her, 42 feet above. Of course, she realised, the line had been played all the way out, but now it was being pulled by the boat. It would make a big arc in the water until the boat stretched it tight in the opposite direction. She only had a few moments to act.

She pulled hard on the line, which now followed her down to the big tether below the platform. Reaching a large metal ring where the tether connected the six chains to the platform, she threaded the end of her rope through the ring and tied an adjustable grip hitch knot. As she pulled the end of the line tight, the rope, tether and whole platform whipped away from her in a violent jolt.

36

SUNDAY

Reg shut the throttles down and frantically steered the Newton to starboard as he watched the pontoon boat disappear in a burst of spray.

"What the hell?" Connery shouted.

"She bloody well did it," Reg whooped.

The cloud of seawater settled, and the pontoon boat emerged from the mist, now facing the opposite way from the direction it had been heading, with the front of the port side pontoon twisted and bent. A line ran into the water from the badly misshapen ring. Jay-P and Mason were both sprawled across the deck and Reg quickly put the Newton back in gear, staying wide of the tether line.

"Quick," Reg shouted to Connery, "I'll get you alongside."

Connery scrambled down the ladder and Macy looked around bemused, holding her radio in her hand but unsure what to say. As Reg swung the Newton around he saw Mason picking himself up, looking decidedly dazed. Reg couldn't tell what wounds were new from the impact, and what had been previously inflicted by his captor, but the lad looked beaten to a pulp. Jay-P rolled over next to him and Mason stepped back. Focusing on getting the boat in close, Reg couldn't tell exactly what was happening.

"Macy," he barked, "look for the gun."

Reg reversed the motors as he swung the Newton towards the damaged pontoon boat. He leaned over the fly-bridge and saw Connery had dropped bumpers over the side and was poised, ready to leap across.

"Gun!" Macy yelped. "Da man still has da gun!"

Reg looked over at the pontoon and watched Jay-P raise his arm from the deck and aim at Mason, who took a step to the starboard side and leapt for the water. Two shots loudly rang out. Jay-P staggered to his feet and stumbled to the port side, aiming at the water and firing three more times. Reg was just about to throttle up the motors to pull away when another figure landed on the deck of the pontoon boat.

"Bugger," he seethed, realising Connery had made the jump.

AJ had swum like a madwoman in the direction of the stretched rope, amazed everything had held against what had to have been enormous forces. She saw the hull of the Newton slicing around and coming alongside the pontoon boat where the rope pierced the surface above her. A dull plunk sounded and water churned from the port side pontoon, catching her attention. From the white froth emerged a figure, swimming blindly down. Above him, odd streaks appeared, and she realised it was bullets being fired into the ocean. Mason was already 10 feet down and she watched two of the streaks go wide and peter out just past him, but one reached his leg and she kicked furiously towards him, sure he'd been hit.

Without a mask, Mason's surroundings would be a blurred mess of shapes and colour and AJ knew his first reaction would be to fight. As he levelled off, she approached from behind and wrapped one arm around his body while taking her back-up regulator and jamming it into his mouth. He thrashed, but she had his left arm pinned against his body and he missed her reg hose with his other hand. AJ purged the octo reg and let him take in a breath. He immediately calmed when he figured someone was helping him breathe. AJ turned him around and took his hands, placing them on her BCD straps, locking the two of them together.

Hearing someone land on the deck, Jay-P swung around, and Reg could see his face was covered in even more blood than it had been. He'd obviously hit his head in the sudden stop and his right eye looked to be closed. The gun was still in his left hand and he was coming around towards Connery, who stood below Reg on the starboard side of the pontoon boat's deck.

"I have a shot!" Reg roared and pointed his hand at Jay-P, forming a gun with his index finger and thumb.

Jay-P lifted his gun over Connery and fired at Reg above them both on the Newton fly-bridge. Reg closed his eyes and prayed his luck was as good as Connery's.

AJ had Mason settled down, breathing smoothly, and was considering where to surface, when another ball of froth and mayhem plunged into the water above them. Mason couldn't see, but he tightened his grip when he sensed something else happening in the water around him. Out of the carnage emerged Connery and Jay-P, thrashing and clawing in a ball of desperate humanity. AJ watched on in stunned amazement, unsure what to do next. The fight was short lived when Connery forced his arm around Jay-P's throat from behind, and the young man's elbow jabs were powerless in the dense water.

All the motors quietened above and the sudden lull urged AJ into action. Pulling Mason with her, she swam up to where Connery still held Jay-P four feet underwater, the bleeding man's legs kicking against the choke hold. AJ grabbed the back of Connery's shirt and towed him towards the nearest air, which was between the pontoons above them. Connery took a huge gasp as his mouth cleared the water and Jay-P choked and spluttered with his mouth half in, half out. AJ released Mason and pulled the reg from her own mouth, hitting her inflation button, adding buoyancy to her BCD.

"Let's get everyone on the boat."

Connery turned and nodded. "Okay," he said, breathing heavily. "Get Mason up and come back for us."

AJ hesitated. She looked at Connery, kicking to keep his head out of the water. He had tilted back and pulled Jay-P's nose and mouth clear, the young Cuban coughing and gasping but at least breathing.

"Go on now, hurry," Connery urged.

AJ nodded, and swam rearward with Mason, between the pontoons to the stern. Ahead, she saw Reg's upside-down bearded face lean over and look at them.

"Thank goodness you're alright," he bellowed. "Come on, get aboard."

He stretched a big hand out and grabbed Mason, pulling him clear of the stern, and heaving him up onto the deck.

"I'm going back for them two," AJ called up.

Reg quickly leaned back over the stern. "No, no, get up here, I'll do that," he said in a hushed tone, "in case that little shit causes any more trouble. Take your BCD off so I can use it."

"It'll only take me a second," AJ protested, but Reg had already reached down and unclipped her chest strap.

"Get up here and take care of the lad," Reg urged. "He needs some attention."

AJ unbuckled her cummerbund and let her BCD and tank float behind her. Mason swung the ladder down from the stern and AJ climbed up as Reg ducked under the boat, towing her BCD behind him. She went to look under to see what on earth he was doing, but Macy's voice echoed down from the fly-bridge of the Newton.

"Dat was something, right there, girl," she shouted, holding up her radio and pointing to the east. "Da Marine Unit are just about here. I didn't know how to explain what happened down der," she said, shaking her head and waving the radio.

AJ waved up to her. "Yeah, got a bit lucky with the timing. Glad it worked out."

"Thank you," Mason said, sitting on the bench beside her. "You saved my ass."

"Oh shit," AJ exclaimed, looking at his leg. "Didn't you get shot?"

Mason rotated on the bench and twisted his leg around. "I thought I had, but I'm not bleeding."

AJ looked at the dark blue mark beginning to grow on the back of his thigh. "Blimey, looks like it didn't have enough steam to break the skin. Not often you can say you were shot and came away with a bruise."

Mason laughed, then winced as his beaten face contorted.

"Where da others at?" Macy shouted down. "Dem two went in fighting like a pair o' feral cats at the fish market."

"They're..." AJ started, but Reg's booming voice overpowered hers.

"No bloody sign of them I'm afraid," he bellowed, climbing the ladder. "Keep an eye on the water all around, Macy, you got the best view from up there."

"Oh no," Macy replied, scouring the surrounding water. "Can't be losing no one after all dis."

"What the hell, Reg?" AJ whispered.

He put a hand on her shoulder and squeezed, still looking up at Macy. "AJ only spotted this one go in and I just had a good look around. No sign of them, so maybe they surfaced farther away. If not, they're gone, I'm afraid."

AJ frowned at her friend. "Reg, what's going on?" she asked again, quietly.

Reg took a deep breath. His face held an expression AJ had never seen before, like a piece of granite. "There's a line, my girl," he said in a low voice, "and when you cross that line, there are consequences. That wanker crossed the line when he took you and Mads. Now he's facing the consequences."

"Bloody hell, Reg," AJ mumbled, a surge of emotions running through her. If she understood the situation correctly, the three of them would swear they never saw the two men after they went in the water, and Jay-P would never be seen again. She herself had fired a gun at the man, trying her best to hit any part of him she could. What was different now? Removed from the immediacy of the trauma in the apartment, she couldn't help seeing the defeated and pathetic young man in Connery's expert grasp. Jay-P didn't appear threatening at all, but if released, she was confident he would try to kill any one of them to escape. She presumed Reg's role in this was turning the other way and making sure the cover story was convincing. Connery was taking care of the rest. And what about Connery?

The sound of a boat approaching at high speed made AJ look up, and she saw the Marine Unit rigid inflatable boat from Brac arriving. She had to decide if she was willing to lie to the authorities, or tell the whole truth and go against Reg.

"Where's my rig?" she asked, looking around the stern and the water.

"I'll buy you a new one," Reg growled, waving a hand to the police, letting them know they weren't approaching a hostile scene.

The final penny dropped, and she pieced together what was going on. At least one of the two missing people could breathe underwater. She doubted the other would be afforded the option. AJ took a long, soothing breath, and made a decision.

"See anyone?" AJ yelled up to Macy.

Reg gave her a nod, and she could see a mixture of dogged determination and empathy in his eyes.

It was hard to think about, AJ concluded, but it wasn't a hard decision. The world was better off without the likes of Jay-P.

37

SUNDAY

Castillo bellowed at his pilot to stop screwing around with his bullshit pre-flight inspection and get them in the air. The man dutifully hurried aboard and fired up the twin Pratt & Whitney PW617F1-E jet engines, and began taxiing away from Little Cayman's Edward Bodden Airfield terminal building – an unremarkable stucco building that housed a small office, manned only when planes were expected, and a covered roof for the island's only fire engine.

As they trundled the length of the short, 3,068-foot runway to the west end for their easterly take-off into the wind, the pilot made a general broadcast to warn any approaching air traffic of their forthcoming departure. Castillo's Embraer Phenom 100EV was one of only a few jets capable of landing at the tiny airport, his primary requirement when purchasing the plane. The compromise was only five seats and a cramped interior, but being able to fly directly to the island within 90 minutes of Miami was worth it.

The pilot turned the Phenom around the loop at the west end and stopped as soon as they were pointed straight. The plane would need most of the available tarmac to get off the ground. One person lighter would help, he noted, and knew not to ask about the missing bodyguard. He had worked for the man for several years and had learnt quickly to never question the strange packages, odd people and even a wounded man on one occasion. He had to re-carpet the cabin after that incident. Holding the brakes, the pilot scanned his gauges as he throttled up before performing a visual sweep of the skies ahead, and the runway. He immediately pulled the throttles back and his mouth fell open.

"What the hell are you doing?" Castillo berated him from the rear. "Do you not understand we're in a hurry?"

"I'm sorry, sir," the pilot replied, pointing out of the front window. "But we can't leave at the moment."

Castillo leaned into the aisle from his leather seat. Halfway up the runway was Little Cayman's sole fire engine with lights blazing, parked across their path, effectively shutting down the airport.

Dexter, the island's volunteer fire chief, jogged swiftly back towards the terminal building with the fire engine keys in his pocket. The constable had warned him not to confront the fellows, and he had no intention of doing so. As he reached the terminal, he could already hear the whoomp, whoomp, whoomp of rotor blades from the RCIPS helicopter approaching from Grand Cayman.

By one o'clock in the afternoon, with reggae music playing loudly in the pilothouse, Jabari Ricketts, known to his crewmates as Dunno, had travelled nearly 60 nautical miles. Starting west, he had taken a wide sweep around the end of Little Cayman, heading south until the island was a speck in the distance before turning south-east towards Negril, Jamaica. In another four and a half hours, he would dock at the little harbour where his brother was waiting. They had lined up a man who would buy the boat and strip it down, selling the components and getting the scrap price for all the aluminium. Selling rum on the black market wasn't lucrative in Jamaica, but worth the effort. The Ricketts brothers would stay in

Negril long enough to hand over the boat and its cargo, before disappearing into a country that was easy to get lost in.

The open ocean had been void of a single boat, ship or, for the past hour, even a bird. A plane flew over, and although it approached from the west at 1,000 feet above the water, Dunno never saw it behind him. He finally relaxed enough to set the autopilot and head below to wash his hands again, and change his shirt. The bodyguard had never heard him coming. Shoved over the railing, he fell to the water clutching his throat, and bled out before the Rum Chaser pulled away. Dunno had then washed his hands in the stainless-steel sink in his berth, watching the red-tinted water swirl down the plughole. Later, once he was safely underway, he thoroughly cleaned the deck and the railing, throwing his bloodied shirt over the side.

Now, he scrubbed his hands and fingernails one more time, as they reeked of bleach. He'd considered moving his stuff into Connery's stateroom, but what was the point? He already felt like a captain. Throwing on a clean tee-shirt, he stepped from his berth to the passageway and glanced up at the panel near the stairs. Connery had looked a little surprised when he'd told him about the screw, but more surprised when he'd thought it was Connery who had removed the panel. Maybe it wasn't him, he pondered. Dunno walked down the passageway to the storage cabinet at the end and picked up the cordless drill, which still had the Allen driver in the chuck.

The engine noise from the big diesel was loud, merely a few feet away through the bulkhead, but he paused as a different tone joined the steady drone. For a moment he wondered if it was a cooling fan, but it seemed too loud, and certainly different from anything he had heard aboard before. Putting the drill back in the cabinet, Dunno ran down the passageway and up the stairs to the pilothouse. He quickly scanned the waters through the windows, seeing nothing unusual, and could tell the strange sound was fading. He burst out of the door to the rear deck and looked up.

Hovering high above the Rum Chaser was a helicopter with two lines hanging down. When he looked back down, he faced two men in full tactical gear and assault rifles pointed at his chest. The badges on their left chest suggested they belonged to the RCIPS.

38

TUESDAY

The following days dragged by slowly and nobody felt like they were on holiday anymore. Reg and AJ both scrambled to make sure their clients were taken care of back home and Reg moaned about Coop missing him. Which AJ knew was the other way round, as Coop was probably happy as could be being spoiled by Nora and Ridley.

A slew of police showed up from Grand Cayman, and AJ was pleased to see her friend Detective Whittaker was assigned the case. He didn't seem as pleased. He was probably tired of AJ and Reg being in the middle of another calamity on the usually tranquil Cayman Islands, and she couldn't blame him. She was tired of it too. They were all questioned, made statements, then were questioned again. The police searched the waters for two days, looking for any sign of Alejandro Pérez and Connery O'Brien. Neither were found.

Mads couldn't face staying alone in her apartment, so Thomas moved into a guest cottage with Mason and she stayed in the second bedroom of AJ and Jackson's unit. She was shaken over the events, and distraught about Connery. AJ did her best to console her new friend, and pointed out that as long as there wasn't a body, there was a chance. Mads was confident, body or not, the man was gone. In her mind, he may have drowned, or perhaps not. But with the police all over the resort and Castillo being held until all was resolved, she was sure he would have left the island if he could.

Mason swore he was on the boat all the time and knew nothing about the stolen passport or the young man entering the Cayman Islands using it. The video taken at the Grand Cayman airport showed a figure of similar height and build to Mason, who carefully avoided looking at the security cameras at any time. It was inconclusive.

Whittaker stood on the dock next to the Rum Chaser when AJ and Reg stepped from the golf cart to join him.

"You wanted to see us, Roy?" she said, and then wondered if it was okay to use his first name at an active crime scene.

Whittaker wiped his brow, forced a smile, and nodded.

"Making progress?" Reg asked, looking at a couple of police personnel leaving the boat carrying heavy 5-gallon plastic containers filled with nasty-coloured liquid.

"Not as we would like," Whittaker replied. "In fact, we'll be releasing Mr. Castillo this afternoon. Sorry to bring you down here, but I've been rather busy. I just wanted to let you know and tell you it's okay to head back to Grand Cayman."

AJ looked at Reg, then back to the detective. "How can that be? It was his blokes that caused all the mayhem."

"Let me guess," Reg interjected. "Apart from them being under his employ, there's nothing to connect Castillo to anything they did."

"Something like that," Whittaker confirmed. "His lawyers showed up yesterday morning and have made things considerably more difficult, I'm afraid. They're representing Mr. Ricketts now as well."

"Who's Ricketts?" Reg asked with a frown.

"The man who took Castillo's boat, and we suspect killed his guard," Whittaker explained.

"Why would Castillo's lawyer help the man that stole his boss's boat and murdered one of his bodyguards?" AJ asked incredulously.

Whittaker ran a hand through his neatly cropped hair, "They are claiming that Mr. Castillo requested for Ricketts to take the boat offshore when Pérez started his shenanigans," he said, looking at AJ, "that you were unfortunately a victim of. They also claim that Ricketts had nothing to do with the demise of the bodyguard and was in fact unaware of his murder."

Reg threw his hands in the air. "That's bullshit and you know it, Roy," he groaned.

Whittaker nodded. "I'm certainly suspicious, but Ricketts hasn't uttered a word to us since we arrested him. They're threatening a battle over the arrest too, as it happened in international waters. Fortunately, the Rum Chaser is registered in Jamaica, and while en route our chief was savvy enough to garner a request from the Jamaican Coast Guard to apprehend the boat on suspicion of smuggling illicit goods."

AJ leaned forward. "And what did you find?"

Whittaker shook his head. "A lot of rum, legally being exported from Little Cayman."

"That was it?" Reg asked in surprise.

"We found one firearm, which the lawyers say neither Castillo nor Ricketts knew anything about," Whittaker said with a sigh. "We found it hidden behind the medicine cabinet in Connery O'Brien's stateroom. Needless to say, they claim he must have brought it aboard without their knowledge."

"Did the other guard have a gun when you picked up Castillo trying to leave?" AJ asked. "Jackson and Mads said he threatened your constable."

"Not one of them actually saw a firearm," Whittaker replied. "And he didn't have anything on him when our men reached him at the airport. We searched the plane."

AJ couldn't believe Castillo would walk away from this mess. Mads had shared a little more with her over the last few days, and although she had no idea what was aboard the Rum Chaser, she was confident it was illegal, and belonged to Castillo. Connery had told her that much. Mads wanted to say so to the police, but AJ had suggested she hold off. Castillo didn't seem like a man to cross, after all. Now, hearing he would get away with everything, she was beginning to rethink her position.

"There has to be blood on the boat from the guard," Reg said. "He had his damn throat cut."

"We found a lot of bleach, especially around an area by the starboard railing," Whittaker replied, "but no traces of blood. It's not illegal to clean your boat, even if it's in a suspiciously localised spot."

AJ looked at the Rum Chaser and thought about their tour. Connery had been fine showing them around, but not as relaxed as she found him when they ate together or went diving. Perhaps it was the work environment, she considered, or simply stress over the delay with the labelling issue but he hadn't been quite the same.

"Would it be okay if we took a quick walk through the boat?" she asked, watching the last of the police in pale blue protective suits step to the dock.

"Rasha?" Whittaker called out. "Are you all done?"

The policewoman turned and AJ recognised her from other cases when their paths had crossed.

"Hi AJ," she said with a wave. "Hey there, Reg. Yeah, we're done, we've just finished taking samples from the holding tanks so if anything went down a drain or was flushed, hopefully we'll find a trace. Wear gloves and booties if you go aboard, just in case something else crops up."

"Three sets please," Whittaker replied. "I promise we won't disturb anything."

Rasha handed them all nitrile gloves and pale blue fabric booties to slip over their shoes.

The three stood in the pilothouse and looked around. It was much the same as AJ remembered it, with very little clutter and everything neatly stowed. She guessed the police had been through all the items and returned them the way they had found them. If there was no crime proven to happen on the boat, it would be returned to Castillo and go on its way to Miami, once he'd found a new captain. She quickly made for the stairs on the port side and from the passageway looked up at the ceiling. Walking farther along the passageway, she checked out the series of removable overhead panels, all of a similar size and construction. The same Allen head countersunk bolts secured each panel in place. Whittaker and Reg watched her in silence from the bottom of the stairs.

"It's probably nothing, but when we toured the boat, I noticed the bolts holding this panel were more worn than all the others," she said, pointing to the panel nearest the stairs. "Connery was..." she tailed off, realising she would be incriminating the man if she mentioned his odd reaction. "Connery was showing us around the berths, but this panel caught my eye," she finished. "Have you looked behind all these?"

Whittaker frowned. "I expect so, they're very thorough about this sort of thing."

He thought for a second before taking out his mobile. A few minutes later, Rasha was standing next to them and the four of them stared at the ceiling together.

"We removed every panel in both passageways," Rasha said. "This hull and the starboard side. They access the fuel tanks. Complicated assortment of bladders between all the structure."

AJ shrugged her shoulders. "Oh well, sorry to waste your time," she said, feeling deflated. "It was a long shot at best. It must just be to access all the pumps."

Whittaker and Reg turned and started up the stairs. AJ went to follow, but Rasha hadn't moved.

"Wait a second," Rasha said. "What do you mean about the pumps?"

Shit, AJ thought, how could she answer that without mentioning Connery, but then she figured it didn't matter if they'd checked the hatch and there was nothing there.

"It was mentioned that's where the pumps for the fuel tanks were," Reg replied, dipping his head back down the steps.

Rasha walked to the end of the passageway and opened the cabinet. She returned with the cordless drill. It had the correct size Allen driver already in the chuck.

"We used this to take them all down and inspect behind the panels," she explained. "It had the bit already in it. One of my guys did this side, but I came over and had a look when he'd taken all the panels down."

She stretched up and started undoing the series of bolts around the panel, catching each one in her other hand as they dropped. Reg came back down the stairs and put a big hand up against the panel so she could remove all the bolts without it falling on their heads. When she was done with the bolts, he lowered the aluminium panel and set it aside. Rasha and Whittaker both shone torches into the hatch. It was filled with a black fuel cell bladder.

"I don't see any pumps," Rasha commented.

Reg reached up and grabbed the bladder, giving it a shove. Liquid could be heard slurping around inside. He gave the bladder a tug, and it moved an inch or so down.

He looked at AJ. "That's odd. These bladders should weigh hundreds of pounds each unless they're empty, and I hear diesel in there."

He gave it another good tug, and the others stepped back, worried a heavy fuel cell might plummet down on their heads. Reg pulled the dummy cell section through the panel opening and set it aside. Whittaker stood on his tiptoes and shone his torch into the open space now revealed.

"Well, what do we have here," he said with a smile.

Reg picked AJ up by her waist so her head poked through the hatch.

"Bloody hell," she muttered, staring at a bunch of black duffel bags.

39

TUESDAY

Jackson and Thomas released the lines from the dock and AJ eased into the throttles, idling the Newton clear of the shallows. A lot had happened in the past few hours since they had discovered the nine duffel bags filled with cash, but Whittaker released them to leave, and they decided to make the five-hour run home rather than stay overnight again. Everyone was ready to leave.

The police allowed Mason to retrieve his passport from the Rum Chaser, and with no solid proof that he hadn't arrived on the boat, they reluctantly let him leave aboard Hazel's Odyssey with restrictions. Antoine, the customs and immigration agent who had met with Connery and stamped them in, couldn't recall with certainty how many crew he'd seen on the boat. Mason claimed he was there and his passport must have been missed when the stamping was done. As Mason was the only witness left who was willing to talk about the Rum Chaser, they stamped his passport but ultimately retained it so he couldn't leave the Cayman Islands. He sat on one of the benches under the fly-bridge and chatted with Jackson about growing up in California. They came from very different backgrounds, at opposite ends of the state, but shared a common love of the ocean.

Mads and AJ had spent much of their time together over the past few days, and Mads had decided to leave the resort, regardless of Castillo's fate. She couldn't work for the man anymore, knowing what she knew, and once he was arrested when the cash was discovered, her decision was validated. She had also talked to Walker, who didn't have ownership shares in the Bloody Bay Rum Club, but did own the rights to the name Seven Fathoms. He was leaving too, with a plan to relocate over to Grand Cayman, where he would start his own distillery. He told her he'd be delighted to make her the first hire, and she told him she would seriously consider the offer.

Whittaker had gone into high gear when Rasha carefully documented the duffel bags, pulled them down and began counting the cash. All were circulated US $100 bills, not a new note amongst the $12,137,400. Mason explained that the bags they collected in Florida were always heavier than the bags they departed Jamaica with. It didn't take long for the detective to figure out Castillo was laundering the money through his resorts and casinos in Jamaica, where US currency was prevalent. His next call was to his chief to contact the FBI. The Cayman authorities would be more than happy to extradite Castillo and let the US Feds handle the mess.

Interestingly, Rasha noted that the bundle of 200 hundred-dollar bills they found in Jay-P's rucksack undoubtedly came from the duffel bags.

After an hour at sea, everyone settled down to sleep, read a book, or quietly whiled away the time as the Newton steadily churned its way across the Caribbean. Reg told AJ to call him up anytime she felt like a break, and Jackson joined her at the helm to keep her company. Alone on the fly-bridge together, he leaned against the helm seat and she sensed his need to be close after the tumultuous events. AJ welcomed the reassuring feel of his presence.

"I've been thinking," she began, "about some of the things we talked about over the weekend."

"Oh yeah," he replied warmly, "I can't imagine what prompted you to consider major life decisions."

She nudged him with her elbow. "I was already thinking about it a lot before I lassoed a speeding boat to an underwater stash of rum."

"I wonder if they'll sell that batch as 'aged and extra agitated'," Jackson mused.

"I'm just glad it didn't ruin the platform and all that lovely rum," AJ replied thoughtfully. "I wonder what will happen to it all if they convict Castillo?"

"I'm not sure," Jackson said, shrugging his shoulders.

AJ thought about all those barrels potentially going to waste and hoped Walker would be allowed to have them. Or at least purchase them at auction. That would all take time to sort out, but the whole idea was to leave the rum underwater for a long time, so maybe it would work out. It would certainly help Walker make a go of things if he could offer three-year-aged rum right away.

"Well?"

AJ looked at Jackson. "Huh?"

He laughed. "I believe you were about to tell me something profound."

"Oh, that's right," she replied.

Avoiding talking about sensitive subjects was a trait she had inherited from her parents, proven once again by the slightest distraction keeping her from the point. But she had thought about this an awful lot since their discussion Saturday night.

"I should preface this by saying I reserve the right to change my mind down the road," she said, building up the courage to verbalise what she had concluded.

Jackson nodded, allowing her time to compose her thoughts, and avoiding distracting her again.

"I think the life we have is rather good," she said in her typically understated way, "and while I'd love to introduce a mini-us into that life, that's not the way it would happen, right?"

Jackson took a few moments to reply. "That's true, I suppose.

Our lives would be changed in many ways, so nothing would be quite the same again."

"I know much of that change would be wonderful, new, scary, and exciting in a different way," she pressed on, choosing her words carefully, "but I don't think I'm ready to share you, or give up the life we lead."

Her brow was furrowed and she cringed at the idea of how she may sound. "Pretty selfish, huh?"

Jackson smiled. "Realistic, I think," he replied. "Having a child is selfish. It's us that decides to bring a new life into the world. They don't get a say in the matter."

AJ laughed. "I suppose that's true," she said, then thought it over for a moment before continuing, "The thing is, I really want to have a child with you, to share that together. There's probably nothing more intimate than bringing a new life into this world. You'd be an incredible dad, I'd be a scatter-brained mum, and our little person would be some kind of brilliant, planet-saving scuba kid. But, what about Mermaid Divers? And what about U-1026, and diving plane wrecks on Sixty Mile Bank? All that changes with new obligations and responsibilities."

They both stayed quiet for several minutes as the Newton continued across the soft rolling swells towards Grand Cayman. Finally, Jackson spoke. "I really want to have a child with you as well, and you'd be an amazing mom," he said, and held up a hand when she tried to interrupt him. "Let me finish. But, I think knowing it's something we both want badly, and accepting it's not a choice that fits into the life we have, is perfectly okay."

"Really?" AJ said, searching his eyes, worried he was just trying to make her happy.

"Really," he replied, and kissed her forehead.

"Oi, AJ?" came Reg's voice, shouting up from the deck.

Jackson took the wheel so AJ could move to the back railing of the fly-bridge beside the ladder. Reg appeared puzzled, and pointed to a BCD mounted on a tank in one of the racks, amongst the other gear.

"That looks like your rig."

AJ grinned. "Can't be, can it?" she yelled back. "You gave mine away and you're buying me a new one when we get home."

Reg scratched his beard and prodded at the BCD as though it might explain itself. AJ looked at the horizon behind them. They were well out of sight of Little Cayman. She scampered down the ladder and walked over to the door to the bow cabin. Undoing the lock she'd had on there since they loaded to leave, she swung the cantilever door open and stepped aside. Reg's eyes widened in surprise. Mads squealed in delight.

"Hi there," said the Irishman.

ACKNOWLEDGMENTS

My sincere thanks to:
My wife Cheryl and wonderful friend James for their support, advice and encouragement.

Did the rum ageing process seem a little far-fetched? Walker Romanica of Cayman Spirits will show you how it's not! With kind permission, I borrowed Walker's name, rum-making skills, and the Seven Fathoms brand for this story.

Ian Popple of Reef Smart who make the best dive maps – their Little Cayman map is coming soon.

Steven Becker for loaning me his wonderful Kurt Hunter character in chapter one.

'Mr Mako' for his help building the Rum Chaser – it was fun to imagine.

My tireless editor Andrew Chapman at Prepare to Publish.

The Tropical Authors group for their advice, support and humour! Check out the website for other great authors in the Sea Adventure genre.

My advanced reader copy (ARC) group, whose input and feedback is invaluable. This group pushes me to be a better writer, for which I am eternally grateful. It is a pleasure working with all of you.

Above all, I thank you, the readers: none of this happens without the choice you make to spend your precious time with AJ and her stories. I am truly in your debt.

LET'S STAY IN TOUCH!

To buy merchandise, find more info or join my Newsletter, visit my website at
www.HarveyBooks.com

If you enjoyed this novel I'd be incredibly grateful if you'd consider leaving a review on Amazon.com
Find eBook deals and follow me on BookBub.com

Visit Amazon.com for more books in the
AJ Bailey Adventure Series,
Nora Sommer Caribbean Suspense Series,
and collaborative works;
Graceless - A Tropical Authors Novella
Angels of the Deep - A Tropical Christmas Novella

ABOUT THE AUTHOR

Nicholas Harvey's life has been anything but ordinary. Race car driver, mountaineer, divemaster, and since 2019 a full-time novelist. Raised in England, Nick now lives next to the ocean in Key Largo with his amazing wife, Cheryl.

Motorsports may have taken him all over the world, both behind the wheel and later as a Race Engineer and Team Manager, but diving inspires his destinations these days – and there's no better diving than in Grand Cayman where Nick's *AJ Bailey Adventure* and *Nora Sommer Caribbean Suspense* series are based.